Hungry Woman in Paris

MAR 1 7 2009

Hungry Woman
in Paris

JOSEFINA LÓPEZ

GRAND CENTRAL
PUBLISHING

NEW YORK   BOSTON

Copyright © 2009 by Josefina López
All rights reserved. Except as permitted under the U.S. Copyright
Act of 1976, no part of this publication may be reproduced,
distributed, or transmitted in any form or by any means,
or stored in a database or retrieval system, without
the prior written permission of the publisher.

Grand Central Publishing
Hachette Book Group
237 Park Avenue
New York, NY 10017

Visit our Web site at www.HachetteBookGroup.com.

Printed in the United States of America

First Edition: March 2009
10 9 8 7 6 5 4 3 2 1

Grand Central Publishing is a division of Hachette Book Group, Inc.
The Grand Central Publishing name and logo is a trademark of
Hachette Book Group, Inc.

Library of Congress Cataloging-in-Publication Data

López, Josefina
Hungry woman in Paris / Josefina López.
    p. cm.
Summary: "From the celebrated author of Real Women Have Curves,
a young woman, disillusioned with life, runs away to Paris and
enrolls in cooking school to reawaken her senses and mend
her broken heart"—Provided by publisher.
ISBN: 978-0-446-69941-9
1. Mexican Americans—Fiction. 2. Mexican Americans—France—
Paris—Fiction. 3. Cooking schools—France—Paris—Fiction.
4. Cookery, French—Fiction. I. Title.
PS3562.O6725H86 2009
813'.54—dc22
2008022268

Book design and text composition by Greta D. Sibley

This book is dedicated to my parents, Catalina and Rosendo López, who lived their lives in the United States as immigrants with dignity and sacrificed so much to give their children an education and a better life; and to my brothers and sisters, who all have become exemplary models of successful American citizens.

This book is also dedicated to all the women I met at cooking school—in particular, Amy Whitman, Carla Trujillo, Kate Moffet, Myra Coca, Ingrid Wright, Sofia Sarabia—and to all the women in cooking schools who aspire to be taken seriously as chefs. May the fire in their hearts continue to burn bright.

To my husband, Emmanuel, who gave me a wonderful introduction to French culture and continues to surprise me by aspiring to be the man of my dreams.

To my dear cousin Marina, whom I never got to know because there was a border between us, but whose tragic passing haunts me.

Acknowledgments

This novel and my career were made possible by my wonderful and passionate manager, Marilyn Atlas.

I would also like to thank my literary agent Barbara Hogenson for being so lovely to work with.

My editor, Selina, took my underwritten and overplotted story and helped shape it into a real novel. Thank you!

I also want to thank all the other editors who worked on my novel for helping me clarify my story and making me sound articulate in three languages. Gracias! Merci! Thank you!

I couldn't have survived Le Cordon Bleu cooking school without the kindness and support of Kate Moffet, Myra Coca, Carla Trujillo, and Christopher Carlos.

I also want to acknowledge all the sweet ladies in administration at Le Cordon Bleu for being extra kind to Americans, as well as Chef Didier, for always bringing joy and passion to the kitchen.

Thank you to all my muses and friends who encouraged me along the way: my sweet mother, Miles Brandman, Luz Vasquez, Hector Rodriguez, Mercedes Floresislas, Patricia Zamorano, Margarita Medina, Elizabeth Andrews, Angela Wu, Anthony

Villareal, Jay Vincent, Rafael Rubalcava, Jeremy Ackers, Anaïs Nin, Stephen Clarke for writing *A Year in the Merde,* Alisa Valdes-Rodriguez for showing me it could be done, and Sandra Cisneros for clearing the path for Latina writers like me.

Thank you to all the Latina journalists who serve as inspiration for this novel, in particular Yvette Cabrera, Christina Gonzalez, Lorena Mendez, and Elizabeth Espinoza.

A very special thanks to Angel Alcala, who planted the seed in my mind to go to Le Cordon Bleu in Paris, as well as Jennifer Ladder, who had the courage to follow her heart and inspired me to enroll in cooking school too.

Hungry Woman in Paris

Prologue

This is either the longest suicide note in history or the juiciest, dirtiest, most delicious confession you'll ever hear. Call me Canela. That's Spanish for Cinnamon, but don't call me Cinnamon; that's a stripper's name. Not that there is anything wrong with being an exotic dancer. With my lifestyle, I'm the last one to throw stones. Thank God I'm a modern woman living in a so-called democracy and—aside from in Nigeria and some Middle Eastern countries I would be too scared to visit—getting killed by stones is a thing of the past. My mother named me Canela because she loved to make buñuelos and add lots of sugar and cinnamon to them. She would make them from scratch, using none of the shortcuts, like taking flour tortillas and frying them. You do know what a tortilla is, don't you? By now who doesn't? No, she did them by hand, *a mano*. It was probably her sweat and tears that made them tasty. When she saw me for the first time, she was disappointed that I was so pale. Unlike some Mexicans with internalized racism, she thought being dark and indigenous-looking was beautiful, but she wondered if people gossiped about whether she had cheated on my father with an American to get such a white-looking child. I did get her high cheekbones, big eyes, big breasts, black hair, and love of smells. I also got her propensity to be fat, but let's not talk about that right now. My mother spent most of her time in the kitchen and in the bedroom. When she wasn't making beans, she was making babies. Her world was tiny, as was her kitchen, but she made it delicious. So by adding cinnamon to a buñuelo she would make it even browner. With my name she spiced me up and made me brown. She didn't want people to mistake me for Italian or Irish—not that there's anything wrong with that—so she gave me a Spanish name so people would ask, "What is Canela?" More importantly, I hope you ask, Who is Canela? Who is Canela? Thanks for asking . . . My psychiatrist might have an idea. My psychic might have a better idea. My mother probably has a good idea, but after thirty years in my skin and in my soul, I'm still finding out . . .

BASIC
CUISINE

CHAPTER I

Four Gossips and a Funeral

$\mathcal{A}$re you ready to begin your exciting culinary career?" the cooking school admissions agent asked me in her French-accented English. I stared blankly up at her, clutching my admissions application, not believing what I was about to do. Anyone who knew me would think I had clearly gone insane. But what had brought me here? It had never been my dream to attend Le Coq Rouge, the world's most famous cooking school. Yet here I was in Paris about to lay down thirty thousand dollars to be in the kitchen when I had sworn I would never go back there, ever.

Maybe my mother was right: I had gone crazy and I needed medication. Otherwise why would I have broken off my engagement to a Latino surgeon, given up my journalism career, and run off to Paris by myself?

"Is there a problem?" Marie-Hélène, the admissions agent, asked with half a smile.

"Ah . . ." I tried to come up with a line to buy me a few more seconds. I needed to think about my past and whether I was making the right decision.

Maybe it was Luna's suicide that had shaken me out of my senses, or the Iraq war, or the fight with the editor, or the fight with my fiancé, or my mother and father fighting . . . yes, when all else fails blame it on my childhood. All I knew was that I didn't want to go back to the United States, to my home in Los Angeles, and this was the only way to stay in France.

It must have been the fight at the wake that made me realize I was exhausted from fighting everyone, including myself.

Why is it that when someone dies everyone only says good things about her at the funeral? Death makes angels of everyone, I suppose. No, I think it's out of superstition. At the root of every fear is death, so if you speak badly of someone who is dead and they can't defend themselves, then death might strike you. At my funeral I want people to say I was a bitch if I truly was one to them. All I hope is that the people who experienced my kindness will speak up and say, "Yes, but . . ." Maybe then people can have authentic conversations instead of the stupid ones in which everyone knows the person is dead but, aside from this exception, pretends death doesn't really exist, thus freeing them to converse about silly things. Silly things like my broken-off engagement.

"Is it true what I just heard?" asked my mother in her metiche mode. My mother was usually my favorite person on the planet, but also the one that drove me to tears and insanity at the push of an emotional button whose location only she knew.

"You hear a lot of things, including ghosts, so it depends on what you heard," I replied.

"You and Armando—what's going on?" she demanded to know. "Your sister told me she thinks you are depressed. I think you should get on medication. You are not thinking straight. You can't break it off. He's a doctor and he loves you! Do you realize how hard it is to get a good man in Los Angeles? Es una locura!" she hissed at me like a cat about to get mauled by a dog.

I got up from my pew and went to look at the body. My mother did not follow me. Nobody wanted to be first. I was glad to have a few seconds with Luna, my favorite cousin, before anyone else had the courage to go up after me. I smiled at Luna's over-made-up face. She hated pink lipstick, but here she was in pink for eternity. Luna was more of a red. She loved living life in extremes, like me. When we were little girls we played like boys and hated dolls. We were a pair of mocosas, rascals always getting into trouble. We swore that when we got older we would travel the world and never marry or have children because we would always play. We wanted to be a part of history and make history. We wished we could have been born around the time writers and artists hung out in Paris, like Hemingway and Fitzgerald, or in Mexico City during the Mexican Revolution, like Diego and Frida. Luna was special. She could guess things or predict things before they happened. Her family thought she was just weird, but I knew she was psychic. She was silly when she wanted to be, but wise beyond her years. When everyone around me told me I was crazy for wanting to be a journalist covering all sorts of dangerous stories, Luna would join me on my adventures to catch a story.

In female friendships, a man always comes between them— isn't that the predictable plot? In our story, Luna met a guy and I remained single. I was never jealous of him, but he wasn't good enough for her. He was Mr. Now, but Luna was forced to make him into Mr. Forever when her parents grew concerned that "the neighbors were talking." They married her off before she "got knocked up," to this poor guy who could barely afford to support her and keep her gold-plated birdcage locked. Luna couldn't go to college and had to play the housewife, a role she was never born for. She got so depressed she gained weight and developed diabetes. When she wanted to get pregnant she couldn't, because the doctors warned her it might kill her. She tried anyway but had miscarriages, which made her even more depressed. Her world kept shrinking, but her body kept growing. Her dreams were larger than life, too big to exist in this world in a woman's body.

I covered my eyes and started crying. Flashes of my life with Luna exploded like the big bang onto the little movie theater of my mind. I remembered my first bicycle ride with her and all the promises we made to each other. We were ten, hiding in the attic, leafing through a dirty magazine we had found on the street near an alley. We criticized all the couples and laughed together, not understanding what would motivate adults to make such funny faces. We laughed so hard, thinking we were so smart, knowing that we shared true happiness. Luna told me I was not just her cousin but her best of best friends and said that if I were not alive, she would not want to live anymore. I hugged her and said that I would not want to live in a world without her either.

"Is it true what your Tía Bonifacia is saying about you and Armando being over because you couldn't agree on the menu?" my mother, who had joined me at the casket, whispered into my ear, so Luna couldn't hear. Her question jolted me back to the present and I quickly wiped away all my tears. I couldn't believe my Tía Bonifacia knew about the menu. How could she have known? She should work for the CIA or the *National Enquirer*. Maybe she's psychic . . . Actually, all women are psychic. When a man cheats on a woman and lies to her, she already knows; she just lies to herself. This was the case with Tía Bonifacia. She was a poster child for what happens when a woman stays married to a man who is constantly unfaithful: she turns bitter. If she were a fruit she would be a lemon, always frowning like she just sucked on one.

"Yes. It's true," I whispered back. Poor Luna had to endure this pettiness even on her last day. My mother practically went hysterical at my response. She couldn't believe that despite all her hard work, all the guilt trips, all the bad advice about how women are nothing without men, how careers are not as important as family and children, all the scripts in her "Third World Woman as Servant" file in her brain that she tried to install on my mental hard drive, I was not getting married in two months.

"Tú de veras estás loca," she hissed again. "You really are crazy" was her usual response to anything I did that was out of the ordinary. It used to upset me to be called *loca*, but I was too heartbroken by Luna's death to care about what my mother thought about me. When she called me loca it wasn't the fun loca, as in Ricky Martin's "Livin' la Vida Loca," but the "there is really something wrong with you and we should lock you up with the crazies" loca.

"Tell me something I don't know," I wanted to yell back at her to shut her up and respect Luna's memory, but I would be seen as the one disrespecting this sacred rite. I ignored my mother's comment and left a red rose on Luna's chest. My mother immediately followed behind me and cornered me. My older sister Reina, having overheard that the wedding was off, jumped into the conversation.

"But I just bought a very expensive designer dress for your wedding and I can't take it back," she said, getting no sympathy from me.

I ignored their feeding frenzy by changing the subject. I handed my mother several twenty-dollar bills.

"What's this?" my mother asked.

"It's a donation for Luna's parents for the funeral. I know this is going to cost them a lot of money. Tía Lucia shouldn't have to worry about that on top of her grief," I informed her. Her mood changed all of sudden.

"Yes, you may be a loca, but you have always had a good heart. We should ask all your brothers and sisters to put in money también to give to your Tía Lucia. At least this will comfort her," said my mother. "Does anyone have an envelope?" Reina opened her Gucci bag and took out an envelope. She handed it to my mother and then pulled out her designer pen and wrote an amount on one of her Republican checks. Each check order was a donation toward the Republican Party. I didn't know they needed money since it seems only rich people are Republicans. Oh, wait, not true: there are Hispanic Republicans, former welfare recipients who got out, or former undocumented people, or their children, who made it and therefore think anyone who doesn't make it is just lazy; Cubans who hate Castro; Texans whose parents were beaten for speaking Spanish in school; and other Latinos with internalized racism. Yeah, now I remember; I did an article on this for a newspaper I used to work for.

I rolled my eyes when I saw her check, and she came back at me with attitude.

"Yeah, well, at least he's not screwing his interns."

"I'd rather have a president who drops his load on blue dresses than one who drops bombs on innocent people for oil." Then I added something I'd seen on a bumper sticker: "When Clinton lied, no one died."

"Cochina," my mother reprimanded me for my sexual reference. "You talk like a man."

"He's doing a good job defending our country from terrorists!" Reina said.

The whole president-as-father-figure-and-protector thing has Freudian implications, and I did not want to go there with my sister. I just wanted to be left alone to cry for Luna. Reina mistook my silence as a sign that she was right, and went on talking about all the good "W" has done. "So what that the weapons of mass destruction were not found yadda yadda yadda. . . ."

I went to "Lalala land," my safe place where Republicans did not exist, where only people who cared about people and cared to be people peopled this land... Reina had stopped talking and I was about to get away when she got up to me real close and delivered her message à la *The Graduate.*

"Responsibility . . . You need to grow up and be responsible now. You're going to be turning thirty and, yes, you may be beautiful now, but you won't be forever."

Now I got it: she's always been jealous of me. For some reason, being beautiful rendered me an idiot in her eyes and lots of other peoples' too. That must be one of the universal laws I didn't know about. One of those unwritten rules women are unconsciously told: you must be beautiful or intelligent, but you can't be both because it confuses men.

"Is that what happened to you?" I said.

"Bitch!" she spat out. Wow, I wasn't even dead yet and I was getting my wish.

My mother quickly jumped in between us, took my sister's check, and added it to my money. I walked away to go comfort Tía Lucia, who was crying in the corner. On my way to her I overheard Tía Bonifacia, with her arms crossed, telling one of my cousins how Luna died.

"She drank six Cokes. She was a diabetic; she knew what she was doing. It was a suicide; call it what it was. There's no shame in the truth," Tía Bonifacia preached.

The corpulent cousin shook her head and noted, "Suicide is a sin, qué no?"

All right, call me a metiche, but I just couldn't stand back and say nothing. "The truth? You don't know what the truth is!" I yelled at Tía Bonifacia.

"Oh, no, please don't say that movie line 'You can't handle the truth'—por favor, we are at a wake," my stupid cousin said. She was so annoying; that was the most original line she had ever said in her life.

In the midst of our soon-to-be argument, I watched my mother hand Tía Lucia the envelope full of money. Tía Lucia handed my mother another envelope. My mother quickly put it away, folding it and hiding it between her breasts. My mother used to hide a gun between her breasts whenever she and my father would drive back to Mexico. It was a little security measure in case they were stopped by bandits on the empty desert roads at night. Occasionally she lost money in there and would swear that it was like the Bermuda Triangle, but most of the time it was the safest place in the world.

"I do know what the truth is. I was there when she died." Tía Bonifacia raised her voice, not wanting to be outdone. The mourners stopped talking and turned to us.

I defended Luna: "It could have been an accident."

"No! She drank six Cokes. That's like fifty-four spoonfuls of sugar. We did the math; that's no accident. It was suicide!" Tía Bonifacia said it so loud to prove her point, but her insistence made everyone uncomfortable. If someone is dead, that's one thing, but knowing how they died, that's another. And then knowing that they did it on purpose, well that's just TMI, as a shallow acquaintance once said after I shared with her that my toenail looked like the Grand Canyon. "Too much information—I'm eating," she said and looked back down at the *Vogue* she was reading.

Tía Lucia cried out like she had spilled a basket full of flour that the wind had quickly swept away. I wanted to slap Tía Bonifacia. What gave this 250-pound gorilla the right to hurt people with her gossip?

"You're right," I spat at her, "if it's the truth, there's no shame in it. Maybe Luna did want to die rather than live a life as miserable as yours. Maybe for her that was not good enough because she didn't want to end up a bitter old chismosa like you!"

My cousin looked up at me and couldn't believe I was challenging the Goliath of Gossip. Man, I was a dead duck, but I didn't care. The dirt this woman was going to dig up on me, and the comments that she could throw out like daggers, but so what. Truth be told, I was doing the best I could with my life, even if no one else thought so.

"Now I understand why your fiancé dumped you," she said, being sure to make eye contact with her audience. "I thought it was because you were a puta." The aahs and gasps from our audience issued as planned to the ever-popular "puta" comment. What a desperate attempt, how typical to always resort to "whore" for a strike at a woman's Achilles' heel. "Pero now I know it's because of that mouth of yours. Who'd want to be stuck with you forever?" The crowd around us "Ooohed" and "Aaahed" as though they were watching the first round of a De La Hoya vs. Tyson fight. Clearly I was out of her league and her gossip weight class, but I couldn't let her get away with her comments.

I immediately wanted to defend myself, but if I did, I would be validating her comments and I would lose. I took three deep breaths. That's what Buddhist monks do, I've been told, and I let her comments pass like water being flushed down a toilet at a Tijuana bar. Then I went for the throat, metaphorically speaking. I should have bit her ear, but instead I nonchalantly said, "Then I must congratulate your husband for being a saint and staying with you . . . Oh, wait, he's cheated on you with your neighbor, your cousin, and even your own sister." Someone gasped. Yes, I had scored a point. "I guess being stuck with you forever is his punishment, qué no?" I said this with a smile the size of the dam blocking all my rage. I heard small murmurs of agreement from the crowd. I was about to talk about her bastard grandchildren, pothead son, welfare scam, and all the other crap that Jerry Springer and Spanish talk-show knockoffs feed off, but thank God my Tía Lucia stepped in before I went for a knockout.

"Por favor, stop this! Please respect Luna's memory and stop this!"

I lowered my guard and made for the door. My mother and all my siblings hurried after me. I headed to the parking lot, trying to make a fast escape.

"Go apologize to your Tía Bonifacia and your Tía Lucia for that escándalo you just made!" my mother demanded.

"No. Tell her to apologize to me first," I yelled back, marching toward my Prius. My father also walked up to talk to me.

"I knew you weren't going to go through with it. You're not a woman men marry." I stopped for a second, hooked by his mean comment. Then I decided to let it go and kept on walking.

"If you leave like this, you're not going to be welcome at the funeral," my mother warned me. I hesitated and stopped to consider the consequences. I wanted to attend Luna's funeral, but how could she have committed suicide? Why hadn't she called me to let me know things were so bad? Why hadn't she come to me for help?

"Think about what you are doing," my sister Rosie said. "Armando is a good guy. He really loves you." Rosie was my favorite sister, she always came from a good place, but I was in so much pain even her beautiful words annoyed the hell out of me. How come everyone else knew everything I needed to do right with my life except for me? How come everyone knew what was good for me except for me? How come I was supposed to listen to all this crap just because it came from my family?

I jumped in my car and locked the door immediately. If I'd been a little girl, my mother would have yanked me out of the car and taken me back inside to apologize, but I was too big for her to do that anymore. Her last hope was guilt.

"How can I go back in there and face your tías and our relatives after what you have done?" she asked with one of those faces painted on tortured saints you see in the million and one churches in Mexico.

"Tell Tía Lucia I'm sorry," I blurted and drove off.

For a few weeks after that I stayed in bed. "Why didn't I stop her?" and "Why didn't I go with her?" were the two questions that kept repeating in my head. I stayed in bed until my loneliness scared me and La Calaca Flaca sat next to me. She looked like a skeleton lady in a Posada drawing. She would keep me company and remind me why life was shitty and unfair.

"If life is not an adventure, it's not worth living," she would whisper to me. I don't know if I created her or if she created me to keep her company, but I was used to her. She was like Luna, a loyal friend who promised never to leave me, until I finally joined her and died one day. La Calaca Flaca had shown up in my life on many occasions when life had dealt me a blow too painful to overcome. I always thanked her for her company and shared my stories of hardship with her. I purposely kept busy to avoid seeing her around me, but when she did show up to remind me I wasn't alone, I actually felt a tiny bit better.

"Why don't you join Luna?" she asked, as if recommending a solution. I cried in her arms and she hugged me.

"Just go to the bathroom and grab the sleeping pills. I'll start the bath for you," she suggested, like the loving and comforting mother I did not have.

I got up and went to the bathroom. I saw my face and couldn't believe how bloated it was from sleeping so much. I stared at myself in the mirror and wondered why anyone would think I was beautiful. At least the texture of my light skin was still resilient. I reached into the medicine cabinet for face cream and my hand hit the bottle of sleeping pills. It fell and cracked, sleeping pills rolling into the sink, and I picked them up to examine them. I turned around and heard the bath running. Did I turn it on? I asked myself. I stared at the water and knew it was nice and hot, and how wonderful it would be to sleep in bathwater. La Calaca Flaca moved her bony index finger in her direction.

The phone rang, startling me back to my reality. La Calaca Flaca disappeared and I rushed to get the phone, but I stopped in front of it and let it ring until the answering machine picked up. I was certain it was my relentless mother with her desperate attempts to guilt me into changing my mind.

When I finally worked up the courage to start my day and get some underwear, I saw my wedding dress in the closet. I'd designed it to look like a passionate flamenco dress even though it was in ivory. It was so beautiful it made me want to get married. I put it on to see how it would look. What a shame, all the money I'd spent and I wouldn't get to wear it. I tried it on but it would not zip up, not even halfway. Maybe they'd made it the wrong size, I thought, and checked the tag. Before my eyes, I was back to being a size 12. In less than a month I'd gone from a size 6 to a size 12. Women's bodies are amazing: you can be skin and bones one day, another you're eighty pounds heavier and someone is living inside you rent-free, and then six months later you're back to the same body with a tiny pouch that will never leave you. Maybe they should make men pouch-size so they stay in there and remain faithful forever. Reminds me of that joke: "Men spend nine months inside a woman trying to get out and the rest of their lives trying to get back in." God, I was so heartbroken I couldn't even laugh at a stupid joke. What do you do with a never-worn wedding dress? Do you donate it to Goodwill? Do you put out an ad and try to sell it on eBay? Do you keep it around for the next guy?

The phone rang again and, finally picking up, I told my mother, once and for all, "No. I'm not getting married. Please stop calling me about that. If Armando is so wonderful, you marry him!" I hung up and went back to bed. I grabbed a bar of chocolate next to my bed and ate it. I'm convinced God created chocolate to make up for not striking down the Catholic Church when they were burning innocent women accused of being witches and destroying the "sacred feminine." Chocolate makes being a woman bearable—at least temporarily.

The phone rang again; I couldn't believe my mother would not give up. I let the answering machine pick up again and heard my *Modern Latina* editor leave a nasty message. Perhaps I deserved it. Until now I had never missed a deadline, and now that I had, she was stuck writing the article herself at the last minute. I knew she would never hire me again and that if she could help it, she would make sure none of the other Latina publications would either. I was too depressed to care even about my writing career.

"I hate my president," I muttered to myself, risking imprisonment and another mark on my FBI file. Everyone has an FBI file; didn't you know? Whenever I saw his lying-through-my-teeth face I squirmed as if I had a yeast infection. Never mind that he lied, never mind the truth, he was still going to be reelected. He might not be my ideal candidate, but I was sure he was an inspiration to a lot of mediocre people out there. Why shouldn't they aspire to be president too? I guess he really embodied the American dream. Anyone can be president. Anyone whose family has money, oil, and connections can be president. I saw a sign at a war protest that said, "Somewhere in Texas, in a small village, an idiot is missing," and here he was on TV. In less than two weeks he was going to take the oath of president again and there was nothing I could do. I could go throw eggs like a lot of my fellow activists did at the last inauguration, as he tried to walk to the U.S. Capitol. I have pretty good aim. But I'd probably be beaten to a pulp by the time I got done throwing eggs for all the Latina mothers who'd lost their sons in Iraq. I changed the channel and surfed. Yes, TV relaxes you; it does something to your brain that renders you a happy idiot. Some days that's the best you can hope for when another happy idiot is running the country. I got hooked on the Food Network and was enthralled by two chefs competing to see who could make the most delicious meal with rhubarb. I'd thought it was just for dessert. Who knew? A commercial break set me running for more distraction. I came across the Travel Channel and saw a sweepstakes advertised. The winners would get a romantic getaway to Paris.

"Paris! Oh, my God! I have the tickets to Paris, our honeymoon package!" I yelled out. Armando and I had bought the tickets four months ago because it was hard to pass up the deal. Paris in January is cheap! I ran upstairs to my file cabinet and found the Los Angeles to Paris tickets and the itinerary. Four months ago, when we'd bought the tickets, we had purposely timed it so that we'd depart a day before the inauguration, in case he won, but I had forgotten about it. One week at a fancy hotel in the honeymoon suite . . . Sweet.

CHAPTER 2

A Chicana in Paris

*T*hey're dreadful. They're so rude. They're just as bad as New Yorkers."

"Is that before 9/11 or after?" I asked the lady next to me on the plane, who'd just revealed that she was a U.S. diplomat. She thought about it a few seconds and said, "Before."

The flight attendant approached us, speaking French. I didn't understand her, so she spoke to me in English and asked what kind of document I needed to clear customs.

"My French is dreadful," the diplomat confessed once the flight attendant had left. "Whenever I have to deal with French farmers I have to take a translator with me because I got tired of them correcting me and telling me to 'Please make an effort' in their bad English."

"You deal with farmers?" I asked.

"Yes, I handle many things, including the national 'foie gras' fight.'"

"Foie gras?" I mispronounced it and had to ask what it was.

"It's made out of an enlarged goose liver."

"Oh, I think I had some at a Hollywood party," I said, trying to cover up for my ignorance.

"Well, you know how inhumane it is to overfeed the geese. They practically feed them to death, until the liver is so huge they walk lopsided. The U.S. is considering not buying French foie gras to protest the inhumane treatment of animals. Of course, the farmers argue that the geese love it." We both nodded and I sympathized with her struggle.

"Yeah, my French is awful too," I said, showing her my little phrase book. I had tried learning French so many times that I was ashamed to admit it was practically a lost cause. Back when I was a chubby teenager, I saw a show in which my favorite sitcom characters went to Paris for the summer. After that I became a Francophile and swore I would go backpacking through France as soon as I turned eighteen. My first French teacher, God bless him, was more intent on teaching us Chicano studies, back when Chicano studies hadn't yet made its way to the junior high schools. He was a Frenchman married to a Mexican woman and he wanted to empower all his poor, mostly undocumented students with self-love and pride in our culture. He taught us a lot of beautiful and valuable things, but he didn't teach us French. Then he got sick and we got lots of substitute teachers, who just babysat.

My second French teacher was a fun-loving man from Martinique, gorgeous and dark. Any woman could learn French from him. Things were going great and I was even writing comedy skits in French for extra credit, until his car accident. His mouth had to be wired shut for the rest of the semester. A permanent substitute teacher came in and was so strict I wanted to not learn French just to spite him. He was so mean he killed the joie de vivre of our classroom.

The third time, I attempted to learn French from a private French teacher when I was in grad school. I wanted to do an exchange program at La Sorbonne and it was mandatory that I speak French. She was fabulous, an older, sophisticated woman who loved teaching. She swore she could teach anyone to speak French beautifully by the end of her intensive course. I mentioned to her how relieved I was to be taking her course because I'd almost given up trying to learn it. She laughed when I mentioned all the tragedies my past French teachers had encountered and told me not to worry. The second week into our studies I received a message on my answering machine telling me she couldn't teach me that week because her mother was in the emergency room. The third week she canceled because her mother had passed away and she was too depressed to go on. After that she mostly sent substitutes. I took it as a sign and figured I wasn't meant to learn the language.

"Unless your French is perfect, you can't really say you speak French," my seatmate advised me now. Sometimes it's better to ask in French if they speak English and if they do, speak only in English. If you attempt to speak it and it's horrible, they will stop you because they don't want you to 'ruin' their language," she advised.

"Thanks, I'll try not to speak it if I don't have to," I vowed.

Rosemary met me outside of customs. She almost didn't recognize me with the extra weight. She had managed to stay so thin since college. How did she do it? Rosemary hugged me and gave me a kiss on both cheeks, French-style. Her breath stank like an ashtray left to rot in the sun. She helped me with my bags and told the taxi driver where to take us. I was so impressed by Rosemary's ability to speak French and sound and act like a native. She'd even taken up smoking to fit right in. Don't get me started on smoking and smokers—I'll save that one for another time when you like me much better.

Rosemary and I met in college, way back when I didn't know any better and called myself "Hispanic." Rosemary asked me,

"Whose panic are you?" I didn't understand her question. So she proceeded to give me the whole lecture as to how the classification of "Hispanic" had been conjured up by the census and how it didn't pay tribute to our indigenous heritage. After several hours I got it and marched on over to MEChA, the Chicano activist association founded in the sixties to empower Chicanos. I participated in a lot of protests; it was really exciting. Standing for a cause is a real adrenaline rush. I was even willing to go on a hunger strike with Rosemary to fight to get a Chicano studies center at the university. Of course, I had to back down at the last minute when I got real with myself. I loved eating too much to give it up, even for a good cause. I really admired César Chávez and Gandhi, but my form of activism would have to be the written word, not the empty stomach. My parents had brought my family to the United States because of the fear of empty stomachs.

"Stay with me at the hotel," I begged Rosemary. "It's a honeymoon package and I don't want to use it alone."

We arrived at a fancy hotel off the Champs-Élysées and a doorman opened the taxi door. The woman at the reception desk looked at Rosemary and me and had to ask, just in case she was making a mistake, "You're in the honeymoon suite?"

"Yes," I assured her. I could have gone on and on about how I'd broken off the engagement and what a terrible mistake my mother thought I'd made and how I'd decided to use the plane ticket anyway, but I decided to save the story; this woman didn't get paid enough to listen to me.

Rosemary couldn't help but add her two centimes: "Yes, we bought the honeymoon package back when our marriage license was legal in San Francisco. Then the law changed, but we decided to come anyway." The woman put on a fake smile, not sure what to say. We left the counter holding in our laughter.

A bellhop escorted us to the honeymoon suite and flashed us

a kinky smile. It wasn't the first time Rosemary and I had been mistaken for a couple or had men fantasize about us being one. Rosemary gave him a tip and wished him well with all her charm. She was good at small talk and being friendly to strangers. I hated bullshit. I always got to the truth of the matter. What can I say; I sucked at parties.

Rosemary and I hopped on the double-decker tour bus and stayed on it for the two hours it took to go to the Eiffel Tower, Les Invalides, the Musée d'Orsay, Notre-Dame, the Louvre, Concorde Plaza, the Galeries Lafayette, and back to l'Arc de Triomphe, on the Champs-Élysées. During the two hours she gave me a brief history of how she'd fallen in love with a Frenchman named Antoine while studying French in graduate school, and their wild romance that brought her all the way from Berkeley to Burgundy. She didn't know he was part of an aristocratic family until she got to his town. Her future mother-in-law acted kindly toward her at first, but when she realized how serious he was about marrying Rosemary she proceeded to poison the well. My brother used to joke, "Adam was so lucky—he was the only man who didn't get a mother-in-law." Why can't all women get along? Why can't we all just get along?

"But it's over. He chose his château over me," Rosemary said, still hurt by the whole thing.

We got off the bus and walked down the Champs-Élysées like real tourists. We passed a giant store where people were waiting in line in the freezing cold to go in.

"Is there a celebrity in there?" I asked Rosemary.

"No, it's the Louis Vuitton store."

"What's the big deal?" I asked.

The next day Rosemary had to go to work and left me to visit the Eiffel Tower on my own. Even in January, with practically no crowd, I still had to wait half an hour. When I got close to the elevator, two men in military uniforms informed everyone that the Eiffel Tower had to be shut down because of a possible bomb threat. They'd found a mysterious package. Probably another vibrator in a garbage can someone was too embarrassed to carry, I figured, or something equally innocuous.

They say it takes three days to do the Louvre, but I was interested in only three things: the *Mona Lisa*, *Winged Victory of Samothrace*, and the *Venus de Milo*. The hall in the Louvre where the *Mona Lisa* was caged in a clear, bulletproof box was as hot as a sauna. It was packed with obnoxious tourists like me snapping a million photos with our digital cameras. It was like a red-carpet affair at a Hollywood premiere, except the *Mona Lisa* wasn't signing autographs. A crowd of people came in on top of everything else and everyone had to readjust themselves, like an amoeba. A large man with a commanding voice welcomed everyone to the first stop on the "*Da Vinci Code* tour." I got nauseous with all the international smells and sweat and had to run for air.

On the fifth day of my visit I strolled by myself on the Seine and an Arab-French man in stylish clothes walked up to me. He asked me if I was an Arab, because if I was, I was pretty liberated not wearing a veil on my head and therefore was his kind of gal.

"No, I'm Mexican-American," I responded.

"Mexique? ¡Ah, viva México!" he exclaimed. He proceeded to flatter me and call me *jolie* until I made up a lie about being married after he asked me to have coffee. I even pretended my French was so bad I couldn't understand the word for coffee. Silly, but it worked.

Eventually my week was over and I had to check out of the hotel. Rosemary had said good-bye and gone back to her tiny apartment and I was walking toward the door. The Croatian doorman asked me if I needed a taxi. I was about to say "Yes" when a deep voice from within me said, "No." I sat down by the bar to figure out who'd said it. A cocktail waiter came over and asked in English if I wanted something to drink. I asked for a margarita, but they didn't make them, so I just ordered tequila. Three shots later, I was crying for Luna. Had Luna been alive she would have joined me on this trip in a second. We should be exploring Paris together, like we'd said we would. Maybe if I had been there for her she wouldn't have . . . I couldn't even be at her funeral! I looked at my watch and knew I had to leave that minute or miss my plane. I picked up my cell phone and called Rosemary instead.

"I can't do it . . . No, I can't go back. I hate my life. I hate the war. I hate what is happening to the U.S., and I just can't go back."

CHAPTER 3

Hiding Out in the Sixteenth

U*ne chambre de bonne*, explained Rosemary, is a tiny room intended for maids or nannies. She rented this room on the sixth floor because it was cheap. But she hated living in the Sixteenth Arrondissement because it was the most boring part of Paris. Paris is divided into twenty neighborhoods, or arrondissements, and in Rosemary's words, the Sixteenth was the Beverly Hills of Paris. "Avenue Foch has more millionaires than dog shit," she claimed.

When Rosemary arrived in Paris, after she'd broken up with Antoine, she started working as a nanny and was provided that room. She liked that building because she could walk around naked in front of the windows and it wouldn't matter. The Iraqi embassy was across the street, facing her window, but because it was abandoned only the pigeons would stare back.

"I know it's an eyesore, but it's nice not to have to worry about nosy neighbors. Check it out." I went to the window and looked at the embassy. I could swear I saw Saddam Hussein hiding out in the abandoned offices.

"Is that . . . ?" I started to ask.

"Yes, that's a poster of Saddam Hussein from when he was in power, back before they invaded Kuwait. After they invaded Kuwait, France broke ties with them and they just abandoned the building."

"Why are there police officers in front of the building next to this one?"

"Because they reopened the Iraqi embassy."

"I thought you just said it was abandoned."

"Yes, but both of the buildings belong to the Iraqi embassy. That one across the street is still abandoned."

"What about the building next to this one on the other side?"

"That's Pakistan," she casually informed me.

"So this building is between the Iraqi embassy and the Pakistani embassy?"

"Yeah, most of the embassies are in the Sixteenth. That's one of the reasons it's so boring. Well, the occasional bomb threat shakes things up now and again."

"Bomb threat?" I repeated.

"Yeah . . . Oh, that's actually why I lost my nanny job. I used to work for an American couple, but one day they came home and found a device close to the fireplace. They called the police, and the bomb squad confirmed that it was a bomb and everyone was evacuated from the building. Someone, maybe the maid or someone related to the maid, had allowed someone to put a bomb there so they could blow up the Pakistani embassy. I don't remember what political bullshit was happening at that time. The American couple quickly got rid of their apartment and they went back to the U.S. They made the new owners promise them they would let me keep the room and for the same amount of rent."

I put my suitcase down and Rosemary offered me her single bed. I insisted that I could sleep on the floor, so she laid out a yoga mat for me. She covered it with thick blankets and made me a bed.

"You're lucky I'm Mexican-American and don't have issues with personal space, because this apartment is too small for two people," she said. I took this as a hint and told her I would rent a place if she could help me find one.

"No, don't worry about it," she protested. "I love company, and if you don't mind me, I certainly won't mind you. I like being out most of the time. I am *not* a homebody." I settled in and got acquainted with her tiny bathroom and hot plate. She had turned a dingy room into a cosy casita. I asked her where her fridge was and she showed me a little box where she only had room to keep milk and eggs and a moldy cheese.

"Your cheese is rotting," I pointed out.

"That's the way I like it . . . I know, I'm all French now, eating rotten cheese, *n'est-ce pas*?" We laughed.

"Don't buy anything around here. Paris is expensive, but the Sixteenth is ridiculously overpriced," Rosemary advised me, like one barrio girl to another.

She gave me a tour of Victor Hugo Avenue and showed me the McDonald's. "I know you just got here, but eventually you'll break down and have to eat it." I assured her I was against globalization and had started boycotting McDonald's many years ago. Still, we walked past it and I had to laugh when I saw their version of a drive-through window: a walk-through window with at least ten people waiting. And I thought we were the fat Americans.

"Don't go to Bois de Boulogne by yourself at night," Rosemary said, continuing with the tour.

"Where is the Bua de Bolo—?" I tried pronouncing it at first, then just asked, "What is that?"

"It's a big park, but it used to be the hunting forest, reserved for the kings of France. Bois de Boulogne is right around here.

When you get off the Porte Dauphine metro stop, if you cross the street, that's where it is. There are a lot of transvestite prostitutes, drug dealers, perverts, and things you don't want to discover alone." I took a mental note and said to myself, No Bois de B after sunset for me.

"By the way, how long do you plan to stay?"

Rosemary startled me with that question, but I nonchalantly said, "I don't know . . ." She assured me that I could stay with her as long as I needed to, but that technically I could only stay in France for three months before I would be *en situation irré-gulière*—a nice way of saying "wetback" again. Hey, I can use that word because I was undocumented for many years, before I stopped being an irregular situation . . . or a *sans-papiers*—without papers. I told Rosemary that I probably wouldn't stay more than three months and I could pay her rent money. She laughed, saying, "I'd feel like a slum landlord if I charged you rent for my hole-in-the-wall."

I always heard about the French existentialist writers and the American writers who hung out in cafés pondering the meaning of life and having sex with prostitutes and doing all the things they couldn't do in a sexually repressed country like America. I read in my tourist book about Hemingway's hangouts when he lived in Paris, where he and F. Scott Fitzgerald drank. Man, he got around! I had to go to Deux Magots—big disappointment. A fancy place with French-movie-star-looking people and tourists like me trying to pretend they're brilliant artists on the verge of greatness. But unlike them I was really having an existential crisis, and I felt a little superior because my internal suffering was apparent on my face. I sat down and looked at the menu and thought how ironic it was that back then starving artists came to cafés like these because they lived on wine and street pigeons to survive, and now the same cafés are famous because of them and no starving artist can afford to eat there. It's hard to have an existential crisis when a glass of wine costs more than nine dollars. So I took my existential crisis someplace else.

I headed to a café near Notre-Dame and Shakespeare and Company to write . . . Write what? I scratched the pen to paper, hoping words would come out . . . What does this all mean? Nothing. Who the hell cares? No one. Where am I? I'm somewhere between heaven and hell and nowhere on the map of reality. When am I going back? Why am I here? And how the hell am I going to make a living now that I don't have the answer to the five big *W*'s of life? Since I can remember, I've wanted to be a journalist. Being a journalist and going to Paris were the two things I wanted the most in life. I wanted to be like Hemingway and Fitzgerald and roam around Paris writing a novel or a literary work that would live on past my life. As a writer and journalist I wanted to tell the truth and light up the world with it. After "W" got reelected, an article I wrote about the first Latino soldiers to die in Iraq, along with another I wrote about vaginas in a teen magazine, got censored. I realized that a lot of people in America were not interested in the truth. They were interested in . . . something else, something only a Jungian analyst could explain. If I can't write the truth, I can't be a journalist. So if I am not a journalist anymore, then what am I? What am I going to do with my life? Since what I write makes no difference in the world, why bother killing myself for a story? I try to remember what Deepak Chopra and all the other gurus say: "The world is perfect as it is; everything is as it should be—ohmmmmmm . . ." I don't believe that, so why try? The world sucks, the war sucks, and I can't do anything about it. Going to protests doesn't change anything. Writing to Congress doesn't change anything. So what the hell is the point of trying to change the world when it's hard enough to get someone you love to change their point of view?

Maybe I should just go back to L.A. and face my family and go to therapy and then tell my family I broke off the wedding engagement because I discovered . . . I was a lesbian . . . Yeah! How do I explain all the men in my past? I know: I was experimenting. I was compensating . . . Yeah, right! Sure, they'll believe that! Inside I knew I could go home only when I'd come up with a good enough reason for breaking my engagement to a successful surgeon. I just didn't want to go back and face the disappointment on my mother's face.

I looked up at the sky filled with dirty clouds and my hand began to write a sentence: *Clouds above me, clouds all around me . . . is it depression or just my life going nowhere like stale water in a fish tank?* I stopped writing. It hurt to write. I didn't want to write anymore. Every time I tried to write, the stupid editor's voice from my old newspaper would say, "You lost your objectivity," and I would practically throw the pen out of my hand. So what do I do with my life now? I've always said that if I couldn't write anymore, I wouldn't want to live.

Rosemary arrived early from work and found me on the bed recovering from my sightseeing. She announced that she was taking me to the Lapin Agile in Montmartre to see a cabaret that I couldn't miss.

"I love taking people to this cabaret because it truly captures the spirit of Paris and Montmartre."

"What's that?" I asked.

"It's a neighborhood that's on a hill; a little seedy, but back in the eighteen hundreds it was the place to go for can-can dancers and drinking and all the illegal things. I really like that neighborhood, and if I could find a *chambre de bonne* I would move there."

We took the metro and got off at the Lamarck-Caulaincourt stop. We climbed up what seemed like endless stairs to a house with a gate. When we walked in through the front door, the attendant told us to speak softly. A beautiful voice sang in French like Edith Piaf. It was a woman named Cassita, one of the regulars. To hear her sing transported me back in time, back to my teenage years, when I still believed in love. When the song finished we were escorted into another room, which looked like a cozy cabin filled with tourists and real French people. For over 130 years a family of singers has sung traditional French songs every night at this cabaret. We were given a special cherry brandy, or something like it, a few minutes after we arrived. The head singer welcomed us and people sang their hearts out.

After two hours of this I wanted to go home. French is such a beautiful language, almost as beautiful as Spanish, but after an hour it was difficult to remain interested. I pinched myself to stay awake—I didn't want Rosemary to think I was not appreciating French culture at its best. The ensemble of loyal singers would continue until the wee hours of the morning, but Rosemary, who was now beyond tipsy, decided we should go home. I held her arm so she wouldn't go rolling down the hill and tumble down the stairways of concrete. Her cell phone went off; she searched all over herself for it until she finally found it buried in her bra.

"Hello? Rudy? Hey, what's going on? You're serious? When did this happen?" Rosemary hung up and broke down crying. She hugged me, practically falling in my arms.

"What happened? What did he tell you?" I asked delicately.

"My mom . . . she's in the hospital . . . I have to go see her," uttered Rosemary between gasps of emotional breaths.

We took a taxi home because the metro was already closed and it was urgent to get back to the apartment and call for whatever little details would keep Rosemary's hopes alive. Her mother was in the hospital in a coma. She booked the earliest flight she could get and left the next morning for Los Angeles. I should have gone with her on that plane ride back home, but I was a coward and hid out in her tiny room instead.

CHAPTER 4

Bonjour, Carte de Séjour

After two months of living in Paris, I looked out the window and saw snow falling. It was beautiful at first to see snow on the streets of Paris, but then it dawned on me that it really was winter. This was not a California winter, but a real winter requiring scarves and coats and even boots. I walked down Victor Hugo Boulevard past all the shops and was tempted to buy something, but I had promised Rosemary I would never shop on Victor Hugo Boulevard unless it was at the little boutiques that had preowned designer clothes and purses, some located on the rue de la Pompe. She said most of those clothes were worth it because they were worn maybe once, and the designer purses were practically new. Rosemary explained that a lot of those purses belonged to mistresses or call girls who got them as gifts, bought with the same business credit card used to pay for hotels and business expenses. The women in those situations sold them to the boutiques to get fast cash. "Aside from the bad karma, they're good deals."

I got on the metro and took it wherever it took me. When I started seeing African people in traditional African clothes getting on, I assumed I was getting closer to the part of town where immigrants lived. I decided to get off and explore. It was probably cheaper there. Wherever there are immigrants, you know there are bargains just around the corner. I got off on Clichy and walked around the boulevard north of Pigalle, which was packed with inexpensive coats and knockoffs of every type. I bought a black coat. Normally I'd go for a red one, but the truth of it was that I just wanted to hide out. I wanted to be small and invisible if possible. I made my way to another metro stop and an African man wearing traditional Kenyan clothes handed me his business card. He'd looked at my face and figured I needed help. He had been a witch doctor in Kenya and was practicing in Paris. His card said, "Come to me if your husband has left you. I will make him come back to you like a dog." I imagined that scenario. I thought, Yes, but what if he does come back like a dog and ends up drooling on himself and shitting all over your carpet? Maybe if I could ask him to play dead and hide under the sofa until I needed him to mow the lawn that could be a good thing. A large African woman pushed me aside with her fat arms and I snapped back to reality. I was in front of the metro entrance and had to shit or get off the pot because there were people behind me waiting to stick their metro ticket into the ticket machine. I stepped aside and wondered where the hell I should go next. I remembered I still had not been to the top of the Eiffel Tower and thought it was as good as any day to do it . . . Maybe on such a miserable day there would be no line.

There is always a line, unless it is closed, I soon discovered, and waited for half an hour to take the elevator up to the very top. On my way up I saw the Jules Verne restaurant and told myself I would eat there before I left Paris. Who would I eat with? I had no friends in Paris. What if Rosemary never returned? I got off with the rest of the tourists and looked down. It was a long way to fall. There was no way anyone could jump off; it was suicide-proof. I took photos with my digital camera and wanted to ask a Japanese tourist to take my picture.

"Canela? Canela!" someone yelled out from behind me. I turned around and saw a woman I couldn't recognize at first.

"It's me, Margaret. I did the journalism summer workshop back in Los Angeles with you." I smiled, pretending to remember, until her younger face came into focus.

"Yes, now I remember your face . . . What are you doing here? Are you visiting Paris?"

"No, I live here. I've been living here for the past year," Margaret announced.

"What do you do?" I asked.

"I just finished cooking school. I got my diploma in cuisine and pastries just last week from Le Coq Rouge." She announced this proudly, as if awaiting some kind of applause.

"I thought you wanted to be a journalist," I reminded her.

"I did," she answered, sounding a little annoyed, "but I was tired of the bullshit with the editors. I couldn't write the stories I wanted to write, so I said, 'Fuck that.'" I quickly recalled all the fights with my editors over stories too controversial to publish, like my piece on the Latina immigrant mothers in the barrio whose sons were the first to die in Iraq. I remembered my interview with the Guatemalan immigrant mother about the loss of her son José Antonio Gutierrez, the very first soldier to die there. He'd signed up to go to war so he could get a green card.

"You lost your objectivity," my editor had said, claiming that was the reason he had prevented my story from being printed.

"What do you mean?" I'd replied, trying not to lose my temper.

"The fact that you're an immigrant completely paints this article in an unbalanced manner," he'd informed me.

"You don't think I can be objective," I'd asked carefully, "because I'm an immigrant?"

"Yes. It's clear that you can't. You're too emotionally involved. You should be a columnist, but I can't have you doing this. I'm taking you off the story." He'd said it matter-of-factly, not even looking at me.

"You do that and I quit," I'd threatened.

A woman in a wedding dress walked past me now, on a photo shoot, and I was brought back to reality. Margaret had been talking all along and I caught the last of her sentence.

". . . so I decided to take a year off and come live my dream," she confided with a smile of satisfaction.

"That's really wonderful that you had the courage to just go for it," I offered, trying to make up for my previous annoying comment.

"I figured, you only live once. I always wanted to live in Paris, and I met a wonderful man in cooking school who proposed to me. We're going back to the States to start a restaurant together."

"You actually met him in cooking school?" I pictured them frying up eggs together like idiots in love.

"Yeah, isn't that romantic? I was totally not looking for love and we just happened to be in the same cooking group, directly across from each other, and something about the way he cut his onions got me." We laughed. I was curious about what she had to do to stay in France for a year to attend cooking school.

"If you pay for the whole course, the school will get you a *carte de séjour* for a year."

"A what?" I asked.

"A *carte de séjour*," she said, overpronouncing it. "A card to stay—like a visa." Margaret gave me her cell phone number and told me to call her if I needed anything, but added that she was leaving in a week. I wished her well and wondered why I had run into her, of all people. I guess the Eiffel Tower is the center of the world; you're bound to run into someone from your past.

Back at my building, I was about to step into the elevator when an older woman in a designer suit with large pearls around her neck said something in French. She was well kept and impeccably dressed. These Frenchwomen don't know how to get fat and age properly. Since I did not respond, she asked me in English where I was going. I explained to her that I was going to the sixth floor.

"You must take ze other elevator," she explained. "Ziz elevator is for za people who live here, not za servants." I was about to explain that I wasn't a servant and that my situation was different, but I assumed she didn't speak enough English to understand and didn't care to know my situation. I went behind the main elevator and took the dirty servants' elevator. Rosemary had explained to me that because she had been there awhile, the residents didn't mind her taking the regular elevator, but since I looked like an Arab to this woman I'd immediately been rendered a servant. Everyone in Paris thought I was an Arab. Even the Arab taxi drivers would speak to me in Arabic and were shocked to discover I was Mexican. I didn't bother telling them I was Mexican-American because that tends to confuse people in Paris; even Americans got confused.

Earlier that morning, I had stared at the calendar and counted the days I had left before I'd be considered undocumented once again, in another country. Growing up, I was what people called an "illegal alien." I didn't know I was undocumented, because my parents had told me not to tell anyone I had no papers; I'd just assumed they meant toilet paper or something innocent like that. Then, when I was a teenager and needed to think about college, I discovered I didn't have the right papers to apply. Although I was undocumented and could be deported at any time, I thought it impossible because my parents were both legal residents. It was due to a technicality that I was without papers. Eventually my father applied for citizenship, and my siblings and I were able to obtain residency right in time to qualify for financial aid and attend college.

When I got out of the servants' elevator, a woman was already there, waiting for it. Our eyes met and she feigned a smile. She said, *"Bonjour"* with a Spanish-accented pronunciation.

"Habla español?" I asked her. She stopped and smiled with a real light behind her eyes.

"Sí, sí. ¿De dónde es usted?" She asked me where I was from because I certainly wasn't Colombian like her. I told her I was Mexican and that I was Rosemary's friend, staying in her *chambre de bonne*. She explained to me that she was Colombian, from a town just south of Medellín. I gave her the short version of how my family had migrated from a town north of Mexico City to Los Angeles. She explained to me that she was in Paris with her two daughters and had been in France for six years *sans papiers*. I asked her why she'd come to France instead of the United States like most Latin American immigrants. She explained that many years ago Spain did not require a visa from people from Colombia. They came in via Spain and, once in the European Union, they were able to take the train and make their way into France. Why not stay in Spain, where they speak Spanish and life will be a little easier? I asked her. She explained that she had relatives in France already and France is a richer country than Spain.

"There are a lot of Colombians in Paris," she informed me. She was so tempted to move to Levallois, where most of them resided, but she did not want to lose her *chambre de bonne* and her part-time job on the third floor, with an American couple with two children. She asked me about Rosemary and I told her about her mother and her trip to Los Angeles. I had not heard anything from Rosemary in over a month. I didn't want to call and bother her at a time like this, but I was hoping she would call me soon.

"Bueno pues. *Je m'appelle Marina, et vous?*" she said in Spanish and French. I looked at her funny and she quickly understood that I didn't speak French. She sympathized and said that after six years she could only speak it a little, but could understand it a lot.

"You have to speak French here, or no work," she said in Spanish. We said our good-byes and she added that if I needed anything to knock on her door, Apartment D. I wondered who my other sixth-floor neighbors were. Since I didn't speak French I would have to play face and gestures with them, but they didn't need to know me. I didn't even know how to introduce myself. Would I be able to gesture "Hi, I'm from the U.S., but I hate the U.S. right now, so I'm here and I don't know what I am doing with my life or why I don't want to get married. Nice to meet you"? I went into my room and shut the door.

The next day I had to go get groceries and a copy of Hemingway's *A Moveable Feast.* Just because I was depressed and suicidal didn't mean I shouldn't catch up on my reading. I got on the metro and got off at Concorde and crossed the street. A French police officer was walking back and forth in front of a police barricade; I looked over and saw the American consulate. I walked on the rue de Rivoli past souvenir shops and countless tourists looking for or leaving the Louvre and continued down the archways to the English bookstore. As soon as I walked in, I heard American English being spoken, but soon the beautiful sounds of my language were interrupted by an Englishman searching for Voltaire. He was directed to the French classics and headed down that aisle. I know the British invented the English language, but living in America, I'd forgotten that we didn't; we're the ones with the accent; we're the ones that talk funny; we're the outsiders. I realized that my unconscious mind had just assumed we Americans invented everything—everything except the Eiffel Tower. I hadn't realized how Americentric I was until I'd left the States.

I walked down the aisles and got to the *H*'s. All of Hemingway's books were there in paperback, including numerous copies of *A Moveable Feast*. I wasn't original, going to Paris and pretending I was Hemingway . . . So what that I was a journalist . . . I wasn't an alcoholic . . . yet. I had read *A Moveable Feast* back in high school, when I was taking French. Of course I could have taken Spanish to get an easy A, like so many Mexican students, but I'd actually thought that I was going to go to France and would use the French I learned. Why had it taken me more than ten years to finally get here? I'd been busy trying to save the world; but the Mother Teresa in me needed "a holiday," as the British say.

I walked closer to the cashier and saw a bookshelf filled with nothing but memoirs of Americans living in Paris. There is a tradition of Americans living in Paris and doing all the things they couldn't do in their own country. African-American men came to Paris at the turn of the century because here they didn't experience the discrimination they were subject to at home. They could play their music and have sex with Frenchwomen without being imprisoned or lynched. Countless female writers came to Paris because they could rent an apartment on their own without a husband's signature. Imagine what life was like back then, when you needed a husband to exist in society, I told myself. So what can I do here that I can't do in my own country?

I ended up buying a book on how to live and thrive in Paris, along with the Hemingway book. I had considered getting a book by F. Scott Fitzgerald just to keep my Hemingway book company, but I had to start thinking about money. I had saved up to help out Armando with the down payment on a house. He said I should hold on to my money because he could afford the down payment by himself. I didn't feel right having him pay for everything. He was such a nice guy . . . Now, don't ask me why I called off the wedding . . . My mother has her theories, but none of them come close. I can tell you what I think, but I really can't say I know. It's just a feeling. Kind of a journalist's instinct I have when I'm interviewing someone and something in my gut tells me it's not the truth. Truth is a feeling swimming in my solar plexus, brushing up against my arms, caressing me under my cheeks.

I stepped outside the bookstore and I was back in Paris again; now it was raining. A rainy day in Paris is beautiful, like a postcard, when someone is there sharing an umbrella with you. But when you feel like the only person in the world who doesn't speak French and doesn't have an umbrella, it feels like a giant dog peeing on you. I walked over to a café and tried ordering in French. The waiter interrupted me as I was butchering his language and guessed exactly what I wanted. At least I didn't ask for a Coke, I thought. I went to great lengths not to be the "Ugly American"; it was exhausting trying to be a decent person in a city where people were not so pretty to you. Rosemary had defended the French, being an unapologetic Francophile. "It's not that they are rude, it's just that Paris is the city with the most tourists, and Parisians get tired of them," she'd said. "Also, all those tourists go home and tell their friends and then the stereotype gets perpetuated. I remember people being rude to me in Los Angeles," she'd added as evidence.

I looked around me and knew that if I ever wanted to graduate from being a tourist I would have to learn French. I've already told you why I didn't learn French and how I am cursed, but there was no way around it. I hated when people criticized my parents for not knowing and speaking English. I would tell them that my parents worked manual-labor jobs and came home exhausted to their ten children and the idea of going to night school to learn English was too much for them. After my mother was done with her day she would turn into a zombie and watch telenovelas and escape into lands where women like her got the fairy tale and not the ten kids. I, however, had to learn French. But what would be the best way? A lot of these language schools were so expensive, and they don't give you a *carte de séjour*. I can only stay here for another three weeks before I have to go, I reminded myself.

In the middle of the night I got a phone call from Rosemary. She had been in the U.S. for almost two months, but I'd only heard from her once. I'd wanted to call her, but figured she was probably overwhelmed, so I'd waited patiently.

"I'm not coming back," Rosemary confessed, waking me up out of whatever dream of serenity I was having. She explained how her mother had died and she was so devastated. At the funeral she ran into an ex-boyfriend—not the one who'd brought her to France, but a high school sweetheart, who won her over by being at her mother's funeral. She cried for two weeks and he stood by her side and was devoted to her at her most vulnerable moments. Rosemary realized that she still loved him, and they had gotten engaged.

"You'll return to the U.S. in December for my wedding, won't you?" she asked me.

"Yes, of course," I told her. "I'll be there, I promise." What else could I say? Someday I would have to go back and face my mother and my family, as well as the fact that I would be thirty and unmarried. I hated all those stupid Hollywood stories about women turning twenty-nine and immediately their life was on a timer that eventually would ring, setting off the biological clock that would cause them to explode if they didn't turn it off by dropping an egg and producing a fetus. "God, what a terrible trick you played on modern women," I said out loud, staring up at the ceiling. I hated those stories, what clichés, how typical, how Hollywood . . . how painful. You don't know how it hurts to be soooo single when you're Mexican-American and your five sisters are already married with kids and everyone in your family wonders what the hell happened to you that you can't get your life together.

It seemed all around me my girlfriends had betrayed me. It felt like this was going to be yet another big personal deadline I would miss. All my girlfriends had met the societal demand of thirty, when supposedly you stop being a girl and you get engaged and finally become a woman by getting married. I remembered all the ideals Luna, Rosemary, and Margaret had had about what a woman's life should be: not just "a room of one's own" but a life of one's own. But then twenty-nine came and the ideals were thrown out the window, along with the dirty-girl purse with the multiple fiesta-colored condoms and the prewritten "Dear One-night Stand" letters.

Rosemary asked me to ship her belongings to her parents' address and told me I could keep the *chambre de bonne* for as long as I wanted by paying her rent. I told her I was glad for her that she'd found love at such a difficult time.

"You deserve all the wonderful things in life to happen to you," I said and began crying.

"Are you crying?" she asked me.

"Yes, I'm just so happy for you," I replied, covering up the fact that I was reminded once again of how wrong Armando and I were for each other. The kind of joy that came out of her was so inspiring that I knew I'd never felt that kind of delight talking about being engaged with Armando.

Rosemary wished me luck in Paris and gave me a couple of phone numbers of American girlfriends and a French friend or two who were actually open to making new friends. According to Rosemary, the typical French person won't let you be her friend until after ten years of knowing you.

"If they didn't meet you in elementary school, they are not interested in getting to know you now," Rosemary had once informed me, explaining why French people were more genuine than Americans. "You see, in the U.S., everybody calls you a friend and smiles at you like they have known you forever, but when you really need them they act like they don't know you. But the French don't ever smile or call you a friend unless they mean it." I considered this and realized that, although I loved authenticity and people being direct with me, in these circumstances when I felt so vulnerable and fragile and completely alone, I would prefer people who smiled at me and didn't like me than people who didn't like me and therefore didn't smile. Yeah, okay, call me a hypocrite. Or an American.

I contemplated the phone numbers long after Rosemary had hung up, and stared at the peeling paint on the ceiling. After a few minutes of following the cracks in the ceiling I looked down and noticed a poster of Anaïs Nin. It had a quote about how your life expands depending on your courage. I stared at this Frenchwoman who'd had an extraordinary life and wondered, If I were Anaïs Nin, what would I do? *I would go have sex with a stranger* was the answer I got back. Okay, if I were Hemingway, what would I do? *I'd kick the shit out of somebody, wrestle a bear, or shoot myself.* So if I were me, I asked myself as a joke, what would I do? *Go to cooking school* was the answer that came back at me, and I had to laugh. I laughed so hard I cried. I cried because I missed my mother. Cooking always reminded me of my mother. Actually, lard reminded me of my mother, but I'm not ready to talk about that yet. She was my first source of food, so my brain automatically referenced her even though I had specifically instructed it to bury all thoughts of her in the back of the closet holding all the painful memories, the ones that only come out when you're really drunk and you've puked everything up and all that is left inside you are the vile, bitter memories.

I had considered calling my mother, but emotionally I was not ready to answer any of her questions. The first thing she would ask me was "Where are you and what are you doing?" I would respond, "I'm in Paris . . . having an existential crisis." That would be my honest answer, but she'd probably reply, "In Paris doing what pendejada?" *Pendejada* means idiotic or moronic or whatever colorful insult mothers can think up that they assume would help their daughters understand what idiots they are. Women of my mother's generation were not allowed to have an existential crisis; you had to be rich and childless to afford to have one. She would not be sympathetic, although she could appreciate the fact that she and my father worked so hard to afford me the opportunity to have an existential crisis. If she were not so embarrassed about my breakup with Armando and my nasty fight with my Tía Bonifacia at the wake, I could see her bragging about my existential crisis in Paris to her comadres at the local beauty salon.

So what was I going to do? Would I keep this room and live in Paris and ditch my apartment in L.A., with all my belongings, or would I go back? I looked around for answers, automatically opening the fridge to get food. I noticed Rosemary's rotting cheese. Since she wasn't coming back, I could finally get rid of it. I stared at the cheese; it looked all disfigured, like a dead rat whose insides had imploded. Poor cheese, I thought. I cleaned the sink and washed my dirty dishes and started to laugh at the thought of cooking school. Then I recalled my sisters laughing at me when I tried making a cream-cheese-and-salsa dip that ended up looking like vomit. I'd be the first to admit it was worse-looking than vomit, but I'd felt so tiny in their eyes. The fact that I was a very intelligent, educated, accomplished, and competent woman who could not make a simple dip was just so hilarious to them. This was the sign that although I could compete with men, I failed as a woman because I couldn't do the most basic thing, like make dip. That was the last time I'd attempted to do anything related to food. As a journalist always on deadline, I considered food simply fuel and not the meaning of life. I saw a movie about a woman chef who had no family, but at the end of the movie she makes a dinner for several passionless people in a tiny village in Denmark and everyone ends up happy and her life has meaning again. I thought how empty her life must have been that making a meal was that important. Just being in Paris for two and a half months had made me see that, for the French, spending more than two hours on a meal and spending another three in the grocery store and in the kitchen gave meaning to their thirty-five-hour work-week. *Life is food; food is life* was a thought that flowed out of the river of my stream of consciousness.

I flashed back to the past and relived that moment, but this time I had prepared a fancy French appetizer. This time everyone was impressed that I could do such a thing, and they didn't laugh because they were too busy trying to say *foie gras* or *terrine* or some other difficult-to-pronounce dish. Hmm, how would my life have been different? I wondered. Then I flashed to the future and imagined myself, having already graduated from the most famous cooking school, as that woman in that food movie making a feast for my repressed and passionless family. Of course a repressed and passionless Mexican-American family will look like a very passionate and enthusiastic WASP family . . . so I prepare this amazing meal and not only am I an amazing journalist, but I can also cook. Now I am complete. I am competent and capable like a man, and sensual and creative like a woman.

Yes, it was a silly fantasy, but it was the best thing I could think of for now. Maybe if I learned how to cook I could transform my relationship to food. I could look at food as food and eat for plea-sure and, like Frenchwomen, not get fat. Maybe I could finally lose these twenty pounds I keep losing and gaining. It would be easier to tell people back home that I went to Paris to study cui-sine than to tell them the truth: that I left to get away from my neurotic mother and kill time until I could figure out what to do with my life . . . or end my life.

Yeah, I could go to cooking school, get my *carte de séjour,* and hang out in France for a year cooking, becoming a food connois-seur, and learning French. At the very least I could become a food critic to make a living. "Okay, I have a plan!" I celebrated. Though I still couldn't call my mother and share my plan because her laughter would crush me.

CHAPTER 5

Le Coq Rouge

I got off the metro and couldn't find the Le Coq Rouge building. I studied my map and, after a few tries, I broke down and asked for directions. I'm like a guy when it comes to directions: I can do it on my own! But I didn't want to be late for my appointment. Finally, a retired man with a beret was nice enough to pay attention to me and point. I found the building and realized that I had passed it many times, but the big red rooster on the window had made me think it was a rotisserie instead of the cooking school. Then, like a big ol' dummy, I went, Oh—*le coq rouge* means the red rooster, the national symbol of France. Somebody please kick me. I went to the front counter and waited as the receptionist spoke to a short American girl with a ponytail who looked like she had just graduated from high school.

"You must fuckus," said the receptionist with a thick French accent. The American girl's ponytail practically stood up, but she stared at the receptionist, not sure what she meant.

"What do you mean?" she inquired delicately.

"Fuckus, fuckus—you know: pay more attention." The receptionist said it louder in her best English and leaned forward to make her point.

"You mean *fo*-cus." The short American girl overpronounced the word to help the receptionist avoid making Americans blush. "Yes, I have trouble with that. I have a doctor's note explaining why I can't focus," she continued, expecting some sympathy, but the receptionist turned her attention away from the girl and asked me if I had an appointment. I nodded and she pointed me to a hallway. I walked past an opened door of a demonstration room with a chef chopping up vegetables before a class of about fifty students, all watching in awe. I continued down the hallway to a tiny courtyard where other foreigners like me waited for their tour. After a few minutes, a representative in a stylish red suit welcomed us in several languages. The woman looked like a Latina and spoke English with a Latin American accent I could not place. She told us how Le Coq Rouge was one of the oldest and most prestigious cooking schools in the world. She pointed at a bronze emblem that stated the date of establishment, in case we didn't believe her.

"Graduating from this school is an accomplishment that automatically tells your future employer you are serious about being a chef," she bragged. She also emphasized the fact that enrolling in cooking school in Paris was the dream of so many people around the world, but only a few special people got to accomplish that dream. Would we be one of those lucky people? Although this was supposed to be the Harvard of cooking schools, the building was tiny and I noticed a few paint cracks in the courtyard, covered up by small palms that needed to be tended to. She took us quickly to the demonstration rooms and the kitchens. There were kitchens with up to fourteen students per class, divided into three levels: Basic, Intermediate, and Superior. She explained how it was possible to get your diploma in both pastry and cuisine or in just one.

I raised my hand. "Are the classes only in French?" I asked.

"They are all in French, but there is an English translator for Basic and Intermediate Cuisine. If you take Superior you must be able to understand French to graduate from this school. But if you start taking French now you will be able to understand by the time you take Superior Cuisine." She smiled after her canned reply.

After the tour we were all handed fancy red folders with the prices and dates. She ended the tour by inviting us to a buffet of food the students in catering had just made. I approached her and told her I was interested in enrolling. She walked me over to the admissions agent, who gave me several forms to fill out.

"Congratulations on your decision," Marie-Hélène, the admissions agent, assured me in her French-accented English.

I asked her to calculate the price for me in dollars and my eyes went blind for a few seconds. My God, I thought, I could be going to Harvard for a year for the price I'm paying at this school. Yeah, but you really can't brag about going to Harvard for just one year, like you can about going to Paris and studying cuisine and getting a diploma in a year. So I'm paying for bragging rights. I can live with that. I asked her if I could pay with a credit card and she said only half of it could be paid that way. I asked her if they would take foreign checks and she said only wire transfers. I filled out all the paperwork; as soon as my wire transfer came in, I would be officially enrolled. She asked me if I wanted to start right away or wait the eight weeks until the next class.

"I can't wait eight weeks; by then I'll have been here for over three months. I need a *carte de séjour*," I confided in her.

"Then you have to start next week so we can start the process for your *carte de séjour*. You're very lucky there is an opening. We just had an American student drop out this morning from the Intensive Basic Cuisine."

"The Intensive?"

"The class I'm enrolling you in is the Intensive Basic Cuisine. It's not the normal class; it's a fast-paced class. You do in five weeks what you would normally do in ten." I stared at her for a few seconds, clutching my application.

"Are you ready to begin your exciting culinary career?" Marie-Hélène asked, trying to reassure me that I was making the right decision. I stared blankly up at her, not believing what I was about to do. I handed over my application, and she quickly snatched it before I had a chance to change my mind.

My little sister Rosie was the only person I trusted to help me with the wire transfer. I would tell her it was money to pay for a journalism course or whatever, and she would send it without asking more questions. My mother must be psychic, because she just happened to be visiting Rosie and was next to the phone when I called.

"So where are you and what are you doing?" she fired at me before I had a chance to disguise my voice and ask for my little sister.

"I'm in Paris . . . and I'm going to be here working until the end of the year," I blurted out.

"¿Estas loca? This is crazy. You will regret passing up Armando. He loves you and he's a doctor. I know you couldn't care less about your future, thinking you'll always be beautiful and young, pero m'ija, life happens to everyone and you're not going to have your health and your good looks forever."

"I know—" I started to defend myself, but she cut me off.

"No, you don't know. If you finally get married, I won't have to worry about you anymore. Now I'll be stressed out even more with you in another country. Come back now!" she demanded, and like a little kid I hung up the phone. I called my little sister on her cell and saved myself the guilt trip.

On the first day of class I arrived at Le Coq Rouge forty-five minutes early by miscalculation and was embarrassed to let anybody see me being so anxious. I walked up to reception, where the welcoming committee was already present, taking names and passing out large folders. A short woman with red hair named Sélange handed me a folder. "Welcome to Le Coq Rouge. These are your recipes," she said, pointing me to the demonstration room on the first floor. I went in and observed all the Japanese students already there, going over the rules and filling out their paperwork. I sat down at the front and looked at all the incoming students. The roster had the names of the fourteen students taking the course and their countries of origin: Holland, Brazil, Korea, Hong Kong, Mexico, Portugal, and of course the United States.

I opened my book and saw there were over ninety recipes. Each lesson was one appetizer or salad, a main dish, and a dessert. All the names of the dishes were in French, but also translated into English. As I went through the recipes I heard Armando telling me he was happy with the menu for our wedding reception. I had told him it wasn't so exotic and interesting. He'd begged me to tame my choices for the sake of his family. I'd gotten him to admit that his mother thought I was too wild to make a good mother. We were opposites and that was great for a while, but after we argued over the menu I knew it was over. Armando was a MAP, a Mexican-American Prince—educated, accomplished, polished, cultured, and loved his mother; but that was the problem. He was a trophy husband, and I needed something meatier. He looked good on the menu, but he wasn't a dish I wanted to order for life. Yeah, it was the menu. His culinary choices were limited to beef and potatoes and I needed something colorful and delicious. I desired one marriage and he wanted another. After the argument I began to go through the motions of a relationship, but eventually I just had to be the courageous one to put a stop to the whole thing. My mother thought it was her fault that I wasn't married; she complained to me about my father too much and knew she ruined my picture of men for the rest of my life. That's partly true, though if I were a man and afraid of commitment, nobody would hassle me about it. But because I have a vagina and healthy eggs, I was constantly put on the fryer for all my choices about the men I dated.

Sélange walked in, along with all the female administrative staff, and welcomed us once again. All the women introduced themselves, including the receptionist, who introduced herself as Françoise, at our service. The fifty-something students from mostly First World countries, or from rich families of poor countries, applauded. Finally the head chef of the school introduced himself as Renault Sauber, a white-haired Robin Williams without all the body hair. He welcomed us in every language he knew and told us that although there was a lot of work ahead we would have fun; he would make sure of it.

Sélange reminded us that it was now time to sign the agreement to the rules and to hand them to her when we were done. There was to be no smoking out in front of the school or lounging around and sitting on cars. There was to be no saving seats and no walking around with knives pointed during cooking sessions. A student could have no more than four absences in order to receive a diploma, and we were required to wear special shoes with metal tips, in case we dropped a knife on our toes, plus a complete uniform; otherwise we would not be allowed to enter the kitchen—or, as we would call it from now on, the practical room. I signed the agreement and for a second my heart jumped out and said, What the hell are you doing in a kitchen? Get out! I handed in my agreement and there was no turning back. Seconds later the schedules were handed out and it was explained to us how the color coding worked: Basic Cuisine was red and we had three classes a day, amounting to nine hours every day. Saturdays would only be two classes, a demonstration followed by a practical. A practical class was the opportunity to experiment, mess up, and get advice or get yelled at by the chefs.

Françoise passed out a flyer announcing the "Get to know your classmates" gathering Friday night at an English pub. Someone complained that they wouldn't go because they were in Group B and had a Saturday morning class at eight-thirty A.M.

When all our paperwork had been turned in we were escorted to the courtyard, where we were each handed a uniform, a lock for the locker, a professional knife kit, a weight scale, a mesh bag, and plastic containers in which to transport our cooked food. After we collected all our new belongings the women descended to the basement to the women's locker room and the men climbed up to the men's locker room. I raced down to the basement to be one of the first to get a locker. I blamed the fact that I had nine siblings for my competitive spirit. When I was growing up, Friday evenings were very stressful, because that's when my parents bought groceries for the whole week. That's when the good food arrived: the fruit, the desserts, the tasty stuff I assumed rich people had every day. In our house, if you didn't stuff yourself with the good food or strategically hide the Twinkies, pan dulce, or apples under the iceberg lettuce, come Monday you were stuck eating Spanish rice and beans for breakfast, lunch, and dinner the rest of the week.

I rushed over to a corner of the locker room with a nook that allowed for privacy and space. There was even a chair near to the top locker I chose. The American girl with the ponytail arrived behind me and asked me if the locker next to mine was taken.

"No, that one is not taken," I assured her. I quickly changed into my uniform but had trouble putting on my red tie. I was about to ask the American girl if she knew how, but I saw she was having trouble opening the plastic bag to get her uniform out. I stuck out my hand and introduced myself.

"Hi. My name is Canela. I'm from Los Angeles."

"My name is Basil, but you can call me Bassie. I'm from Connecticut," she said, shaking my hand and half-looking at me. I tried stuffing my things into the tiny locker and then decided to bring everything with me, just in case I needed it. I struggled past the aisle filled with half-naked women attempting to make their uniforms look better than white-and-red potato sacks.

I walked into the demonstration room again and sat in the center seat in the front row. If I didn't sit in the front, my mind would wander to dimensions unknown to me. Throughout my schooling I would get lost in fantastic adventures until my teachers called out my name and dragged me back down to my boring reality.

I waited a few minutes, and the thirteen other students in Basic Cuisine entered the room and scattered themselves throughout. Chef Sauber walked in, and his male assistant brought in a tray with vegetables. The English interpreter sat on a stool to the left of the chef. He introduced himself as Henry from London, and reminded us that both the Basic and the Intermediate Cuisine classes would be translated, but the Superior Cuisine course would not be translated.

"Hint, hint: learn French by the time you get to Superior or all this will sound like Greek," Henry advised us. Henry was not great-looking, but he had a scruffy, lovable feel to him that made you forget he had suitcases packed for a long holiday under his eyes. Chef Sauber got in front of a stove with a giant mirror above it, angled so that everyone could see the burners and counter where he was going to demonstrate his cooking techniques. Chef Sauber welcomed us and told us he was responsible for the Basic Cuisine class.

"Zis is how you tie it," he said in his accented English, demonstrating how we were to fold our table napkin–looking thing and wrap it around our neck like a man's tie. The students copied him, almost everyone getting it down except for Bassie and a Japanese woman sitting next to me. Chef Sauber opened his knife kit, which included several knives and small tools. He explained how every knife had its special use. Our kit included a cleaver, chef's knife, slicing knife, boning knife, serrated knife, small paring knife, carving knife, and sharpening steel. Chef Sauber demonstrated which knife was to be used for cutting meat and which was for the fish. A few tools specific to pastry were also part of the kit. He picked up his sharpening steel, just like the one in our kits, and told us it wasn't that great, but it did the job. He confided that if we still had money left we should get a real knife sharpener. Chef Sauber sharpened his knife and reiterated that we must never walk around with a knife pointed outward because in a kitchen with lots of people running about it was very dangerous. He advised us to mark our knives with nail polish or a permanent marker because everyone had the same equipment and it would be easy to misplace our tools.

Today's lesson would be simple. He was going to demonstrate which pans and casseroles to use for what purpose; then we would learn to make stocks and a vegetable soup.

The first stock we would be taught was chicken stock. Stock is the strained liquid that results from cooking bones. It's the basis of most sauces and it's what gives dishes extra flavor and juice. Chicken stock is made up of a pound and a half of chicken bones, with two cups of mixed vegetables that include onion, celery, and carrots roughly chopped. You boil the vegetables in six quarts of water and throw in two garlic cloves, six peppercorns, and a bouquet garni.

"The bouquet garni is a French chef's little secret," confided Chef Sauber as he lovingly wrapped thyme and bay leaf together with celery and parsley and put them inside a leek as if it was a miniature taco. He tied up the leek taco with cooking string, leaving a long, loose end, and turned it into a bouquet. "This is what truly gives the stocks and sauces flavor," translated Henry.

Today would be a short and easy day, to give us time to take in all the information. Making rustic soup was an opportunity to learn to cut vegetables.

Chef Sauber turned on the electric burners and explained that all the stoves in the school were electric for safety reasons. He warned us against leaving pans on the burners after we had turned them off, because even though they were turned off it would take an average of ten minutes to cool down—or to heat up to the assigned number. He advised us to set up our system in a way where the hotter settings on the burner would be in the front and anything left simmering for a while could be placed farther away from us. But we could do it however we wanted to, as long as we didn't burn our food. He assured us that almost anything in cuisine could be corrected except for burning something. He told us, "Cuisine is more of an art, and pastry is more of a science. In pastry you have to get all the details and steps right or things don't rise."

Chef Sauber grabbed a tray of uncut vegetables and picked out a celery stalk. He demonstrated for us how to set up the *planchette*—a plastic cutting board—by getting a paper towel and wetting it and placing it under the *planchette* to secure it to the counter.

"We will be cutting vegetables in four different ways," translated Henry. "The proper way to cut and the technique we prefer to teach is one in which you fold your fingertips in and the knife barely touches the back side of the fingers. When the knife comes down it slides alongside the back of the fingers and the knife is permitted to move forward only by the back side of the fingers. That's how I can look away and not cut myself." Chef Sauber looked up at us and cut quickly, showing off his technique. Everyone oohed and aahed, like children watching a magician.

"*Mirepoix* is a mixture of vegetables cut into large dice, used mostly for aromatic flavor. For our soup we will be cutting our vegetables in two ways: *brunoise* and *paysanne*. *Brunoise* is cutting vegetables into two centimeters and *paysanne* is cutting vegetables into sticks or triangles, then thinly slicing them into three-centimeter segments." Henry translated effortlessly while checking me out. I looked away, trying to take legible notes. You would think that since I was a journalist my handwriting and note-taking abilities would be developed, but I was having trouble keeping up and understanding my own writing.

Chef Sauber toasted slices of baguette and put them on a small platter next to the soup in a large soup bowl.

"*Et voilà!*" the chef announced as he finished his demonstration. Everyone applauded. A few of the students got up and took pictures of the soup. The soup was then taken away by the assistant and distributed into tiny paper cups for everyone to have a *dégustation*—a taste. I drank from the cup and tasted the magnificent soup.

It was now lunchtime, and we were allowed one hour to eat. I wandered around the neighborhood. I didn't know the Fifteenth Arrondissement very well, so I walked for a while, until I came across a tiny boutique shop that looked like a café. I was about to go in but I saw no customers. I was also not confident that my signs and gestures would get me a nice lunch. There were shelves all along the walls, but instead of books there were wine bottles.

On a few of the walls were paintings of green and red grapes and maps of all the wine regions in France. At the very far end sat a man reading *Le Monde* and drinking a glass of wine. Later I would come to know the owner as Jérôme, a former businessman who got burnt out and started this wine bar, called C'est Ma Vie, to bring knowledge of wine and joy to his customers. I decided that on another day, when I was brave or had a friend who could speak French, I would return.

After lunch I went to my locker to put away my purse. I put on my little red cap, which had a tip higher on one side and made us look like roosters. Perhaps a bit more sophisticated than that, but you get the idea.

I looked at my schedule and tried to make sense of where our practical class was supposed to take place. I went to the large practical room and recognized no one from my class. An American woman with auburn hair told me our class was across the hall. The big practical room was only for the fourteen pastry students in the Intensive course.

"What group are you in?" she asked, being friendly. I looked at my schedule and I still could not figure it out. It was either Group A or B, so I lied and said, "A" until I could confirm which group I was really in.

I walked across the hall and saw two students in what I believed was my group. I was the third student to arrive. Punctuality was so important that you had to arrive at least twenty minutes before the chef got there to look like you knew what the hell you were doing. The other two students had already settled themselves in, picking the ideal spaces of the tiny kitchen: next to the two tiny sinks at each end of the room. I settled myself next to the guy closest to the door. We opened our tool kits and took out our knives and stirring spoon. A Korean woman with a name too complicated for me to pronounce set up across from me. I could tell this wasn't her first time cooking because she took out her knives and everything she needed quickly and without hesitation. I smiled at her and knew if I got lost she would be the woman to trail behind. Six more students arrived soon after, and Bassie stationed herself next to the Korean woman and looked at her tools as though she were about to have a philosophical discussion with Sartre.

Sartre could have written *No Exit* about the tiny kitchen in Le Coq Rouge with fourteen students all about to make one another's life hell for the next five weeks. But why jump ahead of the story?

A Brazilian woman named Janeira with large Chanel eyeglasses set up camp next to me. She wasn't late, but she complained about how the waiter at the restaurant had taken forever to bring her the bill and caused her to almost be late. We all pretended to listen, but no one cared. I looked around to see who was smiling out of nervousness and who really knew what they were about to jump into. It's just soup, how hard can it be? I thought.

Just then the chef entered. He was not Chef Sauber. He was Chef Frédérique—in his thirties, tall, slim, juicy, just the way I like my fish. He introduced himself with a simple *"Bonjour"* and asked, *"Qui sont les assistants?"* Everyone looked at one another, not sure what he meant. We looked around for the translator and quickly realized the practical classes would not be translated. He made a comment in French and then asked a question. I couldn't tell what he was saying, but when he raised his voice at the end of his sentence I could tell he was asking a question. Only the real French speakers responded. The Brazilian woman said she had not been told anything. A tall and athletic American guy with red hair named Rick responded that they had not been informed, but he would volunteer to get the supplies for our practice. Chef Frédérique said the assistants are usually in alphabetical order. The Brazilian woman sighed and went down to the basement, where the kitchen of the school was located, along with the freezers and the stockroom. Rick informed us that assistants were chosen in alphabetical order, so we all announced our last names; I said, "Guerrero." It was soon discovered that Bassie was the assistant this week along with Janeira. Chef Frédérique, who spoke hardly any English, advised us to get all our pans ready and sharpen our knives while we waited for the supplies. Rick automatically became the translator for Chef Frédérique. Chef Frédérique commended him for his near-perfect French pronunciation and Rick explained that he'd gone to a French school back in New York City. His mother was a Francophile who wanted her children to also have her love of French culture.

Bassie and Janeira distributed the vegetables to everyone by putting them in metal bowls. Two people across from each other were to share the one bowl with all the ingredients. They left the pot of chicken stock by the sink closest to the elevator, which would be used to bring the trays of ingredients from the basement to the many floors at the school.

I grabbed a carrot and I peeled. I grabbed some celery and I peeled. I looked across to see what the Korean woman was doing. She had already peeled everything and was preparing the bouquet garni. She cut a large piece of cooking string with her paring knife. She was so precise, not afraid of cutting herself. My biggest fear was cutting myself. I was a klutz. I had five scars from knife cuts I'd made on my index finger from the various times I'd tried trimming tree branches back when I was a tomboy.

I cut my carrot into long rectangles and then I tried cutting them into *paysanne* and *brunoise* pieces. Chef Frédérique walked around smiling and telling us we were all doing well. I took my onion and started cutting away. It didn't quite end up looking like the onion Chef Sauber had cut up. Chef Frédérique watched Arthur, a small-framed guy who looked like he was in the closet. He admired the way Arthur handled his onion and commended him on his precision cutting. Chef Frédérique pointed to my onion and said to the class that we shouldn't cut our onion like that. I was the bad example for the class. My jaw dropped in embarrassment and I tried to hide my onion. Seeing my discomfort, he put his hand on my right shoulder and smiled. He winked at me to show me he was only joking.

"*Je plaisante,*" Chef Frédérique said apologetically. I think he meant it, but he probably thought I was a delicate American student who should be treated with soft baking gloves. I didn't know if I should smile or apologize, but he proceeded to massage my back and said, "No problem," in his limited English to put me at ease. When I finally looked up at him with a smile, I continued with my onion and made the best of it. As I cut the onion I fought back the tears. I think I was so moved by his touch because it reminded me of how long it had been since a man had caressed me. At that point it had been at least four months since Armando had had sex with me. He had stopped making love to me a long time before that.

I continued cutting my onion until I couldn't stand my watery eyes. I wiped my eyes and thought to myself, I want to be touched again and again and again.

Just then Janeira screamed. She had cut her finger and had to let everyone know it. The chef pointed to the first-aid kit in the hallway.

I proceeded to remove the ends on the haricots verts. After doing a few green beans I decided to cut off the ends by doing it to the whole bunch at once. This, I thought, was smarter than one by one.

I saw an old onion, partly rotten on one side, abandoned on the marble counter in front of me and looked around to see if it had an owner. Everyone was done cutting his or her onion, it seemed, so I figured it was there for the taking. I cut off the rotten part and was about to cut it in half. I couldn't remember if you were supposed to cut it horizontally, then vertically, or the opposite. I put it back in the center of the counter and figured, It's just soup. Next time I will get it right.

Janeira returned to the practical room with practically her whole hand bandaged. She reached for her onion and inspected it.

"Who did this to my onion?" she demanded, wanting to shed someone else's blood. I was about to say something when Chef Frédérique shot me a look. I kept silent, and we both smiled. I looked down and said nothing. He told Janeira that it didn't matter how the onion was or who did what. She had more than enough onion to finish her soup. Janeira complained in Portuguese, saying how could there be thieves in such a refined school, loud enough so that anyone who understood Spanish or French could figure out what she was saying. I felt so ashamed of myself for messing up my onion, stealing someone else's onion, and then not admitting to it. It reminded me of the times my mother would rub a chile pepper on my mouth for lying and swearing when I was a little girl back in our pueblo in Mexico. She did it so much that I began to love chiles and hot food. My mother stopped doing it when she saw me salivating just before she was going to punish me. She just cursed me by saying, "When you have children, I hope they do the same to you."

I told myself that after we graduated from Basic Cuisine I would confess to Janeira, give her a gift, and apologize to her for taking her onion.

"*Allez, allez,*" Chef Frédérique said to encourage us to work a little faster. The Korean woman asked the chef in French where the soup bowls were located. He went to the pastry practical room and came back with fourteen soup bowls. Everyone grabbed one and a few of the faster students proceeded to fill up the soup bowls and present them on the standard white plates, which they'd found in a cabinet above the sink, next to the cooking wines and spirits.

Another student, Martin, a lanky American with thinning hair, called the chef over and said he was ready. Chef Frédérique went over to him and set up his grading station on the center of the counter between Martin and Bassie. He tasted Martin's soup and said it was *"bonne."* Martin smiled and turned to the side so the chef could inspect his ID badge and get his name right. Chef Frédérique wrote a score in the roster. Martin proceeded to clean up, and then Rick and the Korean woman presented their soups. One by one everyone took his or her plate to the chef. He tasted mine and said it was too salty. I didn't want to admit that I'd added salt and forgotten to taste it. He took a spoon and swirled the soup. He uncovered an haricot vert with the tip still on it. He pointed it out to me and told me to pay attention to all details. I wanted to tell him it was his fault I was distracted. How could I concentrate with a wet vagina? But I saved my excuses and nodded, practically bowing to him after he was done. I turned to my side and he inspected my ID.

"Jolie photo," he said, complimenting my picture. He pronounced my name and asked me where I was from.

"Los Angeles," I said.

"Mais vous êtes méxicaine, n'est-ce pas?" He could tell by my high cheekbones and full lips that I was not really an American —a typical one, that is.

"Oui, Mexique," I replied, trying to sound like I knew enough French to handle a conversation with him.

"Viva México," he cheered. I looked down, trying not to smile too much, and took myself and my mediocre soup out of his presence.

As I washed my knives, I discovered a sore spot on my finger. I'd ended up with a little cut and I didn't know how I'd done it. I hadn't even felt it. I must have put too much pressure on the knife, so much so that I'd torn my skin. I packed my things and saw Bassie struggling with her soup. Janeira would take occasional breaks because her cut was bothering her. I left with a smile, wondering if all the chefs were as delicious as the two that I had seen so far. "One recipe down, twenty-nine more to go," I sighed, hopeful that I had found a new profession.

CHAPTER 6

Like Water for Canela

I sat in the front row again and the Korean woman sat next to me. I introduced myself and she said her name. I still couldn't pronounce it, so she said, "Call me Ale, like ginger ale" and made it easy to remember. The chef's new assistant in the demonstration worked diligently setting up all the vegetables and ingredients. Chef Chocon, a stocky man with a red nose, perhaps from drinking too much, walked in through the door—one reserved exclusively for the chefs—carrying his metal briefcase. He opened his case, took out his tools, and began sharpening his deboning knife, which looked more like a stiletto heel than a knife. *"Bonjour,"* he said to the few students already there, in a high, nasal voice.

He chopped up bones with a cleaver and explained how we would roast the bones in the oven for forty minutes at 450 degrees; add the vegetable *mirepoix,* with the vegetables cut at half an inch halfway through the roasting; and then add water to deglaze. Janeira turned to another student to ask for the quantity of water, but Chef Chocon raised his voice and told her to ask him, not her fellow student, because she could be getting the wrong information. Janeira apologized in French and explained that she hadn't wanted to interrupt him. Chef Chocon explained that he was here for his students, and after working at three-star restaurants, he wanted to be of service to aspiring chefs. That was why he taught at the best cooking school in the world.

Chef Chocon proceeded to cut an onion, first horizontally, then vertically. Got it, I thought. He finely sliced all the onion and put it in a pan with olive oil. We were to make a "tart," translated Henry, but under his breath he said, "It's really just a fancy French pizza." The chef emptied the rest of the oil into the anchovies, throwing the bottle into the garbage.

"You must put the anchovies in milk to help remove the strong taste," translated Henry. Henry muttered, barely audibly, to the front row: "Too bad you can't do the same to women." I looked up and stared at him, unsure he had actually said that. He was glad he'd caught my attention. He smiled at me and winked. I looked away when I realized he was flirting with me. I looked down at my notes. This is going to be a pizza, I thought; so much for gourmet food.

In practical, Bassie was the only one concerned about the steps. She studied her notes carefully and took out her tools. I grabbed my onion and paid attention to the way I cut it this time. I couldn't get fine slices. I looked next to me and instead of Janeira, now the woman from Hong Kong was slicing an onion effortlessly. I'm sure Janeira suspected me and had decided to move to another station rather than risk losing her onion again. I poured olive oil into my pan and warmed up my onions on a slow burner. The smell of onions hit my nostrils and the memory of pulling out onions from the earth massaged my face. The dirt buried itself in my fingernails and the smell of onions on my fingers seemed like it would never, ever go away. I smelled my tiny ten-year-old fingers and asked my mother if the smell would ever fade.

"When we pick a different vegetable, it will go away. Maybe the next vegetable will not be so smelly. Maybe when we move to the city we won't smell like vegetables or dirt anymore," my mother said.

"When will that be?" I asked.

"Someday, when we have picked enough vegetables, we will be able to afford an apartment for all of us." My father came by and told us to stop talking or the rancher might complain and fire us. I shut up and continued pulling out onions.

The chef assigned to our practical entered with a *"Bonjour"* that commanded attention. We all turned to acknowledge him and I was immediately disappointed that it was not Chef Frédérique. Chef Tulipe resembled Santa Claus. He walked around inspecting what we were doing and stopped next to Bassie. He looked her up and down as if wondering if she was even eighteen and allowed to be in the kitchen. Bassie turned away from him and sliced her onions. She cut her finger and quietly exclaimed, "Ah, shit!" to herself. Chef Tulipe took her knife and studied it.

"It's the dull knives that are the most dangerous," Chef Tulipe said in French. He ordered her to sharpen her knives before continuing. Bassie went to the first-aid kit and then to the sink. I walked past her to collect my can of anchovies and asked her if she was okay. She looked up at me with a smile, surprised that I'd noticed. She pretended to be tough and said it was nothing.

I went back to my onions, stirring them and taking in their pungent smell once again. This time I was in my mother's kitchen, during a party.

"Come here and help me with the food," my mother ordered me. I was thirteen and braless. My nipples were barely showing, but I always tried to prove my point.

"No. How come the men aren't in the kitchen? How come

they're drinking beer and laughing and we are in this hot kitchen doing all the work?" I demanded.

"That's the way it is. We cook for the men. Men eat first," my mother said unapologetically and without concern.

"We are not in Mexico anymore," I reminded her.

"Just because we are in Los Angeles doesn't mean you are American. Pay attention to the chiles . . . They are supposed to be roasted, not burnt."

I pulled a chile off the fire and burnt my hand. I yelled, "Ouch," but instead of my mother sympathizing she said, "Ya ves, for not paying attention." She pushed me aside with the roundness of her body and demonstrated how it should be done. She ended up doing all of them by herself.

"You have to do it right or it won't be worth making it. Go peel some garlic."

I peeled garlic and ended up with some of it buried in my nails. She chopped up the garlic and threw it in the pan along with an onion and diced tomatoes. She added rice and made me stir the rice back and forth to roast it. My Tía Lucia came in with a recipe and read it out loud to my mother.

"I got this recipe for mole negro oaxaqueño from my neighbor. We're going to need to buy the chocolate." She left the recipe on the counter next to the stove and I read it while they debated what kind of chocolate to add.

My mother came by and saw that the rice was burning. She slapped my hand so I would pay attention.

"Mira! You're burning the rice! You really are good for nothing." I stirred the rice as if I were slapping her back.

"Stop that!" she commanded again. I continued throwing the rice back and forth; if I wasn't going to get to eat that rice, why should I care if it got burnt? She grabbed the stirring spoon and took it away from me. She pushed me aside with her big hips and told me, "If you are not going to do it with love, then don't do it at all. Get out of my kitchen!" She made a scene and humiliated me in front of all the women at the party. Tía Bonifacia shook her head at me as I grabbed a soda and left the kitchen with my head held high.

I sat next to the men. My father looked at me but didn't say anything. None of the men spoke to me, and I didn't eat mole that day. I had gotten very sick the first time I'd had red mole, when I was five. Even though this was supposed to be black mole, it would taste bitter to me. I swore after that experience that I would not go into a kitchen to cook for a man. I swore I would someday marry a man who would love me for my mind and not for how I reminded him of his mother or for the cooking and cleaning services I provided.

I recall Armando's mother complaining to him that I might be exciting and fun now, but that he was going to go hungry and so would his children. A man like Armando would never go hungry. If his wife didn't cook for him, you know his mother would be there, serving up his favorite meal. A man doesn't get to go hungry the way a woman goes hungry. A woman will give away all the food she needs to nurture her body and her soul to the man she loves and her children before she thinks of herself. I had gone hungry for so many years. I had never had a mother who cooked for me the way she cooked for my brothers. In my home food was not for pleasure; food was the way you told somebody you loved them and that they were worth something. I remember being hungry when I was growing up. My mother said we never lacked for food. There was always beans and rice and, if I was woman enough, I could cook myself something.

Why do these onions bring back all these memories? Why does it still hurt that my mother never cooked for me? Why does my mother's kitchen always remind me of hunger? I was hungry for her love and affection and encouragement. I was hungry for a life that was not promised to me the second I was sentenced a girl. I was hungry for an adventure forbidden to me as a Mexican woman. I was hungry for a world where women like me could be seen as creators and not just pieces of meat. I am still hungry for my mother's acceptance. I am so hungry that it hurts, because I can't explain how someone as hungry as me can't keep these twenty pounds from disappearing. I want to disappear, but the hunger I feel and the pain in my gut makes me feel alive. I know hunger; she is my friend. She has been with me on all these journeys where there was never enough to go around. Hunger was there in my college days when I could barely afford tuition and had to live on Cup O' Noodles and Top Ramen. Hunger has been with me for a long time, even when I called it off with Armando after our fight over the menu.

Chef Tulipe walked behind me and startled me by barking, *"Vous êtes en train de brûler les oignons!"* My onions were burning, and I immediately removed the pan from the burner.

Many more mistakes were to follow. I turned a fish fumet into a green glob when I threw parsley into the butter sauce too early. I overcooked my carrots, ruined the skin on my delicate fish, and tied up my chicken like it was ready for S & M instead of roasting. I kept telling myself that I was glad I'd made those mistakes so I would never make them again. So what if my fish had a few scales left on it? No one died. Yesterday was too much salt; today I reduced improperly; not enough butter, et cetera, et cetera. The big thing I had to remember was to taste, constantly be tasting, tasting, tasting.

"Cuisine is sensual," translated Henry for Chef Sauber during one of his many demonstrations. "You must always be touching and tasting and smelling and having all of your senses completely open. You can follow a recipe, yes, but you must also feel your way through it." He added, "You have to be like an Italian; you have to touch everything. To truly be a great chef you must love to give pleasure to people." The second he said this, I swear I could feel the hearts of the female students jump. Chef Sauber was old enough to be my father, but in front of the burners he was the chef, the sexiest man alive; the man who could take dead materials and give them life with his beautiful hands, holding the meat and carving out our fantasies. He was an alchemist, turning simple food items into golden delicacies that melted in our mouths, leaving us wanting more . . . Oh, my God, I'm starting to sound like a cheesy romance novel.

In Paris, chefs are revered the same way rock stars or auteur filmmakers are in Hollywood. The cuisine chefs were sexy, but the pastry chefs were the ones with the Adonis bodies. There were a few with doughboy bodies too, but the head pastry chef was charismatic and had muscular arms. He spent all day slapping and punching dough. One day, when I arrived too early for my Basic Cuisine class, the pastry demonstration was finishing up. I snuck a peek and saw that Chef Guillaume had several female pastry students around him. Maybe they were just really impressed by his pies, but they were like little birds flocking to him and eating out of his loving and muscular hand. He grabbed the dough and shaped it like a big breast.

"Now, you must caress it like a beautiful woman's breast," he said. The women blushed. "This dough needs to be like love— the more you beat it, the more it loves you back," Chef Guillaume advised. He slapped the dough with such intensity it was hard not to imagine him slapping you on the ass as he penetrated you doggy-style. Even some of the heterosexual men had to look away. I had considered taking a pastry class, but Luna dying of diabetes, having several uncles and tías who had also lost out to the disease, and knowing how Mexicans in general are prone to getting it had killed that idea.

CHAPTER 7

I'll Always Have Butter

*A*t every demonstration we got a new chef. Some tried to be funny and keep it lively, and others didn't care whether you liked them; they just wanted us to go back to our home countries knowing their techniques and pronouncing French words correctly.

Chef Plat had no personality, but despite being so young he was the most talented. He showed us how he turned a regular mushroom into a work of art. With the paring knife, he gently scraped the mushroom as he pivoted his knife with his fingertips, creating a spiraling design like the inside of a sea conch. We were so amazed. If we could master that technique, we too could be amazing chefs like him. It reminded me of the student in kung fu being told he would be ready when he could take the pebble from his master's hand.

"The soufflé is one of the most difficult dishes," translated Henry for Chef Plat, "because there are certain steps you must follow or it may not rise." After Chef Plat was done whisking air into his egg whites, he added the egg-yolk batter and, in a scooping and cutting motion, folded them together while keeping in the whisked air. He took the prebuttered and floured soufflé bowl and scraped off a fingertip's worth of butter from the center of the bottom of the bowl.

"This little scrape is my little secret. If you do this to the bowl it ensures that the soufflé will not rise lopsided," translated Henry for Chef Plat. When his soufflé was in the oven he was careful not to disturb it. He saw it rising and bragged about how his techniques *always* worked. Ten minutes later, when the soufflé refused to rise past the bowl, he was forced to admit that his techniques worked *most* of the time. The great chef was humbled by a cheese soufflé.

At the end of the demonstration we were told to get ready for our class photo. I ran to brush my hair and put some makeup on. What a hypocrite I am! I complain about how Latinas and women spend more money on makeup than on a college education, but the minute they say "photo" I scramble for the foundation and lipstick. Okay, I could have gone without makeup, but I wanted my proof that I did attend and complete a culinary program from the most prestigious cooking school in the world to show to the nonbelievers, like my family, and I wanted to look "puuurty."

I sat down at a table with Bassie and a blonde who was putting on makeup and pearl earrings.

"He got an American girl pregnant," said Becky, a tall blonde from New York City.

"Which chef?" I interjected.

"Chef Sauber," she replied.

"But isn't he married?" asked Bassie.

"Like that ever matters in this country. That's how the women here stay thin," scoffed Becky.

"What do you mean?" asked Bassie.

"A husband cheats on his wife. The pain causes her to not

want to eat or to go on a diet so she can be thinner than the mistress. I read that somewhere."

I added my two centimes: "I thought it was the cigarette smoking." It's amazing to me that in a country with the best restaurants in the world, Frenchwomen prefer to eat cigarettes for breakfast, lunch, and dinner. I knew it was being an apple-shaped woman in a country full of pear-shaped women, or no-shape women, that made me say that bitter line. Or could it have been that the secondhand smoke was affecting my brain?

"So did she keep the baby?" asked Bassie.

"I don't know—ask him," Becky replied. "They flirt with all the blondes, they think we're all easy, but I like pussy." I missed being around Americans; our potty mouths always distinguished us.

A pastry student who'd finished his practical dropped off a cake at the table closest to the coat racks at the entrance of the courtyard. My "munchies" radar got activated and I turned to Becky, who knew more about the protocols of the school, and asked, "Is that cake for everyone?"

"Yeah, the pastry students leave behind all kinds of failed experiments and sometimes great stuff that they have no one to share with," she explained. I was about to rush over to get the cake when Sélange came into the courtyard and arranged the chairs for our photograph. She clapped her hands and made an announcement.

"We are now ready for the Basic Cuisine photograph. All the girls please sit in the front row and all the tall people in the back."

"Hmm, what to do, what to do," joked Becky and got up and positioned herself in the back at the center. I sat on the sidelines next to Bassie. Since I was wearing black chef shoes, they asked me to sit in the center to harmonize with the black-and-white shoe pattern they were striving to achieve in the photograph.

Sélange thanked us for our cooperation and we were dismissed early so we could rest and then go to the pub later and get to know our classmates.

"Why don't we go to a pub now?" suggested Rick. In seconds there was group agreement and all the American students ended up at C'est Ma Vie. Janeira tagged along to complain about the chefs or anything that reminded her of her French ex-husbands. Rick translated for us, and Jérôme recommended a red wine from Bordeaux and gave us a two-minute history of the wine.

As we commiserated about our first week in cooking boot camp and compared knife and burn wounds, everyone took turns confessing, as only Americans can, why they were spending so much money to learn French cuisine.

"I made a lot of money, but I was miserable, so I quit," said Francis, the lady originally from Hong Kong. "This is my reward for putting up with assholes for many years. I guess I'm in transition." Everyone had their individual stories, but they were all the same story. Everyone had graduated from college or business school or law school and wanted to do something fun and pleasurable before they sold their soul to corporate America or to a law firm. The single guys were interested in earning points with dates by being able to slip in the fact that they'd studied cuisine at Le Coq Rouge. One named Roger was actually there to be a head chef. He had come from Boston and was determined to be a chef. He was not satisfied being a short-order cook at a diner.

I considered going home after two glasses of wine, but realized that by the time I got home I would have thirty minutes to rest before I had to get up and go to the pub. I decided to hang out around the Fifteenth and look for a cheap restaurant. Nothing is cheap in Paris except the baguettes, so I treated myself to a nice meal. I ordered a chicken with sauce *suprême,* and I smiled to myself, knowing that I could actually make that sauce, if I wanted to.

I took several metros to get to St.-Michel and walked around looking for the English pub. Although it was freezing and it threatened to snow, people were out wearing their designer coats and scarves. I was forced to buy a scarf and mittens to function in that weather. I was never this stylish back in L.A. It's so hard to look BCBG—*bon chic, bon genre,* so cool—in hot places.

The pub was hidden away in an alley. A couple French-kissed —or should I say kissed, since they were French—under a streetlight, and watching them got me horny. I hate it when that happens. Especially when I enter a bar. I swear men can smell it on a woman, so I tried not to be too obvious. I entered and I was one of the few Le Coq Rouge students already there. There was a group of female pastry students in the back room comparing the horrors of yeast; they sounded like they were in a gynecologist's reception room, anxiously waiting for their friends.

I smiled at them and killed time by making conversation with a woman from Portugal. She was an American who had come to Paris to study French and ended up falling in love with a Portuguese man and moving there. This was a very common story. It seemed Paris was the place single women came to find love or have a midlife or quarter-life crisis. I was not original calling off my wedding and coming here alone to find myself, but I was unique in one way: I wasn't looking for love. Maybe I would be like Audrey Hepburn in *Sabrina* and return from Paris all "ladylike" and unrecognizable. Maybe Paris was a finishing school for wild women like me.

Bassie walked in with a Band-Aid on her forehead. She had tripped and fallen at home and almost set her apartment on fire, but she was happy to socialize with her peers. She kept talking about her dysfunctional relationship and how many boyfriends just didn't understand her. I was listening sympathetically when I noticed Henry out of the corner of my eye. I looked over to him and we shared a glance, which then turned into a long stare. I wanted to look away and hide from any male attention, but because I was almost drunk I just stared right back and, using my feminine superpowers, hooked him like a savage swordfish. Henry, a couple of drinks already in him too, approached me. "You look so beautiful with your hair down. It's always in a bun, hun," he said, and I could tell he was fishing for a way into my panties. Normally when a guy came up to me with a line that came from horny desperation, I would give him one cold look to freeze his action, but the nights in Paris had been cold and lonely, and if it snowed that night I wanted the extra heat.

"You look sexy out of your translator's uniform," I whispered in his ear.

"You look very nice without yours on . . . I bet you look beautiful with nothing on."

"I do," I said and walked away to another part of the pub, hoping he would follow like a little puppy. He did. We went to the end of the bar and I asked for a margarita; dumb place to ask for a margarita, but the little scenario about to unfold required tequila.

As the night went on, all the students in my group slowly said their good-byes. Around closing time Henry and I were some of the last people there. I debated whether I should take him home or go home with him. We walked out of the pub and he kissed me under the same streetlight where the other couple had kissed. I kissed him back and we smelled like drunks.

The taxi dropped us off at Henry's building on rue du Seine, a street full of galleries. Since there was no elevator, Henry helped me up the stairs by carrying my breasts. We kissed on the staircase and disrobed each other. He was so white he glowed in the dark. I followed this ghost of a man and pretended he was whipped cream when I buried my face in his hairless chest.

"You are so ... so ..." I was about to say "white" when he interrupted me.

"Don't believe all the rumors about me ... Okay, they're all true, but you haven't heard my side of the story." I didn't know how to respond to that, but I followed him into his tiny apartment. I could smell all the women who had been there before me, but I got closer to his mouth and his beer breath silenced all my inquiries about him. I told myself, don't try to psychoanalyze them, just fuck them.

We gave each other sloppy kisses until he pushed me onto his bed and I felt the toughness of his hard mattress.

"Oh, I love your round face. You've got amazing luscious lips." He showered me with compliments like only a drunk, horny man could.

He licked my nipples and I began to giggle. Never giggle when a man is making love to you, I told myself. It really makes them self-conscious. He was too drunk to care about my giggling. He giggled with me and we went under the covers. I wanted him to turn on the heater, but I figured things would be getting hot enough soon. I took his penis in my mouth. My fingers smelled like onions and garlic. That smell was so hard to get rid of with just soap and water. I held my breath and took him in all the way. My coordination was off and I took him in too far. So far I had to gag.

I ran from the bed and vomited into his kitchen sink. I was sure he'd be so disgusted by this, he would not want to continue.

"Hurry back, love!" he shouted.

I rinsed out my mouth with tap water. It tasted dirty, so I opened his refrigerator and looked for bottled water. Searching for a napkin, I opened all his drawers. In one drawer there were many small silver cans with no labels. I finally found a roll of paper towels on the floor.

I drank from the water bottle and brought it back with me to the bed. I continued with the fellatio and he purred when my cold mouth touched his penis. He begged me to do it again. I drank more cold water each time I licked him and he would let out a moan. I drank some more water and I spat the water at his chest. He moaned harder. I finally just threw the whole bottle of water on him. He grabbed me and poured the remaining water on me. It was so cold it instantly made my nipples and clitoris hard. We wrestled for the bottle and flapped like fish out of water on the wet bed. We continued wrestling and fell off the bed. He kissed me, but my buzz was wearing off and his breath was stinky. I slipped away from him and ran to the refrigerator to get ice. I put an ice cube in my mouth and we kissed. He grabbed some ice and slid it down my body to my vaginal lips. I moaned. He put an ice cube inside me and I yelled and moaned. He licked the ice wedged in my vagina. I melted and came all over his face. He pushed me onto the bed again and shoved the tiny melting ice inside my vagina with his penis. Each time he humped me I could feel the ice getting smaller and smaller, until it became water. Minutes later he fell over to the side. After we caught our breath he grabbed my hand and we decided to make the carpet our bed. He pulled a throw blanket from his sofa and covered our naked bodies with it.

"With American women you have to beg them to show you their titties or to do anything . . . But you're different. You don't tease or play stupid; you just get to the meat of things." We both laughed.

"I didn't know Englishmen could be so nasty and rough," I confessed. "I always saw you guys as so polite and with no penis."

"May I fuck you again, please," he said in an overly exaggerated, polite British accent, making fun of me.

"You may, mate," I said, imitating him.

* * *

An alarm went off and I saw my naked butt by Henry's hand. He slapped it and told me we had to go.

"Aren't you in Group B?" he asked me.

"Ah . . . Yes . . . I think so . . . ," I answered, trying to hide my morning breath.

"You have a demonstration in forty-five minutes," he said in a serious tone.

"Oh, I can't go, I'm so tired. I probably can't make it," I whined.

"Yeah, you can. If I can make it, you can make it. I'm supposed to be the translator for that class. Come on, mate, get up." Henry said, pulling me up from the carpet. He threw me my dress and I got my clothes on in a second. Thank God for polyester dresses that don't wrinkle. I was freezing as I tried to get my coat on, and I wondered if the ice inside me had completely melted or had turned into a Popsicle.

"Do you have your knickers on?" asked Henry. I looked down and realized I had forgotten my panties. He threw them at me and I slipped them on over my tights.

We jumped on the metro, then off, and I followed him. As we approached the school he told me to cross the street so we wouldn't be seen coming in together and have people make the connection. I wanted to ask him why, but figured either the administration had warned him not to mess with the students or maybe he was messing around with too many female students and he didn't want to make them jealous. Whatever the reason, it was none of my business; I didn't care. This was just a one-time-thing fling.

I changed quickly in the locker room, then ran into the demonstration room, arranged my tie, and sat in the front row. Henry passed a hand through his hair, combing it down. He called names on the roster and I said, *"Oui,"* looking down, so as not to make eye contact. Ten minutes into the demonstration my mind began to wander. Chef Chocon was carving and boiling artichokes that would soon contain hollandaise sauce, like tiny saucers. Being hungover and about to catch a cold made it impossible to concentrate. I felt like a sundae melting in the sun.

"Is everyone sleeping all right?" the chef called loudly in French to wake me up. I did everything I could to write the steps down, but I couldn't keep up. I just wanted to survive the class. I felt bad for Henry, who not only had to translate but put up with Chef Chocon's mediocre jokes.

Before practical I drank a caffè latte from the vending machine. It woke me up and I told myself I would just have to follow Francis or Ale, but an hour of trying to follow Ale and Francis just got me lost. I looked at the recipe for hollandaise sauce and didn't remember the demonstration. I figured that I would just mix in all the ingredients and it would magically turn into hollandaise sauce. I poured the water into the eggs and Chef Papillon, a giant of a man who looked like Popeye, stopped right in front of me and asked in French, "Were you paying attention in class?" I wanted to tell him "NO! I want to go home" and cry in his arms like a baby, but I just stayed quiet. He mumbled things in French. At least I didn't hear him call me an *"idiot."*

He commanded me to follow him and said, in his limited English, "Look me," and pointed to his eye. I watched closely as he set up a bain-marie, a metal bowl over boiling water, to whip my eggs over it. He told me to whip for six minutes nonstop, then to add the melted butter slowly. Then, finally, salt and pepper and cayenne.

"God, this is like jacking off a guy," complained Becky as she took a little break from whipping her eggs. "Why don't they just let us use a blender? They come out just as good."

Despite my horrible experience with hollandaise sauce, I managed to finish second. Chef Papillon gave me a good note for my filet mignon and boiled artichokes and then gave me a hug. I was embarrassed by the attention, but maybe he felt bad about losing his temper with me.

Thankfully, the next morning was Sunday, our day off, because I couldn't wake up. I felt so tired I just wanted to sleep and rest. I wasn't looking forward to school the next day; I was tired of screwing up recipes and feeling like a loser. If this was only the first week, how was I going to make it to the end?

CHAPTER 8

Pardon My French

I tried not to look at Henry. When no one was watching he would slip me a dirty look—an invitation to his apartment for another night of wine and roses . . . or at least wine.

The admissions counselor walked in and dropped a letter in front of me. I quickly opened it and could make out an appointment for my *carte de séjour*. I had to bring a lot of documents, including proof that I had enough money to stay in Paris for a year. My appointment was tomorrow morning, and I could not miss it.

I got up very early the next day and presented myself at the police precinct. I approached the African-French receptionist and told her I was there for my appointment. She didn't know a word of English and had no patience for my lame attempt at forming a sentence in French. She pointed to a chair and ordered me to wait for my name to be called. I sat there looking at the many foreigners, all equally mistreated by the receptionist.

As I waited, my mind wandered off to the time when I had to wait many hours in line just to get an appointment to come back another day. Thousands of Latino immigrants waiting like cattle to be allowed into Plaza del Sol Immigration Center for a chance at the American dream. When I finally got to the front a woman not in line wanted to ask a question, and the white security guard ordered her to go to the back of the line. He didn't speak Spanish so he assumed she was trying to cut in, and when she tried explaining he couldn't care less about her sad story. I shook my head at him for being an asshole and he threatened to kick me out of the line too. I kept quiet and felt sorry for him. Here he was, the powerful, big man among all these helpless undocumented immigrants, but I bet he would go home to his boring apartment to wallow in his mediocre existence—to a life not worth documenting. I'd always found it peculiar that the immigration officers at the INS I encountered had thicker accents than I did and had been in the United States for less time than I had, and yet I was the one who had to prove my existence in the United States, my qualifications to become a resident, and my English-language ability to eventually become a U.S. citizen.

I returned to reality when my name was finally called and I followed a female officer to her station. She made me sit while she went to get my file. Next to me were an older Frenchman and his ethnic-looking beautiful young wife. I couldn't tell what nationality she was—possibly Peruvian. I could hear him arguing with the male officer about his wife. I couldn't understand their conversation, but finally the Frenchman started raising his voice and saying, *"Ma femme!"* "My wife!" The officer probably didn't believe they were a real married couple and was giving them a hard time. He probably figured this Latina beauty was using him to get her papers, whether the man realized it or not. I felt bad for them, but wondered if there was a MacArthur Park in Paris where they could go to get a fake *carte de séjour* like we did in Los Angeles. I remembered having to go to MacArthur Park to get a fake Social Security card with my father back when

I was undocumented. I returned for a second time when I was going to do undercover work and needed another identity to do my stories. I was "Maria Fuentes" and passed myself off as just another Maria while doing a story about human trafficking.

The female officer returned to her station. She quickly grew impatient with me because I didn't speak French. She spoke in an annoying, nasal voice; even for the French her voice must have been grating. I presented all my documents and passport to her, hoping they would do the talking for me.

"You are not really American—where are you from?" she inquired, staring at my face. I'm sure my cheekbones were a dead giveaway that I wasn't a typical American. God, here I was again, being an immigrant in yet another country that didn't want me. After I'd been sworn in as a U.S. citizen five years ago, I'd been certain I would never have to go through this type of indignity again. What did I do in my past life to deserve this? Maybe I was a racist white guy and now I have to see how difficult life is being one of the people I hurt.

"I am an American," I insisted and slid the passport closer to her for inspection.

Her eyes looked down and she read that I was originally from Mexico.

"Ah, but you are really a Mexican . . . Hmmm, I like Mexico. Nice people, nice country," she said with a smile.

"I am going to cooking school because I want to learn French cuisine and open a French restaurant back in Los Angeles so all my friends can experience France, at least this way. I can't do that if I don't get my *carte de séjour.*" I said my lie as sincerely as possible. I could tell it had an effect on her and she nodded, agreeing with me that my goal was a noble one. She stamped my photo at the edge onto a blue card and told me it was temporary. In a few months I would have to go take tests and continue the process. I gave her a quick *"Merci"* and got the hell out of there.

As I walked to the metro, an older Frenchman wearing tie-dyed clothes and an African hat approached me. He spoke to me in French, but I couldn't figure out what he was saying. Realizing I was a foreigner, he then spoke English.

"You have a woman following you," he said. I turned around and saw no one behind me. "She is not a person . . . she is a spirit . . . she is around you . . . I see her following you."

"What are you talking about?" I asked, waiting for him to ask me for money or to reveal his scam.

"She needs to tell you something." He looked to his side, as if talking to someone next to him.

"Who is this woman?" I asked.

"She says she's your cousin," he informed me. I stared at him for a second and then I just walked away, holding in my tears. I ran into the metro and hid from him.

During the third week of classes we were informed that there would be a written exam in a few days. I couldn't imagine what to study. We had covered so much material. I couldn't even keep track of the sauces, much less the fish. After class the last thing I wanted to do was study. I just wanted to go home, pig out on the food I'd made, and go to sleep. Despite my ravenous hunger, I was actually losing weight. Being on my feet for many hours each day and sweating up a storm had already made me drop ten pounds. Who knew going to cooking school would be a great diet? You get to eat all you want and lose the weight; this was a story worth including in the *National Enquirer*! Maybe I could write about my experience and submit it to a women's magazine, I considered; but then I quickly remembered that I didn't care about being a journalist anymore.

Whenever I burnt anything in practical, the smell always took me back in time to either the smell of burning corpses coming from the Evergreen Cemetery when I was a teenager growing up in the 'hood or the burning rubber of a car taking off after a drive-by. Not that I would burn a lot of food; it's just that working on an electrical stove takes time getting used to. I had to remember to take things off the stove or they would continue to cook and would burn. My brain was also burning; I could smell the smoke coming from it. Although I would follow each step as best as I could, I still could not keep from making a mess and getting distracted by other people's work. I would try to focus on something, but then I would see someone else doing something and want to do that instead, and I'd end up burning something or overcooking it or forgetting to add salt and pepper. I was so exhausted; I didn't care anymore. It was just food!!! I had never worked so hard to end up being so mediocre. I felt like such a loser.

At the end of the week I got on the metro with my many bags of food. Everyone in my group was either going out because it was Friday night and they didn't want to be burdened with their food or they had simply not wanted their monkfish. That poor fish has a face only a mother monkfish could love. When I arrived at my stop at Charles de Gaulle–Étoile I collected all my bags and walked out of the metro. Ten seconds later I turned around, realizing that my purse was back on the floor of the metro. I ran back, but the doors closed on me. I looked around for my purse, but it was gone. Then some French ghetto wannabe rappers in their twenties started laughing at me. I ignored them and peered into the metro car to see who had it. These boys kept laughing as though it was the funniest thing they'd seen in their lives. My suffering was just so amusing to them. The metro took off. What a wonderful way to end this day: I felt like a loser and I'd lost my purse—how poetic and pathetic. That purse contained everything, except my passport, thank God. I went to the ticket vendor's window and explained in my horrible French that I'd left my purse on the metro. She tried cheering me up and said that people were very good about returning purses. She handed me a small piece of paper and instructed me to call in two days to see if anyone had turned it in; if not, then maybe I could check the Paris lost and found.

I felt as lost as a child waiting to be found by her parents after being separated from them in a crowd. That there was nobody in Paris who cared if my purse was lost or found hurt worse than actually losing it.

I walked toward my building and saw police cars blocking the entrance to my street. A policeman informed me and an old woman walking her poodle that we had to wait because a package had been found in front of the Iraqi consulate and the bomb squad was studying it to determine whether it was a bomb. I secretly hoped that some kind soul had found my purse and left it at the consulate door instead of my building. I waited fifteen minutes with my leaking plastic bags of smelly monkfish before I decided to sit on the sidewalk. I couldn't wait to go to my bed and cry. After half an hour it began to rain, and I let my tears bathe in the rain. Another fifteen minutes later, the package turned out to be nothing more than magazines in a box someone had forgotten, and the police allowed us to enter the street. I took the servants' elevator, hoping not to run into anyone, but when I reached the top I saw a Muslim woman with a tattoo of a cross on her forehead waiting there. I automatically smiled, but she didn't acknowledge me. I realized again that smiling was such an American thing to do and people here frowned upon it because it was inauthentic. Fine, I won't smile anymore unless I mean it, I told myself.

I took a shower and sat on my bed. I had lost my cell phone

too and couldn't call anyone. I debated whether to use my last minutes on my international calling card in a public phone to call the credit card company and my bank to cancel my cards and get a replacement immediately. I didn't want to do it right away because I held on to the hope that someone would find and return my purse. But after a few hours hope gave way to reason, and I called my credit card company and found out that the bag was now officially stolen. The thief had gone to Hugo Boss on the Champs-Élysées and bought himself a new wardrobe. Maybe now this thug could get a real job.

I cried, wondering how I was going to make it without money for almost two weeks, until my ATM and credit card arrived. I could eat just the food I made at cooking school and walk to school, but I couldn't do much else. Classes would end in a week, so what would I do for the seven days before Intermediate Cuisine began? How would I survive?

I unpacked my food and saw that my notebook containing my recipes was soiled with sauce. I cleaned the plastic sleeves protecting my recipes and saw Henry's phone number written on one of them. How had he gotten it on my recipe without me noticing? He must have written it down when I slipped out to go to the bathroom.

Since misery loves company, I called Henry, hoping that at least one night of satisfying sex would make him remember me and care that my purse had been stolen. When he answered I heard a woman laughing in the background. I wanted to hang up, since he apparently already had booty for the night.

"Hello," he said in his cute British accent.

"Henry, it's Canela," I announced, trying my best to sound cheerful and sexy. He hushed the laughing woman and took on a flirtatious tone.

"My purse was stolen. I have no money," I confessed, almost embarrassed to reveal too much. He remained quiet for a second and then told me to get ready.

In a few minutes, he came over in a taxi and picked me up. I knew this evening would probably end up in sex, but I didn't care. I just didn't want to be alone. I have always been afraid of being alone. I don't trust myself when I am alone. Sometimes food substitutes as company, but the monkfish was not creamy enough to keep the thoughts of suicide away. Until now, whenever I was not busy doing a thousand things under the guise of saving the world and I ended up alone with my suicidal thoughts, I would call Luna. Every time I would have a major life crisis—which happened often since, according to my family, I'm a drama queen—I would call Luna and she would listen or go meet me at the weirdest locations and oddest hours . . .

Wait a minute: she never called me, and now that I really think about it, I was always doing the calling. I never stopped to ask, "How is life with you?" since I already knew it was fucked up, but I'd assumed Luna was strong enough to take it. On so many occasions I'd told Luna to leave and be my roommate, but she wouldn't leave him, so I'd stopped asking. And then I'd stopped calling . . . Oh, God, I'm a self-centered bitch! Why hadn't I called her? Why hadn't I saved her? Why hadn't I been a good friend? I missed Luna. I started to cry and wanted to die . . . Henry would have to be my Luna to keep me from thinking of death.

"Where are you taking me?" I asked. He pulled my hand and led the way past the Algerian teenagers and black rapper wannabes hanging out by a French burger joint on one of the corners of Place de Clichy, and past the rowdy crowds of tourists and locals with mischief on their minds.

"I'm going to educate you, Ms. Canela. I'm going to give you a cultural experience and then some," he said with a devilish grin.

"Yes, educate me, teach me the ways, O great pale one," I joked.

We arrived at the museum of erotica and he paid my admission. We walked up the stairs, admiring every form of erotic and sexual expression on paper, oil, photograph, and papier-mâché. He rubbed his hand on my butt when no one was looking. Other times he would rub up against me when there was another couple looking. They smiled at us wickedly, but we just kept moving up the stairs. Henry knew his way around the museum. This was not a tour for him; this was foreplay. I stared at the photographs of women posing in front of their brothels in Montmartre. Brothels had been outlawed in 1946, and there were black-and-white photographs of brothels closing and prostitutes being "rehabilitated." There were ledgers showing how much straight intercourse cost in the 1900s . . . Henry translated for me, wishing he could have been around back then when life was simple and all a man had to do was pay instead of pretending he loved women and put up with their drama.

"Let's go get a drink," he said, pulling my hand. I followed him like the black sheep that I am to my family; as long as he was paying, I was along for the ride. Wow, so this is how it felt to be a woman on a typical date: the guy pays, and he gets sex at the end. I never really dated. I was always running around chasing stories and didn't waste my time dating. Armando was the only man who'd been patient enough to chase after me. After he had caught me, he'd done what every man loves to do when he has found the woman of his dreams: take her for granted.

Henry pulled me into the Sexodrome mega-sex toyshop, all the way back into a private dance room. Two African-French immigrant women came onto the stage and started undressing each other. Henry kept looking for a waitress, but the tiny room in the giant porno shop did not serve drinks. The tall, skinny woman coughed and whispered something. The poor woman had a cold, but she had to pretend she was so turned on by the other woman, whose teddy was a little too tight on her chunky body. In whispers, even I could tell, they commiserated about how shitty this work was. Nobody was fooled by their passion-less acts of foreplay. I felt sorry for them and wanted to interview them instead of fantasize about them. Henry took my hand and we walked out. The cashier at the door told us to wait, saying there would be male-female couples coming up, but I shrugged my shoulders and smiled as we left. Henry and I walked around Pigalle looking for a bar. Pigalle was the red-light district where Le Moulin Rouge and the Black Cat resided. It was the closest thing to Vegas in France.

"Have you ever had sex in an alley?" Henry asked me.

"Yeah," I lied. Technically, I didn't lie; I just didn't want to explain how I'd tried. At first the idea is pretty erotic, but doing it is another thing. When I realized that my butt could freeze in the cold, it completely spoiled the mood. Even on a hot summer night, the wind blowing up my butt is not erotic.

Henry looked into a bar and in seconds he knew he didn't like it, so we didn't bother walking in. Down the block an attractive mixed-race couple entered a different bar, and we decided to fol-low them in. A man dressed in black looking like Zorro, minus the mask, stopped us at the door and told us we had to have membership. We were about to walk away when he stared at me and called me *"jolie"* and said something in French to Henry, as if complimenting him on his choice of woman. Henry translated and told me it was a libertine club—a swingers' club. The man in black invited us in. I looked at Henry, who was waiting for me to say yes. All eyes were on me and my heart skipped a beat. Could I really do this? Yeah, I could talk dirty and tough, but could I really go through with this?

"Do you want to go in?" I stared back at Henry, hoping he would say no.

He cleverly threw it back at me: "Do *you* want to go in?"

I paused to consider what this decision meant, and I thought about all the times I had said no to my sexuality because I wanted to meet a deadline and how each time I did that I'd deadened my senses. I'm in Paris to revive, I realized.

"Yes. Let's go in," I told Henry. Henry looked to Zorro and he opened the door and said *"Bienvenu."*

We went into the dark club with barely a sign on the front.

The smell of cigarettes welcomed us. The night was still early and there were only a few faces hiding in the dark.

"What do you want to drink?" Henry asked.

"Do you think they make margaritas here?"

"I can ask. What else would you like if they don't make them?"

"Anything . . . fruity," I responded.

Henry left for only a few minutes, but I was anxious for him to get back. He stopped to talk to Zorro and they conversed privately in French.

"What were you asking him?" I asked Henry, trying to stay close to him to avoid making eye contact with anyone.

"He explained a few rules. Basically, women have carte blanche and the men just have to sit around like chumps waiting to be picked. It's up to you to initiate things, dear." Henry handed me a margarita. I took a sip; the tequila was pretty strong.

"I got you a double shot just to inspire you to get started," Henry explained.

"I just want to watch. Can't we just watch?" I asked, intimidated by the whole thing.

"Don't tell me you have never done this before?" he asked in disbelief.

"This is my first time in a place like this," I confessed and took another sip.

"You're a virgin again!" Henry got excited. "Maybe you need me to coach you a bit so we can get something juicy started," he suggested.

"I don't know if I can do this, Henry. Maybe we should go." I started chickening out.

"Canela, you are the hottest thing at this club. We're all counting on you to get the party started."

"I didn't agree to be the party hostess. I just want to watch," I interjected.

"So you're going to play journalist and let life pass you by like it already has."

"What do you mean pass me by?"

"Canela, if not now, when? This is Paris—it doesn't get better than this, darling."

Henry was right. I had been living my life as though someday I was going to live it. "Okay . . . You're right . . . I just don't know if I can do this . . ." I sheepishly apologized. "I can't do this; I didn't bring any condoms." I came up with an excuse and headed for the door. Henry stopped me.

"No worries, I have plenty," he reassured me. He saw the worried look on my face and put his arm around me and said, "Sweetie, look around . . . If there is no one here that catches your attention, then we'll go to my apartment and do the nasty. But look around first," he advised.

I didn't dare look at first. I tried burying myself in Henry's eyes so he would notice that I wanted only him. When I saw his wandering eyes surveying the salon I didn't continue fooling myself into thinking Henry cared about me. This was just sex,

I told myself. After I said that I felt liberated. This *was* just sex. How many times had I wanted to have sex but didn't have the ovaries to just go for it? Yeah, I wanted to experience sex with a stranger, and the tequila in my veins was finally letting me admit it to myself. So many years of being a good girl and a good little reporter, but now I wanted to be a bad little girl. Maybe Henry would spank me at the end of the night.

I tried downing the rest of my margarita without getting brain freeze. Halfway into my drink a man's face from across the room caught my attention. I wondered if he was part of the couple who'd watched Henry fondling me at the erotic museum. Had they followed us into this club?

"Don't they look like that couple we saw earlier?" I asked Henry, but he was too busy checking out the few women in attendance.

"Hey, the woman he's with has nice boobies," he said. "Do you like him? You want to go talk to him? Maybe she'll reciprocate and come . . . talk to me."

I took a final swig and finished my margarita. This is what it must feel like to be a man who has to initiate things and try out his luck; except the odds of getting laid are pretty good here.

I walked across the room and said, *"Bonjour."* I don't think language is ever a barrier when you are trying to get sex from a man. Both the African-French man and the Frenchwoman said *"Bonjour"* a little too anxiously, and I got all intimidated again. I just wanted to get his attention, so I walked close to him and said boldly in my best French, *"Voulez-vouz danser avec moi?"* Would you like to dance with me? I know you thought I was going to say, *"Voulez-vous coucher avec moi ce soir?"*—Would you like to sleep with me tonight—but even I am not so bold. I extended my hand to him to invite him to the dance floor. He gave his lover a flirtatious look before taking my hand. He quickly grabbed my waist and we slow-danced on the dance floor. I couldn't believe I was initiating sex with a total stranger; then again, in some way this was a man I'd known and lusted after for many years.

Yes, a black man. Call it jungle fever or a *Mandingo* fantasy, but I remembered that after I'd accepted Armando's proposal for marriage I'd thought that my one regret I would take to the altar would be never having had sex with a black man. I knew I was going to get punished for stereotyping—he probably has a small penis, I thought—but this was my politically incorrect sexual fantasy and I loved it. He talked to me in French and I tried not to say anything because I didn't want to ruin the fantasy with my bad conjugations. He just thought I was being mysterious. He moved his chin to indicate his belt. I got the hint and slipped his belt from his pants. I put the belt around him and pulled him close to me. I lifted my blouse and exposed my breasts to him. He buried his face in them and I leaned back holding on to his belt. He licked my nipples and we slowly made it down to the floor.

Now we had an audience. We undressed each other and my nipples got even harder when I saw Henry dancing with the man's lover close to us. He looked at me and then licked the woman's nipples. I stared at Henry until he looked over to me and I buried my face in my dance partner's humongous penis. Henry danced her to the floor and now we were all putting on a show. My partner plunged his tongue into my mouth and we slobbered each other with our wet tongues. His tongue made its way back to my erect nipples, then down to my pubic hair. He brushed his mouth on my pubic hair and stuck his tongue in my vagina. He wiggled his tongue inside me and then outlined my vagina with his vibrating tongue. Time stood still and I saw myself running in a field of daisies, like in those douche commercials I hate. This was the most pleasure I had ever felt. I was about to come and I opened my eyes. Henry was licking one nipple and the black man was licking my other nipple, like two babies breast-feeding.

I looked down to my vagina and there she was, licking me like a man on a deserted island who had just found a tiny spring and was having water for the first time. It made her so happy to do it that I was about to say something, but the guilt of ruining their fun made me keep quiet.

Then I couldn't just lie back and take it. It was too much. I pulled away as she licked her lips and I shook my head. I threw my clothes on and walked out of the club. I could hear Henry staying behind to apologize for my bad manners. I walked to the metro, straightening out my clothes, and I bumped into a woman wearing too much makeup who was making a living on the streets. She gave me a dirty look, but I kept walking. I couldn't believe how distressed I was. What bothered me so much? It wasn't that a woman was giving me sexual pleasure . . . What bothered me was that there were so many people giving me pleasure. I couldn't receive it. I felt I didn't deserve it. Oh, my God, my low self-esteem even shows up at a time like this!

CHAPTER 9

Casseroles of Fire

Y ou either get fish or you get meat. There is always one easy one and one difficult one for the practical exam." Janeira claimed that's what her friend who had already graduated with her *Grand Diplôme* in cuisine had told her.

Françoise passed out the written exams and said that although the written exam was worth only ten percent of our grade, it was very important that we do our best. We were told to sit apart from one another so we wouldn't be tempted to copy.

"I heard just a year ago there were no written tests. This is bogus giving us a written test," said Rick to anyone who would listen.

I quickly started my test and was immediately stumped when it came to describing the steps to make a soufflé. Nor could I explain all the precise steps to making the stocks. I felt like an idiot—how could I not know all this stuff? I did know that the secret to keeping green vegetables green when you boil them is to take them out and place them in ice water for a few minutes to hold the chlorophyll. At least that was something. I was one of the first students to turn in my test. Everyone assumed I'd aced it since I'd finished it so quickly.

"No, I just knew I didn't know most of the answers so I quickly guessed rather than torture myself trying to figure them out," I confessed to Rick and Bassie.

Later that day, in practical, Chef Chocon chastised me for running into him. He got in my face and said that I must never do that again. He warned me that it was dangerous. His icy blue eyes pierced my wide pupils as he said in French, "If I were to be holding a pot of hot water and you were to run into me we would both have been scalded." I apologized and slowly walked away from him, back to my station, where my green beans were already too dark to call "green."

The day of the final, the Basic students waited in the courtyard. We sharpened our knives and studied the ten recipes we'd been told to have committed to memory. The chef would choose two recipes from the list and we would be assigned to make them without help from anyone. We would also have to clean two salmon and filet them to demonstrate our technique. Chef Tulipe called us up to the second floor, to the smallest practical room. We waited in the stairway for the assistants to finish distributing the ingredients. When the chef left the room I looked in and Becky, who was the assistant, whispered to me the two recipes we were getting.

I rushed over to my classmates and told them the recipes were *blanquette de veau* and *filets de daurade*, veal stew and fish fillets. I was so anxious with too much adrenaline that I blanked out and could not remember *blanquette de veau* and Bassie quickly went through the steps with me. I prayed to get the fish; that was the "easy" dish.

Chef Tulipe entered the hallway and explained that our recipe would be left to chance. He held up two poker chips; the red chip represented the fish and the blue chip represented the veal. He then called us into the practical room one by one and we each stuck our hand into a pot to select a chip. Chef Tulipe mispro-nounced my name, but I rushed in before he had a chance to cor-rect himself. I closed my eyes, stuck my hand in, and picked out the blue chip. I instantly yelled and lowered my head, knowing I was doomed. Chef Tulipe thought I was crazy and pointed me to my station, where a sheet of paper with only the ingredients and quantities waited for me.

I put down my knives and immediately filled my pot with water and put it on to boil. Then, grabbing my fish scaler, I got my salmon and cleaned them up. I gutted the fish and tried not to look at their eyes as I did it. I was trying to be perfect, but then I remembered that the veal would take an hour to cook, so I quickly removed the filets and stuck them in the cooler. I stared at my ingredient list.

⇜ *Blanquette de Veau à l'Ancienne* ⇝
Traditional Veal Stew

1.2 kilograms boned veal shoulder
80 grams carrots
80 grams onions
100 grams leeks
1 celery stalk
2 garlic cloves
1 bouquet garni
salt, peppercorns
3 cloves

ANCIENNE GARNISH
250 grams button mushrooms
200 grams pearl onions (about 20)

20 grams butter
1 lemon
salt, pepper

SAUCE
White Roux

30 grams butter
30 grams flour
500 milliliters of the *blanquette* cooking liquid
150 milliliters whipping cream

Thickening Agent

50 milliliters whipping cream
2 egg yolks

RICE PILAF

Half an onion, finely chopped
30 grams butter
200 grams long-grain rice
1 small bouquet garni
salt
Cooking liquid: One and a half times the
volume of rice (water or chicken stock or
a mixture of half of each)

I swear I had sharpened my knives, but I could barely cut through
the veal. It was taking me so long to cut the meat into morsels I
wrapped a third of it in paper and threw it into the garbage when
no one was looking. Yes, there were people starving in Africa and
here I was in Paris wasting meat. I prayed to God for forgive-
ness and to remove all the guilt. If my mother were to see me

she would have reminded me how hard my father worked to put meat on the table. I would have argued with her that the meat was only for the men so what did I care, but there was no time for a feminist debate now. I had only a few seconds to finish preparing the meat before I had to add the carrots, onions, leeks, celery stalk, two garlic cloves, bouquet garni, and salt, peppercorns, and three cloves to the pot of water with the veal chunks. While the meat was cooking I started on the mushrooms and onions. I looked up at the clock, calculating the good hour it would take to cook. There was no room for error. I made the rice with no problem following my notes.

An hour passed and I took the meat off the burner. I put my feminist pride aside and asked Rick, who was next to me, to please help me with the heavy pot of water so I could remove the chunks and vegetables yet save some of the boiling liquid. I hated asking anyone for help, but I was not strong enough to pick up that hot pot. I thanked him, but he was too busy making the fish dish to wait around for compliments on his chivalry. I set aside the cooking liquid for the sauce. I tried to make the roux. I forgot the steps and threw the flour into the cooking liquid with the melted butter and whipping cream. The flour popped into little globs when it hit the liquid and I gasped, holding in a scream.

Down to only ten minutes. I decided to pass the sauce through the colander to remove the globs. I threw tons of butter and salt into the sauce, hoping to salvage it. It ended up tasting like milky, buttery water. I looked around to see how the others were progressing. Ale was decorating her dish with carrots, a minute away from presenting her entrée platter to the chef. With five minutes left I splattered the veal mixed in the white sauce onto the platter and threw in some carrots. I compared my presentation to Ale's and realized I had forgotten to include the rice pilaf. I grabbed spoonfuls of rice and tried cupping it into little domes, but because I hadn't planned ahead the rice fell apart, like a sand castle being stolen away by a wave. I had one minute left when I announced to the chef I was finished, and he covered it up with plastic wrap and wrote my number on it. He announced in French, with Rick translating, that time was up and that whoever was not finished would have points taken away for every minute they were late. Bassie, Janeira, and an older American woman were still ten minutes away from finishing. I cleaned my knives and wiped the sweat off my forehead. Bassie asked me for a hand with her pot, and I did my best to help her. I gave her some of my rice when the chef wasn't looking and she ended up being only five minutes late.

I sat in the courtyard and took a few minutes to breathe. When I was doing investigative reporting, I had been chased by gang members, shot at, harassed by drug dealers, and threatened by men from every ethnic group, but this was the best adrenaline rush of my life.

"So how did you do?" asked Henry, undoing the red tie of his translator's uniform.

"Awful, but I finished on time," I admitted.

"Hey, it's just Basic. Once you get the fundamentals, it gets easier," he reassured me. "What dish did you get?"

"The *blanquette de veau*—"

"You don't need to know how to make that dish, it's not all that great. Stupid dish," he said arrogantly.

"Have you ever cooked it?" I asked.

"All the time. I worked as a sous-chef here for many years before I told those frogs to go fuck themselves. They wouldn't promote me to chef because I'm not French and I hadn't studied to be one."

"Why is it that English food has such a bad reputation?"

"Have you ever tried English food?"

"Hmmm, no, not really . . ." I said honestly, trying to remember the last time I'd gone to an English restaurant.

"It's hard to get respect from French chefs when you're British."

"Do all chefs go to cooking school here in France? How come there are no French people at this cooking school if it's supposed to be the best one in the world?"

"Yeah, that's what the marketing people wanted you to believe . . . French chefs either work their way up, inherit the restaurant from a family member, or go to real cooking schools just outside of Paris. This school is for foreigners."

I nodded and instinctively reached for my imaginary journalist's notebook to write a mental note: Don't ever again believe what you read in a beautifully designed brochure.

There was a minute of silence as Henry looked at me with his puppy dog eyes.

"I'm sorry about the other night. I thought you were enjoying yourself and then I guess you freaked out—"

"No, I'm sorry . . . That was pretty immature of me to run out like that . . . I guess I got shy . . ." I lied.

"You? Impossible, not you . . . I think you liked it too much and don't want to admit it," Henry smirked, putting his arm around me. "Let me be your guide to your erotic zones. I'll help you find your G-spot and anywhere else you didn't find with your ex-fiancé," he boasted.

"I don't need you to be my guide," I interjected. I was too proud to admit I could learn a thing or two from Henry.

"Your mind may be saying no, but your erect nipples are saying yes," he whispered into my ear.

I got up and grabbed my knife kit. Henry's perceptiveness disturbed me and I wanted to get away.

"So what are you doing next week, since you're off?" Henry asked.

"I have no money," I confessed, "so I guess I'll stay home and—"

"Maybe you can come with me to London. I can take you to a decent English restaurant."

I looked at him, wondering if I'd have to have sex with him in exchange.

"Yes, you'll have to have sex with me, but only if you want to . . . " he said with a wicked smile.

I debated whether to get dressed up and make a big deal about completing Basic Cuisine. I couldn't imagine any chef finding pleasure in having to taste my cooking final. I pictured an old retired chef making the face of a baby who's just eaten spinach when he tasted my dish to score it. Shaking the image from my head, I slipped into a dress and swore I'd be happy for the winners.

Since this was a crash course, there were fewer students than usual and the graduation took place in the courtyard. The pastry students were the first to be given their diplomas and awarded first through fifth place. I was convinced Ale would win first place for our class. Chef Sauber presented our diplomas in alphabetical order. To my great dismay Ale got fourth place and Paolo, the Portuguese guy in Group A, was awarded first place. Rick came in fifth. I was happy for him, but wondered how he could have come in fifth when he'd been absent for one class. As bad as I was, I was never late or absent. Judy, a perky blonde from Seattle who came in second, had also been absent from a class. It didn't make sense that they were awarded a place if they'd been absent. When Paolo went to accept his diploma, pin, and first-place certificate, Becky whispered to Bassie and me that he'd had a couple years of restaurant experience. After I received my diploma and tried to look at the photographer with a smile, I read my scores and felt worse. Then I remembered my promise and tried to be happy for those who really wanted to be chefs. Getting a place meant that a serious student could end up getting a nice internship. If I'd have gotten first place it would have been a nice ego trip, but I wasn't planning to do a *stage*—internship—at some fancy restaurant with three Michelin stars that would be the springboard to a fabulous and exciting career as a chef.

At the end of the graduation ceremony our tiny class of fourteen students took a photo and drank champagne. I pigged out on the dessert trays and tiny appetizers. Henry stopped by to congratulate us and flirted with anyone who would flirt back. Chef Frédérique also stopped by between his classes and thanked me for the bottle of tequila I'd left on his desk earlier that morning. I had debated whether I should do that, but I'd said in the thank-you card that I was giving it to him so he could experiment with it and try making sauces with the tequila; I'd written that just in case my letter was opened by anyone in the administration. I thanked Chef Frédérique for his kindness and he said he was very "touched" in French and let his hand linger on my shoulder, caressing me slightly. He looked at me with longing in his twinkling eyes. I started turning red and made the excuse that I had to go to the ladies' room. He said it was nice having me as a student but he was leaving the school to work full-time at a three-star restaurant. I took his phone number and he said he would save the tequila and maybe I could call him and we could drink it together. I shyly agreed and ran away before anybody could hear us conspiring to meet. Bassie was already in the bathroom and started talking about Chef Frédérique.

"He was always flirting with me," complained Bassie. My jaw dropped and I tried to nonchalantly say, "He was? I never saw him flirting with you" without revealing how jealous I was.

"Oh, yeah, I considered telling the administration," she said, making a big deal out of it. "He has a Peruvian girlfriend and here he is flirting with me!" Oh, great, he has a girlfriend, I thought to myself. I felt like such an idiot. Man, he had me. Okay, give it up to the French: they know how to seduce and they do it so well. I guess I won't be drinking tequila with him after all. I liked Bassie, but that minute I hated her for ruining my little fantasy. I tore up the piece of paper with Chef Frédérique's phone number and flushed it down the toilet.

When I returned to the graduation party, people were already leaving. I exchanged addresses with Ale and Rick and I was about to tell Janeira about the onion, but she was too busy complaining about her stove, saying that it didn't work properly and that was why her veal didn't get cooked all the way. Janeira was not returning for Intermediate, so I would never have to see her again or hear her complain, ever. Bassie, Paolo, Roger, Becky, and me were the only ones coming back for Intermediate and, hopefully, Superior, with the hopes of getting our grand diploma before Christmas.

Later that night some of us gathered to celebrate together one last time. Bassie was drunk and hitting on Rick. He was a gentleman about it, but when she went to the bathroom he flirted with me. Becky came and sat next to us.

"Rick, is your girlfriend coming to join us?" she asked with a big smile. Rick smiled back at her, knowing she was just trying to cock-block him. My throat was hurting and, as much as I wanted to see what Rick's girlfriend looked like, I decided to go home and rest. Bassie decided to go home too and was threatening to walk. Although St.-Germain-des-Prés seemed pretty safe, I walked with her to the taxi stand while she rambled on about how Rick really wanted her—too bad he was returning to the States tomorrow. I borrowed money from Bassie for the taxi. I was grateful to have her as a friend. I was probably as drunk as she was, but even in this state I could sympathize with her delusions and still kick some ass if I had to. Not that growing up in Boyle Heights, a barrio that people thought was rough, had prepared me for that. I just knew I could look pissed and intimidate people. Plenty of men had told me so, but the brave ones with substance usually made it past the stare.

I was sad that I was going home by myself. Flirting with Rick had gotten me all *caliente*. When you touch and feel and smell things all day, it's inevitable that you want to eat something too. It's sad that as a woman I feel like I always have to apologize for wanting to eat—I mean, have sex. Men are horny most of the time and for them there is no shame about getting sex. "It's like being hungry," a guy friend once told me. "You don't feel bad about satisfying your hunger; you just have to eat."

I walked up to a taxi and looked at the driver. He looked up and acknowledged me and gestured for Bassie to get in. I waved good-bye and took the next taxi in line.

"Rue du Général Rueben, c'est pour la Porte Dauphine," I said to the taxi driver, using my routine line that would get me home. He nodded and added in his Spanish-accented French, "Isn't that by Giscardistan?"

"*Qui?*" I asked in French.

"The former president of France. He lives on the next street. He's one of the head people responsible for writing the European constitution."

I just nodded my head since I didn't know enough French to further the conversation. That explained why there were police guarding his house all the time. I had assumed it was just another embassy.

"Are you from South America?" the taxi driver asked me in Spanish.

"No, I'm North American . . . Mexican-American," I clarified for him in Spanish. I wanted to tell him I was a Chicana, but then I would have to give him a cultural and historical lesson that included the Treaty of Guadalupe Hidalgo, and that required more brain cells than were available to me in my inebriated state.

"You're Mexican?" he asked.

"Yes, I'm Mexican-American," I reiterated.

"It's a shame that you should want to call yourself an American. I like that you are Mexican, but I guess you can call yourself whatever you want. But I like South Americans better. Mexicans are fine people. I like them better than Americans."

"Me too. I like Mexicans better than Americans, and look, I know Americans are not liked anywhere these days. I was born in Mexico, and at five years old my parents took me to live in Los Angeles. So yes, I am Mexican, but I am also American. Mexicans are also American because we live in North America and we are part of the Americas."

He didn't say anything for a few seconds, but he stared at me through the rearview mirror. "When you get home you should look up a map and you'll see that Mexico is not North America," he advised me.

"Yes, it is," I replied.

"No, it isn't. Just check," he shot back at me confidently.

"Hmm . . ." I really thought about it for a few minutes and wished I wasn't drunk so that I could argue back with certainty. "Wait a minute: yes, it is North America, because it's not in Central America. All my years living in the U.S., Mexico has never been referred to as Central America."

"Well, it is."

"No. You know how I know Mexico is considered North America? Because I remember that the price for a U.S. postage stamp for Canada, the U.S., and Mexico was the same amount; it was the same amount for all of North America. The government runs the U.S. Post Office. How can the governing administration of the U.S. make a mistake like that—?"

"Look at the war in Iraq. That's where your government made a mistake," he said righteously.

By now I was used to hearing everyone, from taxi drivers to waiters to bakers, complaining about the war and the evils of America. I wanted to tell them to shut up and let me get on my soapbox and give them better and more specific facts about how bad it was, but right then I just wanted to get to bed. He continued talking about how proud he was of being Spanish.

"I have been in France for over twenty years and my daughters were born here. But if you ask them what their nationality is, they will tell you that they are Spanish."

"How old are they?" I asked.

"They are eight and six."

"Well, just wait until they are teenagers and they will tell you that they are French. Spanish-French if you are lucky. You may always be Spanish, but your daughters are French too," I informed him.

"No, they are not," he replied firmly.

"It won't be up to you to determine their identity; it's up to them. They'll probably marry Frenchmen and for sure they will call themselves French."

"Never," he responded, completely dismissing me.

"You may not understand what it means to grow up in two cultures and form a new identity, but your daughters will," I said, tap-dancing on his nerves.

"Well, we'll see."

"Your grandchildren will only speak French," I said, pushing his last button. He got quiet and said nothing.

Ten minutes later the taxi arrived on my street and I handed him his money, which included a tip.

"Gracias," I said and he said nothing back to me. I knew he wouldn't be able to sleep that night thinking of the day one of his daughters would shout back, "I am not Spanish! I am French!" Would he slap her and tell her she was Spanish until the day they died or would he understand? None of my business—it's for him to figure out in the next few years. Or maybe someday they will all just be "European Unioners" or whatever would be the appropriate term if they all agree to pass the European constitution.

I told Henry I would pay for the Eurostar ticket once my ATM card arrived. He insisted it was a gift. I was excited to finally get on the Eurostar and cross the English Channel underground.

About three and a half hours later we arrived at the Waterloo train station in London and quickly took a taxi to his friend Max's flat. It was Max's thirtieth birthday party and we were getting there empty-handed. I pointed to the liquor store.

"Shouldn't we get your friend a present?" I insisted.

"I'm already bringing Max a present," Henry replied. On our way there I told Henry that I actually appreciated his offer to be my "erotic guide" and was open to learning and trying new things with him. He kissed me, told me he knew I'd agree, and grabbed my ass in public. I blushed and pushed his hand away, but after a few seconds I grabbed his hand and put it back on my ass. We marched up to the fifth floor and when I arrived I was out of breath. Henry knocked and a tall guy with glasses opened the door. Henry hugged him and introduced me. A skinny blonde with long hair kissed Henry on the cheek and immediately looked me up and down. I hate it when women do that to me. I do it too, but I don't do it viciously.

After looking me up and down, the blonde spoke: "Hi, I'm Max. Welcome to my little ol' flat and my birthday party, sweetie."

We entered and saw there were a few friends of hers staring at us. We drank wine and passed around a joint. I shook my hand and turned it down when it was offered to me because pot turns me into a horny Chihuahua. Before I know it I end up on someone's leg moving up and down. I was about to fall asleep on the couch when Henry whispered in my ear to go into Max's bedroom. I fell asleep—I don't know for how long—and I woke up with my eyes covered by a blindfold. I could smell Henry's alcoholic breath as he kissed my neck. I tried to hug him, but my wrists were tied to the bedposts.

"Henry, did you tie me up?" I asked, pulling my legs and answering my own question.

"Just lie back and enjoy it, darling." His hands touched my whole naked body. I felt my nipples and my navel being licked. Then I felt something cold on my nipples.

"Is that ice?" I asked Henry.

"No, it's a beer bottle. Do you like it, doll? Does it turn you on?" Henry half-laughed and pushed air out of his mouth as if hushing someone.

"Yeah, I really like it. Keep doing it," I ordered him. Henry rolled the cold beer bottle around my stomach and I got goose bumps. My vagina got wet and I let out a loud gasp. He then grabbed my breasts with his hands and squeezed them like they were running away from him.

"Ouch," I uttered.

"Sorry, love, I'll be gentle." I could feel nails scratching my chest and long hair brushing against my cheeks.

"Henry, is someone else here?" A woman's giggle grew louder. Henry hushed her, but the pussy was out of the bag. Max got on top of me and stuck her tongue in my mouth. I spat her tongue out and she slapped me. Henry pushed her away.

"Didn't you say she was my present?" demanded Max, who was very drunk and talking like a baby.

"Henry, untie me," I ordered.

"No, Henry, you promised we were going to have fun with her," she squealed.

"Untie me right now or I'll scream," I threatened. Henry untied me and Max grabbed my breast again like I was a blow-up doll.

"Come on, Henry, I've never been with a Latina. I thought this was my fantasy," she begged. I pushed her hands away and started to put my clothes on.

"Canela, I'm so sorry. I should have told you about my plans. You said you were open to trying new things so I figured—I wanted to surprise you."

"Well, you did." I was about to walk out the front door when I remembered I was in London and had no money. Henry begged me to stay and I did, but I told Max she was going to have to settle for a scented candle for her birthday or whatever Henry could buy for her at the liquor store next door, but she was not getting her sloppy hands on me. Max grabbed Henry by his cock and practically dragged him to her bedroom. He followed her to keep his family jewels intact, but when he had a chance he pushed her onto her bed and tied one wrist to the bedpost. In the morning she would not remember how it happened, but Henry felt good knowing she wasn't out on the street harassing other men and potentially getting herself into trouble.

On the sidewalk I walked ahead of Henry, trying to ditch him, but I couldn't get far without him. I finally turned around and let him have it. I didn't care that he was my ride back; I was pissed.

"Look, I know this is just sex and we're just having fun! I know I'm disposable because there will be another stupid American girl in the next class who will play along, but I can't believe you were using me like that! Why didn't you tell me your intentions? You should have given me the choice—"

Henry kissed me and shut me up. We fell against a chain-link fence and kissed until we ran out of breath.

Henry and I ended up at a cheap motel that night. I find cheap motels so romantic. I'm a migratory soul and, like a maxipad, my soul has wings. I have fond memories of cheap motels. Maybe it was because I made love for the first time in a motel so cheap it made the whole experience richer: two young people so in love we could transform the pastel peeling paint into our palace.

"Canela, I do care about you. I'm sorry I tied you up without your permission. I thought maybe you'd appreciate the surprise and find it a real turn-on. I wanted to continue what we didn't finish at the libertine club." When I saw the sincerity in his eyes, I was touched by Henry's words.

"Max is pretty sexy . . . I just didn't like the way her nails carved into me. I literally felt like a piece of meat," I confided to Henry. I then wondered if the African-French man at the libertine club had felt that way being my fantasy doll. No, I think most men don't take issue with being "objectified" like women do; lucky them.

"You know, I was almost ready to come right before I heard Max giggling," I confessed to Henry. "I was pretty turned on when I was tied and blindfolded. I was frightened at first, but I . . . really enjoyed it." What I really wanted to say, but didn't dare, was that I'd felt so peaceful surrendering to him when I was blindfolded. Henry jumped off the bed and looked through his carry-on suitcase and pulled out a few ties.

"Canela, may I?" he asked, holding up the ties. Henry tied me up again and he made love to me. I didn't fight him at all; I felt completely connected to him and safe. When we came together

I had my eyes closed and said, "I love you." Two seconds after it accidentally slipped out, I muttered, "Shit" and wanted to take it back. I regretted saying it and felt so naked beyond naked; I felt vulnerable and weak telling him that. Only a minute of silence had passed, but I already felt the miles of distance he'd run while lying next to me in bed. He untied me and quickly went to the bathroom. When he came back clean, he was another man: a stranger who had unloaded all his attachments to me and flushed them down the toilet.

INTERMEDIATE
CUISINE

CHAPTER 10

Blood of the Earth

By the time we returned from London my credit and ATM cards had arrived. I had been in Paris almost five months and I was finally feeling like I had found my groove. Now armed with my credit card *and* my groove, I knew I could let myself feel settled. I was ready to take on even more adventures. I had heard about how essential it was to take a wine class and enrolled in the introductory wine course, hoping it would work out with my Intermediate Cuisine class schedule.

"Yves is such a good teacher. He is one of the best sommeliers in France," the administrator in charge of registration assured me.

I got to my first Intermediate Cuisine demonstration early, but most of the front seats were already occupied by young Korean women gossiping. I managed to squeeze in and sat next to a square pole. The class filled—there were almost sixty students in Intermediate. Most of them were continuing together from the last class and had been on break while the crash courses were happening. I turned around and saw the United Nations behind me. Students from all over the world were represented. More Americans and Japanese students were present, but to my surprise six Mexicans were also there.

Chef Chocon, the chef who'd reprimanded me for bumping into him in the practical room, welcomed us. He said he was the chef in charge of our class. He was very happy about overseeing the Intermediate course because he personally felt this was the most important one.

"Intermediate Cuisine is a culinary tour of France," translated Henry, who didn't make eye contact with me. I had considered moving to a row in the back to avoid Henry, but I needn't have bothered. He had already erased me from his radar.

"We will cook specialty dishes from the many wonderful regions of France. We are so lucky to have such an amazing country because we are able to produce the best products in the world. We are blessed there is no other place like this on earth," he said with a smile as if Saint Peter were giving him passage through heaven's gates.

A student raised his hand. Henry pointed to a tall blond guy with a nice tan.

"What about California? Aside from the cheeses, California is an agricultural capital with the most variety—"

Chef Chocon, who did not speak English, but could understand "California," cut him off with a shake of the head. He wagged his index finger to the sides and said, via Henry, "No, no, no. It does not compare. What you take pride in saying is 'organic' is just natural food for us. Everything here is cultivated with respect for the animals and land and with the best methods." Chef Chocon did not care for a rebuttal and quickly moved on with his lesson.

"Today we will be cooking three dishes from Normandy: fish stew with dry cider, pan-roasted guinea fowl with Calvados sauce, and an apple tart with honey butter," translated Henry. The chef explained the importance of apples and cider and Calvados to cuisine from Normandy. He reminded us that before we left France we should visit Mont-St.-Michel in Normandy and go to a restaurant that makes *l'omelette à la crème de la Mère Poulard*, omelettes the size of cakes. "Do you want to hear a story?" he asked, knowing that we would. We answered yes and via Henry he explained how he'd learned cooking and gained an appreciation of food from his grandmother.

"My grandmother sewed me a cooking apron that said, 'I'm the chef and what I say goes in my kitchen.' She assured me that if I ever pursued cuisine I would be a great chef," translated Henry. Chef Chocon wiped a tiny teardrop from the edge of his eye when he recalled that, on her deathbed, he'd made her a soup that was so delicious she'd told him after she ate it, "Now I can die." We all practically cried too. He quickly cheered up and recalled more memories of his exciting culinary career.

"When I was sixteen, I studied cooking and won many prizes for my aspic decorations. I have pictures," he said. A large photo album circulated with pictures of Chef Chocon's prize-winning buffet presentations. Looking at the pictures I realized that all the decorations had been created with vegetable peels and clear gelatin. I appreciated seeing him in the photos as a thin, handsome young man who'd once had joy and hope on his face. Wow, he was actually young and happy once. He wasn't always an abrasive know-it-all jerk, I thought to myself.

The chef poured the cider into the sauce and asked us, "What is the difference between champagne and cider?" Everyone threw out responses and then he said, "The price." He got caught up in his joke and a story and burnt the tart. His face turned red and he made excuses. I secretly smiled inside, knowing that even a chef who has worked at the best restaurants for over twenty years burns the occasional tart.

After the demonstration, I put away my things in my locker in the corner and sat down on the chair next to it to put my socks on. Bassie expressed her disappointment at having been put in a group where she knew no one. I could sympathize; I also didn't know anyone in my group and didn't look forward to being the odd man out. I went upstairs and was the first to arrive in the practical room. I quickly stationed myself closest to one of the sinks and the service elevator. I would have the advantage of being close to all the ingredients and the sink, where the mixers and Robot Coupes (high-priced blenders) were kept. I immediately placed my plastic *planchette* on the counter to reserve my cooking station. More students arrived and no one said "hello" or *"bonjour"* to me; they just got their *planchettes* and placed them at their stations. I recognized a young Japanese man named Yoshi from the demo and we exchanged a quick smile. He placed his *planchette* next to mine and I explained that I was at the end. He moved to my other side and settled in.

Everyone had arrived and it was a room full of men and three women: me, a Turkish girl, and another American woman, whom I would later know as Sage, who entered casually. She had lots of hair and a pointy nose. Sage asked around to see what cooking station was left and I could tell from her accent she was from the Midwest. She informed me that in the Basic Cuisine class most of this group had previously been in, they'd had a certain agreed-upon setup. Since this group had fourteen people, the extreme capacity of the practical room, I had to move down and work on the stove next to the other sink. I looked at the station I was going to be relegated to and was about to move when I said, "No. I'm not moving. I want this work station." She stared at me with wide eyes, as if unable to believe I wasn't automatically doing as she'd instructed.

Stuttering, she explained further that the group already had their groove. I explained to her that since there were two new students and I'd gotten there early, things were going to be different.

Her expression shifted from disbelief to anger, and I thought we were going to have it out right there, but then Yoshi said he would move to the stove next to the sink; he didn't care.

I finished the first practical in Intermediate and was exhausted, regretting having signed up for the basic wine class. I ate my guinea fowl and studied the next recipes on my tour of France. The African custodian finished cleaning up the small reception room on the second floor and then he brought in bottles of water and platters of cheeses. I followed him in and sat at the very front. I liked getting to my classes early because as a journalist I was always late. A story would happen and by the time I arrived on the scene it was all about catching up and getting neighbors and witnesses to tell me what they'd seen.

The introduction to wine students arrived at their leisure and this time I made an effort to say hi to people. Yves, the instructor the registration woman has raved about, arrived a minute before class started. He was a middle-aged man with charm and presence. A representative of Le Coq Rouge gave him a glowing introduction that made us feel grateful we were in his presence. I was lucky to be so close to him that I could smell his subtle yet expensive cologne. I sat in the front and my inquisitive mind kept wondering, if a sommelier became an alcoholic, would he have to change professions or would he just qualify for disability in France?

"Bonjour," Yves boomed, the Le Coq Rouge representative translating for him, "I love to teach this class. On one end I can teach you that wine is a gastronomic Kodak of a day in the life of the earth, the land. With one taste we experience *la terre;* wine is the blood of the earth. At the other end, at its simplest, wine is just fermented grape juice. For me wine is science and poetry coming together and exploding in my mouth." As Yves's spicy scent

filled my nose and his silky voice filled my ears, I wondered what it would be like for me to explode in his mouth.

"*Homard à l'Américaine*, lobster American style, comes from Marseilles and is one of the dishes of Provence. It was created on a cruise ship going from Marseilles to the U.S.; hence the name," translated Henry for Chef Chocon. To avoid causing the lobsters too much pain, Chef Chocon would work faster.

"The best method to kill lobsters without causing them too much pain is to stick their heads in the boiling water," translated Henry. The chef grabbed the lobster and forced the head down. The lobster kicked up its tail and, even after the lobster was technically dead, the muscles still stretched and moved as the tail and legs were cut off. Most of the women around me flinched. "*C'est ça la cuisine*," Chef Chocon explained via Henry. Cuisine is this way. "I watch television shows about doctors performing surgery and cutting up people in all sorts of places and there is blood and guts everywhere . . . you suffer just watching it. Well, in cuisine there is a little bit of suffering and blood, but at the end you get great sauce," translated Henry.

Who knew the guts of a lobster would make great sauce? But they do. The chef fried the aromatic vegetables and threw in the lobster's shell. After the pieces of shell were red, he added cognac and struck his lighter. In a split second the casserole was on fire and he looked like a magician instead of a chef. The whole class gasped, "Wow." He then confessed that you do that cooking trick only for the cameras, because the alcohol in the cognac would evaporate on its own as it proceeded to get cooked; but this was the thing audiences wanted to see celebrity chefs do. He went on, complaining about celebrity chefs preparing designer dishes that were more chemistry than cuisine. He criticized the very famous Chef Bocuse and called him "Chef Beaucoup" for the *beaucoup*—lots of—money he made off his frozen meals and his private cooking school.

The lobster ended up finger-licking good. I hated seeing that poor lobster die before my eyes but, damn, did it taste delicious. I was always one of the last students in the demonstration room because I waited until the food paparazzi finished taking their pictures of the food and then I took mine. I also made sure to get my demonstration *dégustation,* and then seconds and thirds if possible. There is a word that describes someone like me: *gourmand.*

In practical I looked at my knives and then at the lobster. I am a hypocrite. I will not kill my lobster, but I will gladly eat it. I felt bad about the time I'd sat in the courtyard during lunchtime next to a woman from California studying here who proudly claimed to be a vegetarian; I'd made her think twice about her choices.

"You know plants scream when you cut them," I informed her with a serious tone in my voice.

"How do you know?" she asked.

"Ask any psychic and they will tell you they can hear the trees crying after they have been chopped down."

"I don't believe in psychics," she said, dismissively.

"They've conducted scientific experiments where they had someone cut up part of a plant and abuse it. A week later the same person came back and this time they were measuring the electrical responses of the plant and found that when that person came close to the plant the plant remembered that person and was scared." I delivered the line as a matter of fact.

"Really?" she said, finally believing me.

"Yeah, I think if you really want to be sensitive you shouldn't eat plants either . . . but then you would have to starve and die . . . I know, it's a difficult decision . . . That's why I accept that I am a hypocrite and I really enjoy my food." I confessed all this to her and then left, like the Lone Ranger. She probably looked at her food and wondered, Who was that bitch who ruined my appetite?

Chef Lucas stared at me, wondering why I hadn't killed my lobster yet. I handed it to him and asked him if he could kill it for me. He looked at me and smirked.

"You women want equality in the kitchen, but you don't want to do the dirty work or have the strength to get the job done," Chef Lucas said, shaking his head.

"The day you can pop out a bun from your oven I will bow to you," I responded in my horrible French. He wiped the smirk off his face and tore the lobster in half. I was so shocked I had to turn away. He handed the still-moving lobster back to me, but I just pointed for him to put the pieces on the counter. He had no patience for a girl like me. I said, *"Merci"* and he continued inspecting everyone's work without turning back.

I poured the cognac on my lobster shells and aromatic vegetables and stuck in my long fancy lighter and *boom,* it was a beautiful fire. Sage asked Benino, her friend working at the station next to hers, to lend her his lighter but he'd forgotten it in his locker.

"Do you need a lighter?" I asked Sage. She turned to me and paused for a bit before uttering, "Yes" and snatching the lighter from my hand. Sage poured the cognac and flicked the lighter, but the casserole did not catch on fire. She tried a couple more times before she gave up and handed me the lighter back. She took too long and the cognac had probably evaporated.

"I need a beer," she announced.

"Do you want to get one after class?" I offered. I hated beer, but I wanted to buy her one and somehow make it up to her for not being so nice on our first day of Intermediate.

She paused again to consider my offer. Eventually the doubt left her eyes. "Sure. I don't have much time, but we can get a quick one."

After class we ended up going to C'est Ma Vie. As usual, there were not that many customers during the day.

"I'm sorry about the other day—" I began to apologize.

"No sweat," she cut me off. "You're funny thinking you did something bad. I've been in New York City kitchens and the kind of shit men do to you . . ." She drank her wine. "I'm used to getting shoved and mistreated. It comes with the territory. I know, I could be doing something else with my life, but it's hard getting chosen as a female firefighter, so this is the closest thing," she admitted, almost laughing.

"You want to be a firefighter?" I asked, not sure if she was joking.

"When I was younger and liked playing with matches," she replied, mellowing down and letting the wine soothe her nerves.

"So you want to be a chef?" I inquired, trying to see where that would take the conversation.

"Of course, don't you?"

"I just want to own a restaurant. Manage it, let someone else do the cooking in my kitchen," I lied. Then I felt bad about it and figured that over Bordeaux you should tell the truth. "Actually, I'm just killing time. Maybe I'll be a food critic, since I can't go back to being a real journalist." I stuffed myself with cheese so I wouldn't reveal more.

"It's a pretty expensive way of killing time. Why don't you just hang out at cafés pretending to be a writer like all the rich kids I know?"

"Because this way I get my papers to stay in the country and at the end I get a diploma, so I won't feel like I wasted my time."

Sage got real close to me and whispered, "Hey, that guy behind you is a famous author. He has a book on the best-seller list at W. H. Smith. He wrote a novel about stepping on dog shit for a whole year in Paris, or something like that." I turned carefully and studied his face.

Sage whispered, "You would think the first few days after stepping on dog shit he would have looked down."

I was not about to add blood as a thickener to my rooster sauce. I didn't mind eating cooked blood if I found out afterward, but the mere thought of blood in the sauce brought back many memories. Like the red mole we had that included my pet rooster back when I was eleven. My friends hated it when I admitted to growing up with chickens and roosters in my backyard in East L.A., but some stereotypes are true. Of course not everyone had chickens, or a sweet rooster like Ricky, in their backyard, but we did and the day Ricky went from pet to plate I sobbed. I might have to make rooster again now, but I draw the line at adding blood.

Chef Fournier, the first female chef I had ever encountered, came up to me and inquired why I wasn't working. I liked her very much and from the rumors I had heard about the last female chef at Le Coq Rouge, I truly admired her for whatever bullshit she had to put up with to be there, so I didn't want to give her a hard time. She was about to tell me something when the fire alarm went off and she commanded all her students to take everything off the burners and leave the practical room immediately. We all marched down to the street level and walked across the street and watched students pour out of the building. Some of the pastry students had flour on them and were annoyed at having to wait outside, knowing that their soufflés were disasters by now. Two American girls from Intermediate, Cynthia and Persia, were happy about leaving the building so they could take a cigarette break. I caught bits and pieces of their conversation.

"She is so stupid, I don't know why they put her in our group. She's only studying cuisine and isn't pursuing a *grand supérieur diplôme* like us."

"I think it's because Trevor left."

"What a loser. I can't believe he left because he couldn't handle a chef calling him a fag," the tall girl said to the Indian-American girl.

They enjoyed their cigarettes more than food. These were the two students in demonstration who never ate the samples afterward. They would instantly leave and talked about how they were determined to lose weight; they were going to win this fight. After Chef Sauber complained to the students that they were required to taste the demonstration as part of their training, Persia was forced to eat, and during the break she was so disgusted she vomited. Once I was waiting by the bathroom door when she did it. When she came out of the bathroom she avoided looking at me. I thought it was a one-time thing, but I soon discovered it was a regular ritual. I made it a point not to go to the restroom after her because the smell of acid was overpowering. How could you be bulimic and in cooking school? I tried to picture myself as a bulimic or anorexic, and I'm sure there is a Mexican-American woman out there who is, but I couldn't imagine being Mexican and having an eating disorder. Just like I couldn't conceive of being Mexican and on a diet. I was used to fighting with my nine siblings so I could get my share of food to eat. I would eat as fast as I could so I would get seconds and feel satisfied. The thought of wasting food in that manner made *me* want to vomit.

Their cigarette smoke in my face also made me nauseous, and I was about to tell them to point their poisonous smoke elsewhere when Chef Sauber escorted Bassie out of the building, giving her a lecture, in front of Sélange and Françoise, about cuisine being a very serious business. I walked closer to them to listen in as Bassie tried to explain how she was not an arsonist who'd intended to burn up the trash can. It was an accident. She had poured too much cognac into the lobster and when she stuck in the lighter it practically exploded in her face and she stepped back. She probably ignited the paper towels in the garbage can next to her by accident. Poor Bassie looked like a little girl surrounded by upset family members telling her to stop playing with matches. Bassie lowered her head and nodded every time they told her that she was going to be on probation and no more special treatment for whatever disorder or disease she had.

The students were allowed back in and the grades for that day were nullified. I was at my locker when I saw Bassie come in. I tried not to laugh at the image of her setting the garbage can on fire. Poor Bassie; I knew she was trying her best. I'm so glad I had her as a friend because we could both commiserate. I asked her if she wanted to get a drink and, much like her lobster, Bassie's face lit up.

We went to C'est Ma Vie and no one was there except for Jérôme, reading up on his wines. He welcomed us and we ordered two glasses of red. Jérôme recommended the house wine and read off from a book the region it came from. He showed us a map and located the winery.

"They want me to quit," admitted Bassie, holding back tears. "They are willing to give me back my money, but I am going to finish," she said with the determination of an ant.

"Don't they understand what you have?" I asked compassionately.

"I've explained to them that I have ADD and all my allergies, but their answer is that I just shouldn't do it. People like me shouldn't be in the kitchen." Bassie went on to describe all the mistakes she had made and I started recognizing myself in her. Maybe I have whatever she has, just not as bad, I thought to myself.

"The other students are all doing both cuisine and pastry and they think that makes them special. They resent the fact that I am merely a cuisine student and they have to share their kitchen with me. They want me to quit so they can have the extra space and not have to censor themselves with their stupid jokes about the cuisine students in front of me." The more wine Bassie poured into her mouth, the more her frustrations poured out of it.

"I heard Persia and her friend mention you," I revealed.

"Those bitches are mean. They threw a party for our cooking group and didn't invite me." Bassie sulked.

"Can you ask to be moved?" I suggested.

"Yeah, I already tried, but I think this is the administration's way of showing me how incompetent I am by putting me in a class with competitive students who all want to be the next celebrity chef." We both laughed at them, but I secretly imagined myself with my own cooking show. My show would be for single women: how to make a meal in fifteen minutes or less with enough leftovers for the cat.

Jérôme came by and poured more wine into our glasses.

"*Merci*," we both said. We took a sip of the wine and let out a deep sigh.

"I'm so lonely. Paris is the worst city to be in when you're lonely . . . I actually broke down and called my ex-boyfriend," confessed Bassie.

"I thought you said he was a jerk?" I asked carefully.

"He's gotten better," she replied in between swallows. I thought about Armando and wondered how he was doing. On occasion I thought about calling him. When you're dating you think it's so wonderful that your boyfriend is also your best friend. When you break up it sucks double. I knew loneliness very well. Now that Luna was gone and Armando was becoming a distant memory, I only had me; but I wanted to run away from me.

The next day I woke up hungover, again, and quickly threw on some clothes. I couldn't miss the chartered bus to the Loire Valley for my wine tour.

"In my family the first sons always inherited the wine business, but because I was born female it went to my younger brother," Marie-Anne, a translator from Australia who'd joined us on the wine excursion, translated for the winery owner, Véronique. "So I decided to go to school to study winemaking; that's where I met my husband and we decided to start our own winery. We focused on sweet white wines and we are very happy that our business is in continual growth." Véronique then explained how they made their wines and escorted us into their caves. I was not prepared for the cold and crossed my arms and massaged them to generate more heat. Yves handed me his scarf. I looked up at him and was touched by his chivalry.

"*Merci*," I said, looking him up and down. He nodded with a smile and walked ahead to catch up with Véronique and continued asking questions for the benefit of his wine class.

At lunchtime we tested each of their six wines. I'd had a croissant and tea for breakfast, but by then my stomach felt pretty empty. I drank the wine and kept looking around for the meal that had been promised. I'm not good on an almost-empty stomach. I'm worse when I have wine or cheesecake on an empty stomach.

"Are you warm now?" Yves turned to me. He surprised me by speaking a heavily accented English.

"Yes. Thank you so much." I took off his scarf and offered it back to him.

"No, no. Keep it as long as you need it. Have it if you like," he said with a flirtatious smile.

"The wine has made me warm now," I replied, returning a coquettish smile.

"Do you like the wine?" Yves asked me.

"I actually love it." I smiled and batted my eyelashes.

Yves got close to my ear and whispered so Véronique would not hear: "I don't like sweet wines too much, but it's not bad." He tickled my ear in the process. He looked around to make sure no one noticed him whispering. We both swallowed together and stared at each other. We were silent for a few seconds and although we said nothing, I knew he didn't want to leave my side.

"What is the best wine you have ever had?" I asked, attempting to continue our conversation.

"There is no such thing as the best wine, because it may go well with one dish, but not another. It may go well in summer and not in winter. It's all relative."

I rephrased my question: "In your opinion, what is the best wine you have experienced?"

"Well, it wasn't so much the wine, but the food and the woman I had it with," he confided. I smiled and continued with my journalistic probing.

"What wine, which meal, and what woman?"

Yves took a second to reflect, looking at me as if wondering why this was so important for me to know. "The wine was a red 1987 Châteauneuf-du-Pape with beef bourguignon in winter, and the woman was the woman who became my wife and now is my ex-wife," he declared. I looked at his hand; there was no wedding ring or a suntan line revealing there had been one not long ago.

We smiled at each other as we drank. I'm pretty sure I was no longer sober, because he looked like the most handsome man in the world and, without hesitation, I whispered the line to top all lines—the one handed down to me by a saucy Latina friend who swore it would work on any straight man with a pulse. "I wonder what you look like when you come," I whispered into his ear and walked away without a care in the world. I loved how it felt to come on to a man instead of waiting for him to hit on me. Besides, he probably didn't understand my English anyway.

After our liquid lunch we boarded a bus back to the school. When we arrived all the students walked out, and I made my way down the aisle. I was giving the scarf back to Yves when he pulled it to him. I didn't let go of the scarf, so I almost fell on top of him. He caught me.

"Where do you live?" he asked. "Why don't you stay on the bus and the bus driver will take you and me home."

Yves and I hid out in the bus and the driver dropped both of us off at his place. He offered to personally drive me home after making up a story about getting his car keys from his apartment. I followed him like a bad girl, knowing what was to come . . . or who was to come. Yves escorted me into his voluminous white apartment with a view of the Eiffel Tower—the kind of place that made it clear he didn't need to teach.

"Why do you teach?" I asked, assessing his wealth like an Ugly American.

"So I can meet interesting people like you." Yves grinned.

"But you don't know anything about me. How do you know I'm interesting?" I wanted to tease him, first with words, and later . . .

"Oh, I know you are," he assured me. "Would you like me to make you dinner?"

I suppose getting to the sex without dinner would be crude, but food wasn't what I was hungry for. Still, I played along. "Yes, that would be nice." A man was going to cook for me; it made me feel special.

I walked around, studying his library and his art collection, until Yves asked if I wanted to see his wine cellar. I knew he was proud of it, so I obliged.

In the wine cellar he gave me a tour of his collection. He kept his whites and reds separate; I'm sure he never made the mistake of mixing his white laundry with his colors, either. Though if he did, he was the kind of man who would look good in pink. Very manly.

"This is my most prized wine," he said pointing to a bottle. I got close to see the wine label and he grabbed me from behind by putting his arms around my waist. He nibbled on my ear and whispered something dirty in French. I couldn't understand him, but some things don't need translation. We returned upstairs to his apartment and our eyes were glued to each other's. Yves got close to me and held my hands.

"Lick me," I whispered in his ear. We kissed again furiously and tumbled to his plush carpet. The curtains were wide open and the Eiffel Tower from upside down looked like I was looking up a woman's skirt. He practically tore off my dress and fondled my breasts.

"What wine would go well with my *chatte*?" I asked him. He licked my vaginal lips and thought about it for a few seconds, as if analyzing a fine wine, trying to make out all the different flavors. "Let me do it again so I can get a good taste." He smelled them and then licked them again.

"Hmmm, I have the perfect wine for you." He put on his jacket and left me naked on the floor. I waited a few minutes, totally confused, until he returned with a dusty bottle of wine from his cellar.

"Lie down," he ordered me. He poured the wine on my vaginal lips and drank it off me. Seconds later I ejaculated and he drank me, too.

"Hmmm, you are one of the few women I've ever been with who actually ejaculates . . . like a little fountain . . . Do all American women go like that?" he inquired. I looked at him and laughed, "No, only the very special ones who don't ever fake orgasms."

"You are dangerous."

"Mais porquoi?" I asked.

"You don't lie. That's a horrible thing for a woman not to do. You must lie to us; that is your duty as a woman." He continued pouring the wine on my naked body and he cupped my breasts and drank from them.

"I want to be a human food platter and have many men eat food off of me," I confessed to Yves.

"*C'est facile.* Let me make dinner and I'll eat it off of you, *chérie.*"

During wine class I sat in front of Yves and teased him with my eyes. Even though my mind was always distracted with sexual thoughts about him, I managed to learn a thing or two. I always thought the reason why restaurant sommeliers poured a little bit of wine in the diner's glass was so that the person could sample the wine to see if they liked the taste. However, they actually do that so you can make sure the wine cork did not ruin the wine. If the taste of the wine was marred by a bad cork, that was the time to turn it away; otherwise, if you complained after a glass or two, the sommelier would probably take back the wine and just recork it—as Yves admitted to doing on occasion—and return it back to you as a new bottle. The other valuable thing I learned is that in Paris, at most nice restaurants, if you don't finish your wine you can request to have it corked and take it home.

"No one is supposed to give you dirty looks if you do that," Yves said, empowering his novice wine students. Throughout the class Yves and I would pretend nothing was happening between us, but when I walked by the metro he would pick me up in his black Jaguar and we would go back to his apartment. Things were fun, but I knew it wouldn't last. Once you open good wine it has to end or go bad.

On the last day of our wine class we had a test. We had to answer questions like Where do the Beaujolais wines come from? and When are you supposed to drink them? There were also tricky true-or-false questions. When we were done with the written test Yves poured each of us a glass of red wine. We had to taste it and describe it using as many details as possible. The color, the smell, every possible nuance that would give us clues as to where it came from. I looked at the glass of wine and held it up to the light and studied the rich burgundy color. I tilted the glass to see how slowly the wine dripped down the sides of the glass. I stuck my nose in the glass and took in the aroma with my eyes closed. I could smell the earth. I could smell the sky. I could smell my past. The fragrance of the wine took me back to being eight. Everywhere around me were grapevines. On the vine were the most beautiful grapes in California and maybe on earth. My mother picked grapes in front of me and my father picked grapes behind me, with my siblings scattered around me. I imagined that the kind of grapes that made this wine were the kind of grapes that I touched and soiled with my blood once. Being undocumented, my family was used to hiding from the Migra, the INS, Immigration and Naturalization Service, or Homeland Security, or whatever you want to call it now. That one particular day I stopped to admire a bunch of grapes that were hanging so beautifully, as though God had hung them there for me to pick. Maybe it was the way the rays of sunlight hit them during that magic hour that made them so unique to look at amid the many other bunches of grapes. They looked so purple, so plump and soft and just perfect. When I held the bunch in my two hands I felt as though I was carrying a newborn baby or a warm heart. My father came by and tapped me on the head and ordered me to get back to cutting.

"¡Rapido! ¡Apurate! ¡No mas corta, corta!" Fast, just cut, cut, he barked. I quickly grabbed my small knife and was about to cut the stem of the beautiful bunch of grapes when a distant desperate voice yelled, "¡La Migra!" I was startled and accidentally buried the knife in my hand. Blood dripped down my hand and onto the grapes. My blood was deep red; it looked like wine dripping out of me. I yelled and my father put his hand over my mouth to shut me up. I wanted him to hold me and comfort me, but instead he scolded me, "¡Callate!" Seconds later he whispered loudly, "¡Vámonos!" When he took his hand off my mouth I licked my hand to stop the blood. Then we heard everyone running among the grapevines.

"¡Corranle!" my father yelled, ordering his tribe to run away. I yanked the bunch of grapes and took off running with my family. My hand kept bleeding and my blood dripped on the dirt, leaving a trail. I put the bunch of grapes in my bleeding hand to keep the blood from falling out of me. My hand throbbed and the cut felt like it was getting bigger as we ran from the Border Patrol officers in the distance yelling, "INS!" My mother found a run-down shack covered with vines and bushes blending into a hill, camouflaged by the greenery. We all ran toward it and hid inside. We lay low on the dirt. My blood kept dripping on the dirt. No one noticed that I was bleeding and hurting because they were holding their breath, trying not to make a sound, trying to be invisible. We all looked at one another in silent prayer that we didn't get caught or separated. I rubbed my hand against the earth to clog up my cut with dirt. It stung at first, but I finally made it stop.

After an hour of waiting in silence I got hungry and took my bunch of grapes, soiled by my blood, and ate one grape. I didn't care that it had my blood on it; I licked it clean. It could have been that I was just so hungry, but eating that beautiful purple grape comforted me. Since there was no one there to hold me, the grapes comforted me. They numbed the pain of being cut and then ignored. I continued to eat the grapes and each grape I ate was a prayer to God. The largest grape was for my mother and then for my father. I prayed for each one of my siblings so that we would pick enough fruit and vegetables so that we could leave this type of work and get an apartment in the city and never go hungry again . . .

I opened my eyes and saw the wine glass in front of me. I chuckled, because after that memory I did not know what to write down. So I simply wrote on my test: *I smell the earth.* I didn't care about my score on the test since I had already scored with Yves. He had ultimately taught me not to analyze wine but to enjoy it.

A week after the wine class finished Yves and I had agreed to meet for lunch at Ladurée, on the Champs-Élysées. I entered Ladurée and walked up to the hostess. I asked her if she spoke English and, after she nodded that she did, I explained that I was waiting for a friend. She immediately cut me off and moved on to the next person. I clenched my jaw and stifled the urge to yell. Sometimes you didn't know if the French were just plain rude or if their English wasn't good enough to lubricate the social transitions necessary to be respectful . . . which is probably exactly what they say about Americans.

I decided to walk into the restaurant and search for Yves. He might have gotten there early and was already seated at a table. I headed upstairs and found him right away, holding the knee of a beautiful Frenchwoman under the table. I quickly turned away and continued looking at them through a mirror on the wall. My blood rushed to my heart and it beat faster.

Seconds later I felt so cold. I knew he didn't love me, but I didn't have to find out like this! I continued looking at the mirror and observed that he was as charming as ever, fulfilling my stereotype of a Frenchman. The longer I stared, the more I realized I wasn't heartbroken; I was merely disappointed that he didn't laugh as much with me as he was with her. And here I'd thought I was funny. I went downstairs and waited for Yves to meet me as planned. I decided to get in line for the patisserie boutique just to kill time. I was about to order four *macarons* when I turned around and saw Yves kissing his mystery date on the mouth. What a cocky bastard. He knew I would be arriving in five minutes and he was so blatant. So I ordered a dozen *macarons* instead and made him wait for me. I wanted to leave the restaurant and make him wait around all night, but in reality I knew he wouldn't wait more than fifteen minutes. I was his exotic Mexican dish, but not his main meal. I took my beautiful box of *macarons* and stuffed it into my raggedy purse. I knew my purse looked like I had stolen it from a homeless woman, but it was like my loyal friend who had been with me through all the tough times.

"*Chéri!*" I yelled to catch his attention. He turned in my direction and I surprised him by giving him the sloppiest French kiss. The hostess looked at him with disdain and asked him in French if we were ready for our table. Throughout lunch I pretended to be so in love with him. "Kill them with kindness," a priest-turned-politician once told me when I was doing a story on him. "You must lie to us," I recall Yves telling me on our first night together. So I pretended that my life revolved around him and his wine class.

"Yves, you are so funny and amazing . . . I think I'm falling in love with you," I lied, then looked away as though I meant it and felt vulnerable having said it.

He was so flattered by all my attention, but then he started fidgeting with his tie.

"Canela, maybe we should leave," he whispered. He looked around to see what the people at the neighboring tables were looking at since, just minutes ago, he'd been talking and flirting with a blonde. I purposely imitated the other woman. I was cruelly mocking him, but this was the way I spared myself the feelings of being so disappointed by him. I'd known it was going to end; I just hadn't thought it would be that soon.

We strolled up the Champs-Élysées, holding hands. I stopped pretending I was in love with him, and just tried to keep a happy exterior to avoid showing my disappointment. We walked past all the overpriced American franchises, up to the Louis Vuitton megastore. Surprisingly, there was no line that day.

"Let's go in here," Yves said.

"Sure," I said, excited about finally seeing what the big deal was about. I straightened myself up a bit before walking in, as though I were entering the Vatican or the Smithsonian. The designer suit–clad doorman looking like a CIA agent opened the doors to a marble palace. The store resembled a museum; the purses looked like priceless artifacts. There were tourists in shorts standing alongside women in designer outfits. A trio of Muslim women in silk veils, looking as made-up and modern as their veils permitted, walked around escorted by their bodyguard. They looked irked by the fact that it was so crowded. I had to force myself not to stare at them or judge them. They had jewels and luxuries from head to toe, but they didn't have freedom. Sure, they could buy whatever they desired, but they couldn't move free of their bodyguard's watchful eye. They carried large purses and occasionally would remove their Gucci sunglasses to inspect the bags and LV leather bracelets. If I were them I would exchange all my jewels and luxuries for freedom, I thought. I shook my head. None of my business, I reminded myself, and turned my attention to a pack of wild Chinese tourists, scurrying around buying up merchandise as fast as their tour bus would allow.

"No, you cannot purchase two of the same items," the LV saleswoman informed a woman in French-accented English while studying the woman's Chinese passport. The translator for the Chinese tourist explained, and the woman wanting to buy her two identical LV signature bags pointed at a different bag. In the background I saw a Japanese girl named Miyuki from cooking school purchasing several items. I thought about saying hi, but I was afraid to have her see me with Yves, so I turned away before our eyes could meet.

Yves went to the men's section, and then we made our way to the second floor, where it wasn't so crowded. I spied a burgundy crocodile bag, all by itself, radiating. The bag had caught my attention from a distance and I walked toward it until I saw the price and my hand froze. Who the hell needs a sixteen-thousand-euro bag? Obviously *need* is not the appropriate word here. Who the hell wants a sixteen-thousand-euro bag? Ah, but these were not just bags; they were status symbols, archetypal symbols. When the LV saleswoman would open the bags for the customers to see the insides, the shoppers would inspect them, sticking their fingers inside to feel, probing them carefully the way a gynecologist would examine a vagina. As I passed the countless counters I chuckled quietly, imagining hearing: "Yes, this vagina is very sturdy. It never loosens. No matter what you stick in there, the elasticity and firmness will remain intact." The female customer would look at the price and think what a bargain it was. How else could you explain paying five hundred to two thousand to sixteen thousand euros for a mere handbag?

Then I looked up and saw the vagina—I mean the purse—of my dreams. It was a black leather bag with a gold zipper standing high and mighty all by itself. I approached the counter and stared at the bag. Yves told the unoccupied LV saleswoman to bring it down for me to look at. I immediately opened the bag and inspected the suede interior. It was so brand-new, not a scratch or a speck of dust. Just holding it made me feel like a virgin again. The gold zipper looked like a garden snake with a gold line, all curved. Yves saw the genuine excitement in my eyes until I saw the price: 695 euros . . . almost a thousand dollars!

"Can I buy it for you?" Yves asked. I took a moment to absorb his question.

"You want to buy it for me?" It didn't feel like a gift to celebrate our lust for each other as much as a good-bye present. I guess I'd done such a good job of convincing him how much I cared for him that he was now afraid I had serious feelings for him and had to say good-bye.

"Yes. Let me buy you this bag," he insisted.

"Yes. I would love that. *Merci, chéri,*" I said, accepting that whether he bought me the bag or not, whatever we had was over. Yves gave his French ID to the LV saleswoman and she quickly found his account. I took a peek at the monitor when he wasn't looking and saw he had made so many purchases of bags that either his mother was getting an LV purse for Mother's Day every year or he was a serial purse giver and this was his M.O. for getting rid of women. I guess American men take you on a romantic weekend getaway and then break up with you, and Frenchmen give purses. Hey, at least he didn't take me to a Dodgers game to break up with me, like some Latino men do.

Yves's platinum card cleared and the transaction was complete. We were given a receipt and told to wait for our merchandise at the main counter by the entrance. Yves held my hand and told me I was beautiful. Now he was being so sweet. Yves was going to break up with me or not call me again and this was the way he did it. He'd started out as a fine wine and ended up being just fermented grape juice.

Close to us, an American tourist grabbed a purse that a Muslim woman was considering buying. The Muslim woman reached for it and took it away from the American woman. She was shocked by the American's rudeness and pulled it out of her hands.

"Don't you be pulling it out of my hands when I'm looking at it!" screamed the American tourist. The Muslim woman yelled back in Arabic or bad French and a tug-of-war ensued. The LV "CIA" agents quickly escorted the American woman out while she shouted, "You fuckin' French bastards, why aren't you kicking her out too! Kick the veiled rich bitch out too!" Everyone watching shook their heads and silently thought to themselves, "Stupid Ugly Americans."

CHAPTER 11

Eat Woman Drink Man

"Cooking is too serious a job to leave to women," Chef Sauber said via the translator at a demonstration. Sage turned to me and rolled her eyes. That comment was almost as bad as one of Chef Tulipe's—"That is why women should be in the kitchen; for those special jobs that require little delicate hands"—and Chef Plat's—"You have to be strong to be in a kitchen because it requires a lot of stamina and strength, ladies." Chef Chocon was the worst with his comments: "This is the kind of steak that keeps your husbands happy" and "Handle the quail the same way you would handle a young bride."

"Have any of the chefs ever called you 'Chef'?" asked Sage. I thought about it. "You mean refer to me as 'Chef'?" I asked for clarification.

"Yeah, especially after they grade you. I've only heard the chefs calling the men in my group 'Chef.'"

I took a few seconds to wonder why I'd never heard the chefs telling the male students, "This is the kind of fish that keeps your wives happy so they won't do the plumber." Or "When you graduate from here you will go home to your girlfriends and your wives and make them very happy and satisfied." It was clear to me, and to many of the women, like Sage, who were serious about becoming chefs, that for the French chefs the women were there to become better cooks for their husbands. The men were there for a career; the women, for self-improvement.

"There is only one woman who owns a restaurant with a Michelin star in all of France, and she inherited it from her father," revealed Sage. I saw how upset she was and sympathized with her. She had worked as a cook and was tired of the sexism she personally experienced in the culinary industry.

"What does it matter if you are talented and ambitious if you are a woman?" she lamented, shaking her head. "It's just not fair," muttered Sage.

"All the nuts in this school have a rancid smell; even the chefs," Henry once said when he was being a naughty translator. That joke summed up everything. All the chefs who taught at the school, with the exception of Chef Plat and Chef Frédérique, were in their fifties and came from a different generation, one in which sexist comments were perfectly fine; or maybe "politically correct" had no translation or place in France. Henry had also jokingly informed me, "Didn't you know, Le Coq Rouge is the place where old French chefs come to die?"

Nobody studied for the written exam. It was ridiculous to study so hard for a test that didn't matter. In a professional kitchen no one will ask you which fish has four fillets; they will just want to see you filleting them and doing it right. So when the woman giving the test turned around to talk to Françoise, everyone would whisper to his or her neighbor for the answer. I rushed through it and finished it quickly.

I sharpened my knives and went over the ten recipes in my head. Bassie and I were taking turns describing all the steps we had to memorize. Becky came up to us and told us that someone who worked in the kitchen had seen the ingredients and the recipes for *pavé de boeuf* or the *blanc de barbue poêlé,* the beef and the fish dish. Bassie and I disregarded the eight other recipes and focused on those two instead. Sage came over and sat next to me and began sharpening her knives violently.

"So what are the two recipes again?" she asked me.

"It's the *pavé de boeuf* and the *blanc de barbue poêlé*... Man, I hope I get the beef recipe because the fish one has so many steps and we still have to have enough time to make the hollandaise sauce by hand, which is the extra recipe to prove our technique," I admitted.

"If you get the fish recipe, I'll exchange with you. I like the fish recipe," Sage said while scraping her chef's knife against the sharpening steel.

"Thanks," I said, touched that she would do that for me.

Chef Plat came down to the courtyard and asked Group D to come up; they were ready for us. We marched upstairs and waited in the hallway, as was the routine. The chef informed us that a red chip signified beef, and blue indicated fish. When my name was called I said a silent prayer, stuck my hand into the pot, and pulled out a red chip. I smiled triumphantly, knowing I would have more time and could make fewer mistakes.

❧ *Pavé de Boeuf* ❧
Beef Steak

4 rump steaks, 140 grams
peanut oil

CELERY PURÉE
600 grams celery root

500 milliliters milk
salt, pepper, nutmeg

CELERY FLAN

400 grams celery purée
20 grams butter
100 milliliters to 150 milliliters heavy cream
2 eggs
salt, pepper, nutmeg
Decoration for flan: carrot, celery, and the
green part of 1 leek

GARNISH

1 kilogram potatoes (waxy type) turned *anglaise* style
150 grams goose fat
Decoration: 1 bunch chervil

SAUCE

100 milliliters Madeira wine
400 milliliters veal stock
15 grams butter
1 truffle

Chef Plat opened a small tin can with no label and took out the truffles for the beef dish. He handed me a small truffle as carefully as if he were passing me the baby Jesus.

"Take care of your truffle," he advised. "If you lose it or it's stolen you will not get another one." I cut the truffle in half and used half of it for the sauce and the other half to make thin strips for decoration.

Half an hour before the exam was to be over, my flan was still not fully cooked. It had been in the oven for almost fifty minutes and it was not cooked! The toothpick I stuck in came back moist. I checked the oven to see if it was at the correct temperature; there were no signs that it wasn't working. Perhaps I added too much cream or maybe the oven was not functioning properly. I quickly seared the meat and made one piece rare, another medium rare, another medium, and another well done to show that I knew how to cook meat. I grabbed a pan for the meat to rest on, but I dropped it and it made a thunderous noise. Everyone stopped and looked at me. My hands were trembling so much I couldn't make them stop. Chef Plat yelled, "Relax" in French. I had never been that nervous before. On many occasions my life had been threatened, but I had never felt scared; here I was merely trying to make food and I was mortified.

With ten minutes left I started the hollandaise sauce for my technique test. I placed the metal bowl with the eggs over the bain-marie and whipped away like Minutemen were chasing me in the desert. I was dehydrated and dying to get to the finish line. With two minutes left I poured the failed hollandaise sauce into the presentation saucer and added salt and cayenne. It tasted watery and I knew my eggs weren't cooked. I felt like such a failure: not only had I failed to fertilize my eggs by my societal deadline, but I also couldn't even cook them on time. As my mother would say, "¡Ay, que vergüenza!" How embarrassing. What a disgrace.

"*C'est fini!*" yelled the chef, announcing that time was up, ready or not. Sage yelled and begged for more time: "*Une minute, s'il vous plaît!*" I handed him my platter with my beef and my deformed celery flan. I swear I'd done everything I was supposed to do and yet it had turned out like dog doo-doo. Even the beautiful bird of paradise I had painstakingly designed on my flan looked like a cockroach. The chef covered my sauce and platter with clear plastic and wrote a number on it for the judges. Next to the other beef platters my dish looked mediocre. I sucked at turning potatoes and shaping them into perfect little oval things. No matter how hard I tried, I did not have the coordination to get them to look even or professional. This was not one of my talents, and it was painful to accept that even Benino, who was not the brightest guy, could turn out potatoes that could be served at a three-star restaurant.

At the graduation ceremony the graduates of Intermediate Cuisine were called in alphabetical order and their ranking announced after. When they called Miyuki's name, Sage made a face.

"I knew she was going to come in first! It's not fair," Sage whispered angrily into my right ear. Bassie said a little too loudly that Miyuki had originally gotten the fish, but she didn't want to do it so she smiled at the chef in charge of the exam and asked for the beef, and he happily obliged. This only added fuel to the fire. Sage had gotten the fish and was still pissed off at herself for being so nonchalant about the exam and finishing five minutes late.

A snooty British guy named Jason got second place. "He's such a jerk," Bassie whispered in my other ear.

My name was called and I was just grateful that I'd passed the exam and wondered who was whispering things about me. About one hundred students got their diplomas that day; everyone applauded because the ceremony had finally ended. I got my diploma, but I refused to look at my scores on my final sheet. I gave myself a consolation speech in the ladies' room when I looked in the mirror: "I'm proud of you, Canela. For someone who never cooked a day in her life before cooking school, you did good." If that didn't help, two glasses of champagne would make me want to celebrate this and all the other small accomplishments. Bassie had also sought comfort in a bottle. She had already had too much wine, and was rambling about Henry being such a great lover.

"What did you say about Henry?" I asked her, trying to make sure I hadn't imagined what she'd said.

"Ooops. I wasn't supposed to say anything." Bassie covered her mouth like a little girl who had just said a bad word.

"What do you mean?" I asked, trying to show her how non-important the whole Henry thing was to me.

"I'm sorry. I know you were with him and—"

"And you fucked him anyway . . . It doesn't mean anything to me," I assured her.

"I see the way you look at him," Bassie said, too serious for my comfort. Was she accusing me of something?

"I don't care. Have fun with him. He's . . . fun," I said to her nonchalantly.

"You sure that doesn't bother you?" she asked me.

"No. There was nothing serious. Henry doesn't get serious," I confessed, showing too much emotion.

"Ah! See, I can tell you still have feelings for him," Bassie said, proud of her detective work. She giggled like a little sister having caught her older sister kissing a photograph of her latest crush. Although I liked Bassie most days, sometimes I wanted to treat her like a little sister and lock her in the closet or tape her mouth shut.

"No . . . Look, let's talk about something else. I know how lonely it gets in Paris, so I'm happy you have a new friend . . . with benefits." I was trying to get the image of Bassie and Henry in sexual positions off my inner movie-theater screen. Bassie was not bad-looking, but I couldn't imagine her being his type. I bet they were drunk.

"Look. They brought out the *macarons*," I announced and made a run for the dessert table to get away from the conversation. I grabbed a burgundy *macaron* and forgot my problems; the five-second sweet high I got from a few bites was enough to make me forget Henry. It was so delicious and sinful I couldn't stop till

I'd finished all the burgundy-colored *macarons*. Miyuki came up to the dessert table.

"Are they good?" Miyuki asked in her British-accented English.

"Yes. They are amazing. I must leave the table now or I'll eat them all."

She tasted one and giggled. Miyuki was so pretty and petite, with white pearl earrings to go with her outfit. Chef Guillaume, the pastry chef, came up to her and told her he'd made the *macarons* himself, smiling like the big flirt that he was. She complimented him and laughed at his stupid jokes. I left the dessert table and looked around to see all the various groups and cliques; it was like high school again. Sélange came up to me and said that the administrator needed to talk to me; it was urgent. I left the celebration and went into the office. The administrator asked me to sit down, and that's when I knew it was serious. I was expecting her to tell me that I had not passed and I was going to get kicked out or something bad like that when she started apologizing.

"I don't know how this mistake happened, but for some reason you are not registered for Superior Cuisine."

"I paid for all three courses at the same time," I reminded her.

"Yes, that's why it's unexplainable. But you'll just have to wait fifteen weeks until the next course starts."

"Fifteen weeks!" I said, raising my voice. I couldn't hide my anger. Fifteen weeks meant that I would be alone with my suicidal thoughts.

"Well, why can't you just register me back in?" The solution seemed so obvious I couldn't understand why they hadn't already done it.

"Because it's all full. There is absolutely no room left . . . Wait a minute. There is a class starting in ten weeks."

"Great. Then register me for that class."

"It's an intensive class. Is that okay?"

I had sworn to myself never to do another intensive class again, but the prospect of spending fifteen weeks away from cooking school with no real friend in Paris made me reconsider my promise. "Yes. It's all right."

"Maybe you can work on your French in those ten weeks because Superior Cuisine is not translated," she reminded me. I nodded, left her office, and went back to the reception. An hour later I went to clean out my locker. Sage walked into the locker room lost in her thoughts. She was smiling and I asked her what she was scheming.

"Who? Me? Why do you ask?" she said with a big smile.

"You're smiling. Two hours ago you were pissed off and bitter."

"What are you doing tonight?" she asked me, changing the subject.

"I have no plans. As a matter of fact, for the next ten weeks I have no plans."

"What do you mean? You're continuing with Superior, aren't you?"

"No, they screwed up and didn't register me for Superior. Now I have to kill time on my own until Intensive Superior Cuisine begins, ten weeks from now."

I had agreed to meet Sage by the metro next to her apartment in the Maraïs. Sage had urged me to wear something sexy, so I was anticipating a blind date or some kind of setup. I was not prepared for her plans.

"I got an invitation from Chef Sauber to come over to his apartment. He wants to cook dinner for me."

"He wants to cook dinner for you? Why do you want me to come along if he invited you?" I asked.

"I started telling him about how much I wanted a *stage* at a three-star restaurant and how disappointed I was that I hadn't placed. I worked so hard and I didn't place. I practically cried in his champagne, so he felt sorry for me and invited me to dinner to talk about it." Sage seemed a little too eager for me to believe her.

"So what's the problem? Why do I need to go?" I asked, not bothering to hide my suspicion.

"You saw how depressed I was and how much champagne I drank . . . well, I was flirting with him and now I think he expects me to show him some flesh or let him taste me or something."

"So do you want me as a chaperone or am I a two-for-one deal?"

"Look, just come with me," she said, rolling her eyes and not answering my question. "We can flirt with him and play along and see if he can get us both a *stage* at one of the best restaurants."

"But I'm not planning on doing a *stage*. I don't care about that."

"Okay, then do this as a favor to me. Look, how often does a world-famous chef cook for you at his apartment? We'll just eat his food, drink his wine, and laugh at his jokes, and if he starts getting nasty or inappropriate I'll take pictures of him in a compromising position and blackmail him," she admitted, trying to make it sound as innocent as possible.

"Why do you want to do this? You're such a good cook you can probably earn it on your own."

"Canela, come on. We both know it's the guys who get all the respect and that the blondes and pretty girls who flirt with the chefs get higher scores. Look at Miyuki. There's no way she could have gotten first place. I have a friend who was right next to her station and she tells me Miyuki flirts with the chefs all the time and they help her with things . . . I've heard things . . ."

"But it's wrong to—" the feminist in me interjected. Yes, by now you surely know I am a hypocrite, but having sex with a teacher for fun is one thing; doing it to get a good grade or get ahead is another.

"Canela, please save the lecture. Yes, if we were in the U.S., this would be unthinkable. But here in France, seduction is how you get ahead. I'm just playing their game."

"Don't you think it's degrading to—?" I tried to reason one last time.

"No. I really want this. Please help me. It will be quick. I promise."

"Okay, I'll go with you, but the minute anything weird happens, I'm leaving." Sage knew I meant it.

Sage and I rehearsed our roles and we agreed on hand signals and gestures that would help us communicate with each other in case Chef Sauber tried something. Sage asked around in her broken French for directions, and after several failed attempts a little old lady made us follow her and pointed to a tiny street not found on any tourist map. We climbed the stairs to a decrepit apartment building. We rang the doorbell, and as soon as he opened the door it struck me that this was not really Chef Sauber's apartment. A man so successful and creative would have a residence that would rival Yves's apartment. I knew Chef Sauber was divorced, but this apartment was too tiny and unkempt to be his. In demonstration class he was always meticulous, organized, and clean. You could eat off him. This apartment was out of character. He caught me studying the interior design and said he'd just moved in and was sorry the place was a mess. Sage handed him a bottle of Jack Daniel's and he kissed her on both cheeks, commenting on how thoughtful it was of her to remember how much he liked American whiskey. Sage introduced me and Chef Sauber said, "Viva México" to demonstrate that he remembered me clearly. He kissed me on both cheeks and I got a whiff of his fine cologne.

When we sat down on his couch, I could practically feel the sexual tension left behind by other young American female cuisine students. Sexual tension, just like violent energy, leaves an imprint on things in the ether. I've developed a feeling for it over years of covering all sorts of stories. I've reported on everything from rape and gang violence to celebrity gossip. I was a social issues reporter covering immigrant stories, but did a little bit of everything just so I wouldn't get bored. On occasion when I was covering a march or a rally I would get pushed by an anarchist pretending to be an activist or get teargassed by police or shoved and threatened by any number of officials or men in power. Whenever I would return to the scene of the incident, the wind would practically whisper to me all the details that had come before, and the energy would be heavy.

I reclined on the couch and lost my balance—my legs went up and I'm sure I accidentally gave Chef Sauber a peek at my leopard-print panties. Sage looked at me, wondering if I had started flirting already. I shot a look back at her to tell her it was an accident and she should start pleading her case. Sage was about to share with Chef Sauber how she'd dreamed of being a chef since she was a little girl, making pancakes in her play kitchen, when he interrupted her, telling her to save her story. The stuffed quails needed to be taken out of the oven. He left for the kitchen and I got up and looked around. On the floor was mail. I made sure his back was to us, then studied the date on the junk mail: five months ago. I looked around for a few seconds before he returned with two glasses of champagne.

"*Voilà. L'apéritif.*" He gave us each a glass and we drank. I slowly put the pieces together and realized that this was the place where he seduced women. Maybe he wasn't married anymore, but only his real girlfriend would get to be in his real apartment. This was the casa chica, the small house for the mistresses and lovers.

Sage continued her story and he interrupted her again, this time to compliment her on the sexy dress she was wearing.

"The uniforms make the women so unattractive," Chef Sauber said. I wanted to reply that it was supposed to make us look like sacks of potatoes so the chefs would keep their hands off us, but I wasn't drunk enough to just spit it out in my usual uncensored style. Sage took the compliment with ease and flirtatiously complimented him back.

"Chef Sauber, you also look very handsome out of your uniform," Sage commented, using her little-girl voice. He smiled and drank from his wine.

"*S'il vous plaît,* call me Renault. We are now friends," he declared.

"I heard you were good friends with several of the chefs from the three-star restaurants," Sage continued. He waved his head and sort of agreed.

"Yes, it looks good on your résumé to work at these places, but you must also find a place where you will feel comfortable. Sometimes all you do is cut vegetables at the three-star restaurants, but you can do a lot more at smaller and lesser known restaurants."

"Yes, that's true, but I want to go back to New York City with a strong résumé that will get me considered for sous-chef and eventually become a chef," Sage countered.

"If that's what you want, then no problem. I will help you. I will call Ducasse or Savoy or Robuchon. Whichever one you want me to call," he offered without hesitation.

Sage's face lit up as if Santa Claus had just told her she was getting a pony for Christmas. Chef Sauber left our side to attend to the kitchen.

"Sage, you got what you wanted—now let's fake a headache and get out of here," I demanded.

"*Mademoiselles, venez ici,*" Chef Sauber said, calling us into the kitchen. When I saw the table all set up for an haute cuisine experience, plans for a pretend headache vanished. Why waste a free meal? I asked myself. I could fake the headache after we ate. Or, better yet, a food allergy.

We sat down and had a *salade de homard au melon* with strawberry vinaigrette for our first dish, or as our entrée, as they really call it in France. He would join us at the table to eat but would become our waiter and sommelier at different times throughout the meal. When he brought the main dish to the table, my eyes watered and my mouth tingled. On our plates were two perfectly positioned quails stuffed with green seedless grapes and foie gras. So this is what they were supposed to look like done right. When I'd done my stuffed quails in practical, I'd been unable to remove the skin without cutting little holes everywhere. My poor quails had looked like a serial killer had butchered them in an alley and the police were trying to reassemble them to make sense of the crime scene.

"What kind of sauce is this?" I asked Chef Sauber.

"Truffle sauce," he responded. I wanted to ask how he'd made the sauce, but I didn't really care. When was I going to have the money to buy lots of truffles and make sauce like that? I ate the first quail and, feeling as stuffed as the bird, was ready to fake my headache when the chef pulled out a marijuana joint and smoked it in front of us. Sage and I looked at each other, ready to make our hand gestures for "Let's go." Chef Sauber took a hit and made a funny face that broke up the seriousness of our moods and we laughed. He imitated Cheech and Chong and I didn't know whether to be offended or amused by this Frenchman's interpretation of them.

"I am so bad, no?" he asked. "But we are friends, no?" he said with his cute little French accent that would make you forgive a poodle humping your leg.

"I have a headache. I'm starting to feel not so good," I said, trying to sound convincing.

"Try it," he commanded, sticking the joint in my face. "The headache will go away," he advised me. In her inebriated state, Sage encouraged me to take a hit. I told her to do it first, hoping she would not go through with it. Unfortunately for me, Sage took a hit and poured herself some more whiskey. She took another hit and giggled like I'd never seen a tough broad do. They both looked at me, waiting for me to do it too. I didn't want to do it, not because I'm a good girl and I was saying no to drugs, but because I was afraid of my libido. I hardly ever smoked pot, but on the few occasions when I had, it was for medicinal purposes—when I was younger I couldn't have an orgasm because of Catholic guilt, but a couple of hits silenced the chanting comadres in my head telling me I was going to go to hell for having sex before marriage.

I smoked it, pretending like everything was fine, but then I gave Sage the hand signals. She didn't exactly ignore me; Sage was just mesmerized by Chef Sauber and his magical dishes. I ate the rest of my dinner and it seemed like the most delicious food I had ever tasted.

"Are you ready for dessert?" he asked. After a few hits, I was so ready for anything. Our emergency signals were soon forgotten and there was no resistance.

He brought out miniature soufflés and informed us that they were made with pear. The plates were decorated so beautifully with pear sorbet and a raspberry coulis. He carried a small bowl with fresh whipped cream and fed a spoonful to Sage.

"I want you to taste what fine handmade whipped cream

tastes like," he said proudly. Sage licked the spoon, and then he fed me a spoonful.

"It's delicious, *n'est-ce pas*?" he asked me. I stared at him and debated who was more delicious, the dessert or the chef feeding it to me. I finished eating the dessert with my spoon and then I licked the coulis left on the plate. He was so flattered by my gesture that he took out his large cock and put it on my plate and I continued licking. Sage's eyes widened as I put his warm cock in my cream-filled mouth. I was so aroused by the food and his touch and I wanted him to come in my mouth. I wanted to taste him. I licked him like a hungry woman and my tongue explored him. I buried my face in his pubic hair and smelled his essence. He caressed my hair and called me all sorts of beautiful things I couldn't make out in French. I'm sure he called me beautiful; all women are beautiful to men at this moment. I caressed his balls with my fingers and he gasped. I kept doing that and licking him harder, taking him in all the way back to my throat. He gasped louder and even Sage was aroused by now. She got up behind him and put her hands under his shirt and massaged his chest and his nipples. He gasped louder and tried kissing her. I grabbed his pelvis with my two hands and thrust him into my mouth. He went deep and I could feel by his pulsating penis that he was ready to explode. I yanked his penis out of my mouth and gently put my lips around his hole and he was coming. Would he be as delicious as the food he made? His sperm filled my mouth and I could feel my wet vagina dripping. At that second I realized that I love to experience life through my mouth. I was like a little baby discovering the world with my tongue and my mouth again. Flashes of all the men I had loved and tasted came to me like a heavenly menu of forbidden pleasure. Each man was a meal or an appetizer, enjoyed and digested.

Chef Sauber pulled away and sat down on the couch. Sage tried to continue stimulating him, but he was too sensitive. He needed a few minutes to breathe. I left to go to the bathroom and looked at myself in the mirror. Had I wanted something more than just sexual pleasure from Chef Sauber I would have felt ashamed, but up to this point he was the most delicious man I had ever consumed with my mouth and eyes, and I didn't even love him . . . I actually loved food and dessert more than sex. How wonderful that a man who gave me both made me realize that. I washed my face and looked in the mirror again, knowing I couldn't care less if I placed or got a *stage;* nothing meant anything. I had nothing to lose and nothing to gain from this. I was a woman in no-woman's-land.

In the mirror behind me, Luna appeared holding a letter. I turned around and she was not there. I shook my head—the shock of seeing Luna brought me down and I began to think of the ramifications of what I had just done. Would there be rumors that I'd had the chef for dinner, or would Sage get crap for this later? Would this affect Chef Sauber's ability to grade me? I adjusted my clothes and was about to tell Sage to leave with me, but Chef Sauber and Sage were in the middle of a second course. He was on top, humping her and licking her exposed breasts. They were having too much fun to be interrupted. I just hoped Sage had remembered to bring condoms with her so she wouldn't be rumored as the second American girl to have Chef Sauber's bastard child.

I led myself to the door and left before they looked up. I walked around looking for the metro and realized I was in Henry's arrondissement. I thought about going to his apartment and just surprising him, but he was probably getting it on with Bassie. I would hate to have him think I actually cared about him.

CHAPTER 12

Alive and Rotting in Paris

I forgot to drink water and I was hungover the next morning. At about one P.M. I realized that it wasn't a hangover but depression. I had no reason to get out of bed. For the next ten weeks, while I was out of cooking school, I had no reason to even leave my apartment. But if I didn't get out of bed La Calaca Flaca would visit me again, and death didn't look so bad from her perspective.

"You don't gain weight ever again and the pain is gone forever," she would whisper seductively, tickling me if I didn't listen to her.

I had to get out of bed, I told myself, and I scrambled to come up with reasons to go outside. I reminded myself how little money I had and that I was forced to make some money one way or another.

I walked past an American art school in the Eleventh Arrondissement and saw a flyer seeking models to pose nude for the basic drawing class. It was 80 euros a sitting. All I had to do was be still. I walked into the office and the French art teacher looked me up and down. The French art teacher spoke some English, and she told me I would make a good life-drawing model.

"Normally all the models are so skinny, it's boring, but you are interesting with your little balls of fat here and there, nice little circles," she said in her best English.

"Curves? You mean curves?" I said nicely.

"Yes, curves, that's what you Americans like to call them. I like that for my students. They need to draw all sort of bodies, not just pretty petite ones."

The first class was nerve-racking, but after losing my robe and twenty minutes of the same pose, my spirit left my body and floated first over the Seine, then across the Atlantic, and then across the United States to my mother's house in Boyle Heights. My mother was leaving the house sucking on a milk paleta. She went to the local botânica on Cesar Chavez to meet with Doña Elvira, a curandera who would close her eyes and see me naked in Paris. They conversed in Spanish and discussed what I was doing.

"I don't want to tell you this, but your daughter . . . How shall I put it . . . ?"

"You can tell it to me straight," my mother told her.

"Your daughter likes having sex with many men . . . not at the same time, but she—"

"She is a puta, yes, I know that, but will she come back and marry Armando?" My mother kept pressing Doña Elvira for the future. Doña Elvira looked deeper with her mind's eye and I began to shake my head to tell her no, but the art teacher coughed to let me know I shouldn't move and I snapped open my eyes to the reality of many men watching me naked. I stared back at them, admiring each of their manly qualities. They grew uncomfortable feeling naked and exposed in my gaze. I thought, Yes I like to have sex with different men. They are the spice of life. Why settle for just one spice or flavor when your palate is hungry for more?"

My work as a nude model was rewarding. However, I still needed to make more money. I walked dogs and placed an ad in the *FUSAC*, seeking English students. I taught English to old French men at cafés, who were really just interested in flirting with me. As long as they were paying for a drink and a lesson, and kept me company, I would talk to them for an hour or two. Most of them were married and I would repeatedly turn down their requests to take me out to dinner. It was my rule that I would not date married men . . . Okay, I admit it: once I accepted an invitation with a married man, but only because I had promised myself I would go to Jules Verne in the Eiffel Tower.

As an aperitif my date ordered me a kir royal, champagne with cassis syrup, and I was hooked. We ordered the *dégustation menu* for only 120 euros and had seven little courses with *amuse-bouche* after *amuse-bouche*. I drank three kir royals throughout the meal but then my stomach started talking to me. It would make funny noises until it was tired of talking and decided to explode. I pushed down my stomach and quickly excused myself to the ladies' room. I prayed as I rushed to the restroom that there would be an empty stall for me. The horrors of having to wait in line made my heart skip a beat. I opened the door to the bathroom and jumped into the only stall. The bathroom was empty and I opened my mouth. I quickly vomited 200 euros' worth of food and drink. The carbonation in the champagne was too much for my body and my stomach was completely cleansed. When I stood up and washed out my mouth I looked in the mirror and thought, Wow, this is what it must feel like to be a supermodel.

When I was a young writer learning to put sentences together I always fantasized about being a starving writer in Paris. Paris is wonderful when you can share it with someone you love, but it's torture when you're alone and suicidal and see couples walking around making out like they've found their happy ending and women in wedding dresses strutting around as if they own Paris and are the only ones who know romance.

I used to think New Yorkers were rude, and then I moved to Paris. Now I like New Yorkers. Even the pigeons in Paris have attitudes. I'm pissed and I'm walking and the pigeons don't fly out of my way like regular pigeons. New York City pigeons step away, but the Parisian pigeons look at you like they're telling you, "You move. You're the tourist. I live here!" The Parisians hate tourists, but after putting up with Parisians for almost seven months I decided that the tourists were the best thing about Paris. Tourists are usually happy and moved to joy or tears at all the beauty that surrounds them. Parisians who are so used to beauty become ugly and jaded; nothing impresses them anymore.

As much as I wanted to avoid taking a French class again, I broke down and signed up for one. The three-week intensive course was guaranteed to get me beyond the "tourist level." So I paid the precious money I was earning posing nude and walking dogs and teaching old Frenchmen English, and thought this would be the best way to finally learn French.

Surprisingly, I was the only American in my section. There were a few Mexican students in their early twenties, but they hardly showed up to class. They had a reputation of being the rich kids from the Mexico City bourgeoisie who only came to Paris to party. They had to sign up for classes to keep their parents off their backs, but they cared more about dancing the night away at the clubs at Bastille and on the Champs-Élysées than learning French.

For the first few days we worked on the present tense and I could understand a lot of it because I spoke Spanish. The more French I learned, the better my Spanish got. I learned to introduce myself and tried to explain my life's dilemma, but no one understood me, or my French. We were not allowed to speak anything other than French, so the memories of being a child all came back to me. I remembered learning English by watching TV, so I tried watching French TV, but I found it was mostly dubbed bad American shows that I wouldn't watch in English.

One day in class I made a comment about the sexism of the Romance languages and asked all sorts of questions about the status of Frenchwomen. The teacher, being a Frenchwoman herself, defended their social system; she felt that Frenchwomen were not like American women in the sense that they didn't want to be men; rather they wanted to be friends with men. She also added that France had better child-care services and protection for women than the United States did. I tried explaining the feminist movement in my horrible French, but I felt like a two-year-old toddler who kept getting water instead of milk. The teacher said that she understood me, but that my thoughts were considered "feminist" in France. At first I was very happy when she said I was a feminist, but I quickly learned that being called a feminist in France is not necessarily a good thing. You see, Frenchwomen claim that they don't want to fight with men, they want to get along with men, and that they love being seduced. Men are supposed to seduce, women are supposed to keep themselves beautiful and open to men's advances. Yes, women are equal, but they are also different. They don't want to *be* men. They see themselves as women and still have all the rights, like government-funded child care and maternity leave and the other great stuff feminists have fought for in the United States but haven't been fully achieved there.

During one of the exercises I tried explaining what it was like to be an American of Mexican ancestry. The students listened, but very few people could understand what it was like to be a hybrid person, living in two worlds. All the students described their countries of origin, and then we had the opportunity to bring up the stereotypes of each country. Of course, everyone complained about the United States and all the horrible things about the government. Even I added a few things that no one else had brought up. When it came time for each student to defend their country and shatter the stereotypes, I found myself really caring about the United States. I agreed with what everyone said, but I countered that the kind of life I got to live in the States was one that couldn't have happened in any other country. I explained to them about the American dream and what that meant to people like me. I shared how I came from a poor country that offered very little opportunity, and how my parents had had no choice but to leave the country they loved and bring me to the United States. No, I was not welcome, but I found a refuge that eventually became a home.

I explained to the mostly middle- and upper-middle-class students that women like me were supposed to have five kids and be chained down to poverty by their fertility, but that I'd been able to get the opportunities that had allowed me to educate myself. My education had eventually led to a career as journalist, which had allowed me to meet all sorts of fascinating people and write stories that tried to celebrate diversity and the contributions of Latinos to the United States. I challenged them, asking if someone like me could have had the same opportunities in their countries. An English guy said he thought it was possible in England, but no one else said anything. I continued telling them about how all the Americans I knew had voted against the war and George W. Bush.

"As bad as you think we are, you have to believe me that there are so many decent Americans who fought and stood up and protested and yelled and were heartbroken when the war began. We feel betrayed," I said. At that moment God had given me enough French words to speak from my heart at what felt like a United Nations tribunal.

At the end of class I went to the Seine and sat on a bench. I fed the pigeons and thought about all the useless protests I'd attended and all the things I'd done and . . . it was just useless. I'd become a journalist because I'd always wanted to get to the truth. I'd been interested in truth ever since I can remember my parents being cheated on their rent or being taken advantage of because they couldn't speak English. I'd wanted truth so badly because as poor immigrants all we were fed were lies about what a burden we were to the United States and how insignificant our contribution was.

The truth was that I didn't know what to feel; I didn't want to feel anything. It hurt too much to feel the losses. I'd been in Paris almost seven months now and, because I was so lonely, losing Henry hurt like hell. I couldn't believe Henry could be so cold to me, especially when he'd said he cared. I wondered what Henry was doing that minute. I wanted to think of a reason or an excuse to call him and get him to admit he really did care, but like a big ole idiot he had a fear of intimacy, like a typical male. "God, I'm so lonely and desperate for company that I want to turn a meaningless sexcapade with Henry into a relationship. Please send me a friend," I prayed.

CHAPTER 13

Déjà Vu *Again*

I arrived at the immigration center close to the Bastille and showed my letter to a guard. He told me to take the elevator to the fourth floor. When I arrived on the fourth floor it was already full with immigrants from Africa, also trying to get their *carte de séjour.* Many women wore colorful traditional dresses and had brought their children with them. We watched a video that welcomed us to France and explained our rights. The French was spoken slowly and clearly so that even I understood most of it. An energetic Algerian-French woman wearing a casual suit welcomed us and explained that we were going to be given a language exam and a medical exam. We were also expected to take a civics class that lasted an entire day. We could postpone it for another day or do it right after the medical exam.

I forced myself to speak French and asked to get the civics class out of the way. I was escorted to a room where I was asked in French to talk about myself and I couldn't really do it. The officer interviewing me was about to take notes and mark my application when I spoke up and said I was a journalist. I spoke in the present tense because the past tense is a bitch. I began to talk about how much I loved France and how I was studying cuisine and wanted to open a restaurant to share French culture—my prerehearsed packaged speech. He smiled and said my French was at a good level and he would give me the certificate necessary to get the *carte de séjour.* I smiled and gave a sigh of relief when I got out of his office.

As I walked down the hallway I remembered my English conversation with the American INS officer to prove I could speak English well enough to gain U.S. citizenship. He dictated a few sentences to me and I wrote them down. He said, "America is a democracy that guarantees freedom to all its citizens." I thought about the current state of the nation and the ongoing war that had nothing to do with democracy, and the memory made me want to cry. The second time I felt that way was when the "Terminator" got elected as governor of California, and the third time was when "W" got reelected. It felt strange to be an immigrant all over again, searching for an identity and a country to call my own. I felt so lost I just wanted to run into my mother's arms, but I hadn't spoken to her in months. If I ran back to my mother she would eat me up and try to shape my life as if I were a gingerbread woman or a pan dulce.

I waited about fifteen minutes before I was called in for my medical checkup. A nurse examined my eyes and my mouth. Thank God no one looked in my hair for lice like they did when I was going through my checkup to become a U.S. resident. I returned to the waiting room and sat next to a poster warning immigrants that clitoridectomy was illegal and considered a crime in France. Meanwhile a Muslim man argued with an immigration representative about having the right to be present while his wife's breasts were being examined and she was getting her chest X-ray. They informed him that his wife was supposed to be examined without him present. He found it unacceptable and refused to let it happen. They told him he could refuse to let her do it, but that meant she would forfeit her residency and be deported back to Algeria. His wife, hidden behind her veil, kept her eyes to the floor as though she was ashamed of herself for putting her husband through this indignity.

It's funny that my French sucked but I had managed to make out the situation. Shame was the same in any language. My name was called and I was escorted to a very attractive doctor's office. The doctor told me to take off my blouse—none of the American protocols where they give you your space and a paper gown to hide behind. I hate gynecological and breast exams, but I especially hate them when the doctors doing the examinations are hotties. There should be a rule against it. He made me stretch my arms out and held my breasts as if weighing them. I did everything so my nipples wouldn't get hard. I remembered being seven and covering my tiny nipples in front of a doctor in his fifties who was examining four of my sisters and me when my parents were applying for legal residency for us. Years may have passed, but I still felt the need to hide myself.

Next the doctor made me stand in front of an X-ray machine and hold my arms to the side, as if on a cross. He was satisfied that I was healthy and signed the certificate necessary for my *carte de séjour*. I left his office and saw the Muslim woman going in by herself. I wondered how she would remember her experience. Would she be traumatized by the doctor's touch or would she recall this moment as the one time a man besides her husband gave her breasts pleasure? None of my business, I told myself and went to the waiting room. I was given my chest X-rays and allowed to go in the civics room.

A young, energetic Frenchwoman welcomed us and told us to help ourselves to refreshments and cookies. Several African, Algerian, and Arab men, along with an African woman, a Brazilian, and a few Filipina women, sat around the classroom.

The French administrator lectured us about the history of France and about its laws with a PowerPoint presentation. I understood a lot of it, but I pretended to understand everything so she would give me that damn *carte de séjour*. I was fed up with all the hoops I had to jump through and wanted the class to be over. At the end of her presentation she asked for questions.

"There is no equality in France," an African man stated. He didn't have a question so much as a heartfelt opinion.

"In the eyes of the law everyone who is a citizen or a resident is considered French," she tried to explain. An Algerian man practically laughed in her face.

"I have family members who have been here in France for three generations and they still get discriminated against!" he shot at her. I wanted to tell him, "Try being Mexican-American, born in the U.S. before it was the U.S., and being told you should go back to your country." But thank God I didn't speak French well enough to get in the middle of it. The discussion got so heated that everyone was speaking too fast for me to follow all the details. By the resentment in their voices I could tell what they were saying. They were saying exactly what Latino immigrants and African-Americans living in the urban jungle say in the United States. How come if I am an American I am always treated like I am a foreigner/thug/criminal, and so on—not given an opportunity, discriminated against, on and on . . . Just substitute France for the United States and substitute Arabs for Latino immigrants.

"Why is it that when a qualified and educated Arab man applies for a job he doesn't get a call for an interview? How come you have to include a photograph when you apply for a job? It's because they want to make sure they don't hire an African man or an Arab for the job. So there is no equality!" exclaimed the feisty Algerian man with bravado. The young and optimistic representative of France defended her country and talked about the measures to fight discrimination, and the organizations in France set up to investigate discrimination cases. For every one thing she defended, they came to her from all sides attacking la France. I could sympathize with them, but I felt sorry for her for being punished for the evils of la France. They hated France so much because, for a lot of them, this was their only option; as bad as la France was, their countries were too corrupt or economically challenged to even discuss civil rights.

When the Battle for Algiers was over in the civics classroom, I was glad to leave with my final certificate. I handed all three certificates in, and at last a real *carte de séjour* was mine. I could legally stay in France for a year. No need for my backup plan: marrying a French guy to get citizenship right away. Besides, I'd found out while I was in the waiting room that it takes four years of marriage to a French citizen before you can qualify for citizenship. I laughed. I couldn't believe that it was harder to become a French citizen than an American citizen. Millions of people want to be American citizens, many more than French citizens, but it was harder to become a French citizen. Not even being born in France guaranteed you French citizenship, as it does in the United States. My neighbor, Marina, gave birth to her daughter in Paris, but her daughter has to turn eighteen before she can become legally recognized.

I studied my *carte de séjour* and was happy to be out of the shadows. I was happy to be legal, but this moment didn't compare to finally getting my green card. When it was handed to me I practically cried. I remember having to use a fake Social Security card for many years so I could get work, and how my heart would pound when my employer examined it closely. I remembered all the times I walked around like a shadow or a stain in downtown Los Angeles, hoping this would not be the day the raid would happen at the department store I worked at, despite all the rumors.

I left the immigration center with my brand-new *carte de séjour* and thought to myself that at last I was almost French. Now I had three identities, Mexican, American, and French, but I was still as lost as ever, with not a clue about what to do with my life or who I really was.

CHAPTER 14

Not Without My Bag!

I was passing by the Louis Vuitton store on the Champs-Élysées when a Japanese woman approached me and complimented me on my black leather bag.

"I love it," I told her. My purse had become more than an object to carry and store my things: it was a keeper of my secrets and dreams, a companion on my journey to my dark side.

"Are you an American?" she asked me. I wondered how she knew, but by her American-accented English I figured she had studied in the United States.

"Yes," I answered her.

"Would you be interested in making some money?"

"It depends on what you want me to do," I said cautiously. The way she was eyeing me made me a little suspicious.

"I just need you to go in and buy some bags for me," she explained.

"You can't buy them yourself?"

"No. They don't like selling a lot of merchandise to Asian women," she explained. "They limit how much we can buy, more than the average tourist." She offered to pay me a hundred euros if I bought all the merchandise on the list.

"Is this illegal?" I had to ask.

"Yes. Everyone is allowed to buy one of each item, but no repetition," she elaborated to diminish my suspicions. I didn't think it was fair that Asian women were being discriminated against like this, and I desperately needed money, so I agreed to help her.

"Thank you. My name is Hiromi," she said, introducing herself.

I introduced myself too: "My name is Canela."

Outside the store she told me what to say to the saleswomen so they wouldn't hassle me. She handed me a stack of euros and I entered the store and quickly made my purchases, collecting them at the main counter without any trouble, while my new Japanese friend waited patiently for me around the corner. I told her everything had gone smoothly and they'd been very nice.

"They are never nice to me," she said. She turned to me, thanked me, and handed me a hundred euros.

"Why don't they like selling to Asian women?" I asked.

"We resell the bags for more, many in private boutiques in Japan and China. They are afraid we will make fake ones exactly like these new models," she confessed. It was none of my business, but I had to ask.

"Will you copy them?"

"Of course. How else can the regular woman afford these?" she admitted, and I nodded. She appreciated that I was so calm and hired me a couple more times. You might be wondering why, if I am a fighter for justice like I keep claiming to be, I could participate in this. Simple: it should be illegal to pay more than a hundred dollars for a handbag.

Hiromi liked me so much she had me do shopping runs twice a week and she grew to trust me. After each shopping spree I would meet her at Bistro Romain, across the street from the store. She would buy me lunch and we'd pretend to be friends and then she'd leave with the gigantic brown shopping bags with the LV emblem.

One day while working on an order I approached a counter where a Muslim woman covered by an ivory silk veil was crying. I didn't realize she was crying until I saw her digging into her large Chanel purse. I opened my purse and handed her a tissue. She smiled at me and took the tissue. She looked around and saw that the other Muslim women, perhaps the other wives of the same sheikh, were busy getting their bodyguard to get them assistance. The bodyguard followed after an LV saleswoman and was out of sight. She turned to me and said in a low whisper what I could barely make out to be "Help me." I looked at her, not sure what she meant. She said it again with more urgency: "Help me."

"Help you? How?" I asked, but she did not understand or speak English. She just repeated "Help me" as though it was something memorized from a travel guide.

She turned to see if her bodyguard was still away. He returned, but he was far enough away that he couldn't see her easily. "Help me," she begged me quietly. I looked at her and nodded slightly. Then I committed the cardinal sin at LV and reached over and grabbed the bag on display by myself, without any assistance from a salesperson. I put the bag in her hand and made her grab one of the handles while I grabbed the other and pretended to be in a tug-of-war over the purse. I looked at her and pointed with my chin not to let go so they would have to kick us both out.

"Give that back to me, I had the purse first!" I said loudly so the security guard would see us. Immediately the LV "CIA" man came over. I acted as though she was being rough with me and made myself out to be the victim. Then I snatched the purse back. Security escorted us both out immediately. Many of the customers turned to see the commotion and blocked the bodyguard running toward us. They pushed us out the door and I grabbed the woman's hand. We ran as fast as we could, but her veil and her heels made a speedy escape impossible. We ducked into an alley, cut across a block, and hid in a cheap souvenir shop. We went all the way in and covered our faces with maps. We caught our breaths and smiled after a few minutes. She remained in the back and I stepped outside to see if her bodyguard was following us. I went back in and tried speaking a few words of French and English to her.

"Altair," she said, pointing to herself. Her English and French were nonexistent, so I pointed to the map to ask her where she wanted to go. She looked at the map and didn't understand me. I handed her my cell phone and gestured for her to make her call. She shook her head and pointed at me. Did she want to go home with me? Did she not have a backup plan?

"Me?" I pointed to myself.

"*Oui,*" she said. I took a deep breath and took in what I had just done. Now what? I nodded and pointed to my eye. I left the shop and saw a taxi approaching the curb. I took her hand and we ran out of the store and into the taxi as a passenger was just getting out. I gave the driver my address. The taxi driver was a Muslim man who looked us up and down and spoke to us in Arabic. Altair asked him to translate for her. Although they spoke a different dialect, the taxi driver was able to converse with her. She cried as she tried to explain to him, and he translated in French for me. I struggled to make out what he was saying.

"Her name is Altair," he said. "She says thank you for saving her life" was what I could make out. He turned to me and asked what had just happened. I begged him to continue translating. "She says she wants to go home with you until she can figure out what to do next." He turned to me and insisted I tell him what had just happened. Should he take her to an embassy or a hospital? I told him as best as I could that she just needed to rest at my apartment and then she would be all right.

We got out of the taxi and made it into the lobby. Madame Bodé saw me with Altair and raised her nose up in the air and walked up to her apartment on the first floor. We took the service elevator to the sixth floor. I bumped into Marina and didn't bother introducing Altair to her. I told her I would explain later and quickly went to my little room. I locked the door behind us. Altair took in my room and cried. Sometimes when I looked at my tiny little place I would cry too, so I didn't blame her if she hated it.

She cried for an hour nonstop. I remembered when Luna would call me and cry on the phone a lot; I would tell her to leave her husband, but she didn't have the strength to do it. I wondered if Altair was regretting her actions already or if the relief of finally being a "free" woman was so overpowering. I heated up some leftovers and she tried to eat. I handed her my cell phone again and asked her in both French and English if she wanted to call anyone. She shook her head and offered me a gold bracelet. She put it in my hand and folded my hand to show me it was for me to keep. I shook my hand and told her I could not take it. I asked her in English and my best French what she planned to do. Did she have lots of money to rent an apartment or travel somewhere? She emptied her purse and took out a pen. I gave her a piece of paper and she drew a plane. She shook her head.

"No passport," she uttered. For many hours we babbled, until I understood that she was scared for her life because her husband had threatened to kill her when they returned to Turkey because he suspected that she was having an affair with her bodyguard. He'd beat her the night before and she showed me the bruises on her legs. She couldn't run because of her bruises.

I had read that since Turkey was trying to get admitted to the European Union "honor killings" were no longer allowed, but that didn't mean they didn't happen. If she returned to Turkey her husband's family could starve her and force her to commit suicide and get around the new laws. Altair was heartbroken because she could never go back to see her own family again. She was scared for her family and children . . . and I'd thought the life of a Latina in the United States was tough.

The next day we went to a boutique on the rue de la Pompe and she pawned all her valuables. She got back lots of money, but not enough to last her a lifetime, or even a year. I tried convincing Altair to go to the French authorities to see if she could get asylum, but she refused out of fear that she would get deported back to Turkey.

I knocked on Marina's door and explained Altair's situation. She immediately sympathized and took Altair with her to be her assistant on her nanny and cleaning lady jobs. Marina kept her ears open for any new jobs that Altair could assist her with. Altair learned things quickly, and adapted to a new life. She was a new woman, but she still could not take off the veil; even a bird that lived in a cage all his life before he escaped misses his cage.

CHAPTER 15

Boys in the Banlieue

*T*he phone rang in the middle of the night. Altair grabbed her purse and stared at the door, as if waiting for someone to kick it open. I picked up my cell phone and wondered what kind of emergency merited a call at that time.

"Hello," I snapped.

"Canela, it's Gina, sorry to wake you—" the voice said.

"Gina? How did you get my number?" I interrupted.

"I got it from your sister Rosie," Gina explained. Damn, I had told her not to give it to anyone, especially someone from my past.

"How did you know I was in Paris?"

"Girl, I can get dirt on anyone, you know that, so finding you was easy," she bragged. "Listen, I know it's late in Paris, but I wanted to get you on an assignment right away," said my former editor—not the one who'd accused me of losing my objectivity or the Latina magazine editor I'd left holding the bag.

"I'm not a journalist anymore." I replied.

"I heard, but we don't have anyone stationed in Paris right now—so maybe you can cover the riot," she said.

"What riot?" I asked.

"The one happening over the two Arab teenagers getting electrocuted," she said.

"Oh, yes, yeah," I said, pretending to know what she was talking about.

"Can you do it?" Gina asked, almost begging.

"I don't do stories—" I was about to explain how I didn't want to write anymore.

"I know you can do a great job. So can you do it?"

I remained silent, not sure what to say since I was barely awake.

"We'll pay you double," Gina replied, taking my silence as me playing hardball with her. I thought about it for a few more seconds and then my stomach growled, trying to answer for me. I could sure use the money.

"Okay. I'll do it. How many words and when do you want it?" I said, caging in a yawn. Gina explained all the details and I couldn't sleep that night, scheming how I was going to get into a predominantly Arab neighborhood without speaking French or Arabic. When I had to go to South Central for a story I was never afraid, because I acted like I belonged. I was constantly mistaken for an Arab in Paris, but would people in the *banlieue* see me as one of them if I could barely speak French? Like them, I too felt like I didn't belong in Paris.

I called Henry first thing in the morning and he refused to help me. He claimed he was busy, but I quickly caught him in a lie.

"Do I have to tell the police about all the truffle cans in your kitchen cabinets?" I wheedled with a girlish voice.

"Darling, you're threatening me; that's not nice. Is it because of Bassie?"

"I couldn't care less about you and Bassie. But she's a nice kid, so just don't mess with her heart."

"She's a big girl. She does all right for herself," Henry replied, teasing me.

"Henry, just come with me. I need you . . . to help me translate," I begged him.

"Fine. Just so you know, I've already sold off the truffles and there is no evidence in my flat, but I'll do it."

We took the metro to just outside of Paris where black and Arab youths were burning up cars. As we approached the neighborhood I heard loud music coming from cars, including a song in Spanish called "Gasolina," which I would later come to know as a classic reggaetón song. It served as a wonderful anthem even though it was in Spanish because the cars were up in flames and they kept throwing gasoline on more cars and setting them on fire. I took pictures from a distance until a group of teenagers approached us. Henry stiffened up and I said, *"Salut! Ça va?"*—the equivalent of "What's up?"—to them, acting like I belonged and was so happy to see them. I'd dressed down, in jeans, and I pretended I was simply back in South Central during the riots. Let me just add that a riot in Paris bears no resemblance to a riot in Los Angeles. Sure there were fires, but the difference is they didn't have weapons. In L.A. the riots were so violent and vicious even heroes like firefighters got shot. On the fringes of Paris, only cars were getting burned and an occasional person was getting hurt. When my editor had mentioned "riot" I'd seen glimpses of Los Angeles in flames, smoke visible from a distance, looting, violence—the end of the world. Here it was just young dark men pissed, but without enough resources to do much damage. That's how oppressed and poor they were; they couldn't even afford to take the riot into the city and really burn down Paris, like the U.S. media was claiming they were.

"Why are you doing this?" I asked with an open and receptive face, free of judgment. I introduced myself as a reporter from Los Angeles, letting them know that I wanted the United States to know about the mistreatment of Arabs in France. So what if we were mistreating them all around the world? We really wanted to know how bad the French were to their Arabs. They hesitated at first, but I informed them that in Los Angeles the riots in the sixties and in the nineties all started because African-Americans felt the system was unjust and were so outraged by the injustice they saw they had to do something.

They quickly got that I was a passionate sympathizer with their cause and the teenagers felt empowered by my comparison. One whispered to another and they told Henry they had a friend who was a rapper who could really tell it like it is. We went into the *banlieue*. It was worse than the projects my high school friend Maria had lived in. It was mostly a concrete structure with no style. You would think that in Paris, the capital of the art world, they could design prettier buildings to stack up people. The teenage boys knocked and Mohammed, who went by "M. C. Momo," came out. He was twenty-one and good-looking, trying to make himself out to look like a French version of an American rapper. Henry introduced me and he looked me up and down with attitude. I checked him out up and down and smiled, unafraid of his bravado. He wasn't the first rapper I had interviewed, so I knew how to speak his language and asked him what kind of rap he performed. He was impressed by my knowledge of the different rapping styles and I told him my favorite rap group was NWA. To Henry's amazement, M. C. Momo welcomed us into his parents' apartment. The teenage boys excused themselves. We went into his parents' apartment and his mother ignored us and continued watching a Brazilian soap opera my mother had already seen. He escorted us to his tiny room, which was also his homemade studio, with synthesizer and all.

"So why aren't you out there, rioting?" I asked him. He laughed at my boldness, but Henry hated translating my brash questions.

"I wait until it gets dark—I'm not stupid," Henry translated.

"So why are people doing this?" I asked.

Mohammed explained that he'd been born in France, his father had been born in France, and his grandfather had been born in France, but they were not treated with the rights promised to them as French citizens. They would always be treated like foreigners, like scum, he said. I explained to him that I was Mexican-American and what that meant and he instantly had an affinity with me. He understood what it was like to have a double identity: "We don't have any opportunities and we're constantly harassed by the police." He put on a CD of his rap song about *les flics*—the cops—and sang along to it. Henry took deep breaths, wondering how much longer he'd have to endure this urban anthropological investigation. I tried singing along to Mohammed's song and he continued, playing his next song.

After a while, Henry looked at his watch and I told him he could go. He muttered that he wouldn't leave my side because he was scared for me. I assured him that I felt safe singing along to music. He told me to call him if I got into trouble. It was going to get dark soon and anything could happen, he warned me. I assured him I could take care of myself. Mohammed told him good-bye and continued playing his songs and I threw in questions. He got ready to go out that night and I asked him if I could go with him. Mohammed told me to put on a baseball cap and hide my hair under it. I dressed myself as a guy and went out to see the fires with Mohammed. We mostly watched on the sidelines. At the end of the night Mohammed gave me his number and told me to call him if I needed more information. I thanked him for his interview and gave him my number.

I rushed home and found Altair crying. She was discovering

that freedom was not so nice. She spent her days taking care of rich women's children and she missed her own children. Altair showed me pictures of her children, and it broke my heart. I would have cried next to her, but my deadline was pressing. In the morning I sent the story to Gina via e-mail. In the afternoon I got a call from her telling me it needed to be "sexier."

"Americans want the French to be embarrassed and exposed. We want to laugh at them and point the finger back," Gina confessed. I tried to explain to her that things were not as bad as people in the United States thought they were. Yes, they have a race problem, but Paris was not burning up in flames like my little sister Rosie, who had just called to check on me, thought. Yes, the U.S. embassy had issued a threat alert to all the American tourists in Paris, but only because the train to the airport went through the area where the cars were being burnt. Nobody was targeting Americans.

"Nobody seems to be affected except the poor people in those neighborhoods," I explained. "I walked down the Champs-Élysées in the heat of the so-called riot and nobody stopped shopping," I insisted. I finally had to tell Gina I was not going to write lies to save my story. I hung up and turned on the TV.

The minister of the interior, whose last name sounded like a disease, and who would later become the president of France, had infuriated the rioters by calling them *racaille*—scum. The boys in the *banlieue* continued their rioting with more fury until President Chirac felt obligated to say a few kind words that hinted at the identity crisis France was going through. He told the rioters that they, too, were children of France. He promised more opportunity and equality, and assured them that change would come.

A few days after the rioting stopped Mohammed called me to see if I wanted to come over and listen to his new rap song about the disturbances. I knew it was an excuse to get into my panties, and I reminded myself that he was only twenty-one and this could only lead to disaster.

I went over to his apartment anyway and entered his room unnoticed. He played the song and sang most of it for me. I clapped and sang along. Then he kissed me. There are kisses and then there are kisses, the kind that awaken you to your divinity. How could this young guy I could barely understand electrify me with his kiss? I kissed him back and we whispered things in Spanish and English and Arabic and French. I caressed his high cheekbones and rubbed my face on his face. In his dark eyes I could see my soul. When he penetrated me we gasped together and at that moment we were both worshipping the same God.

"Ay Dios, ay Dios, oh God, oh God," I whispered in ecstasy.

"Oh Allah, oh Allah," he grunted in between humps. God by any name in the heat of passion is still God.

Two weeks after I had sex with Mohammed his mother figured out my age and the fact that I was American and said she didn't like me hanging around. Mohammed had to come over to my apartment during the time Altair was working. One day I came to the apartment with him and we found her crying.

"Altair, what's wrong?" I called to her, making hand gestures. She looked up and I introduced her to Mohammed. Mohammed said something and she smiled with recognition. They began a conversation that I could not understand, but I was happy that Mohammed knew several Arab dialects; he'd grown up hearing them in the *banlieue*.

"*Au revoir*," Altair said in her heavy accent and left the room to give us privacy, but Mohammed remained disturbed. He was silent for a while and did not respond to my caresses.

"Why did you interfere with her life?" he asked me, shaking his head.

"Her husband was abusive. She needed to escape. She needed to experience life and have a baby—" I blurted out.

"Baby?" He raised his eyebrows.

"I mean her health was bad and she needed to get out or it would kill her—"

"What are you saying? Who are you talking about?" He asked perplexed.

"Luna—I mean Altair," I corrected myself. "She asked me for help and she finally had the strength to leave and I had to help her escape and she wanted my help!" I talked rapidly, trying to get Mohammed to understand, until he walked up to me and put his hands on my shoulders so I would stop talking and listen.

"You had no right to interfere. You had no right to do what you did!" he scolded me.

"She asked for my help. She was desperate. I had to help. I didn't want her to die!" I yelled and started crying. He shook his head violently and practically spat at me.

"You egotistical American! Can't you respect other people's cultures! What gave you the right to impose your American views about what women should think and be?" I couldn't believe how sexist he was. Yes, I knew he was an Arab, but I thought he was acculturated and a modern Arab-Frenchman.

"What about equality? What the hell are you fighting for? Oh, yeah, equality for Arab men!"

"*Mais de quoi tu parles? T'es folle!*" he exploded. What are you talking about? You're crazy!

I yelled back and pointed him to the door. He was about to say something when I shook my head and kicked him out.

I waited for Altair to come back that night, but she never did. In my dreams she would come in through the door and explain that she'd run into a friend. I would wake up and see if she was back, but only her belongings were still there. Had Mohammed found her and convinced her to go back to her husband? Had she been deported? Had she killed herself? I walked around the *arrondissement* looking for her at night, but she had vanished. Maybe she went to the Turkish embassy in the neighborhood and turned herself in. I kept imagining every scenario, and all the answers I came up with were more frightening than the last.

One day I arrived at the apartment building and saw police officers interviewing Madame Bodé. She had been robbed; all her jewels had been stolen. She cried as she explained that she'd stepped outside for only an hour and someone had broken into her apartment.

Several neighbors came down to pay their condolences and informed the police that two Arab girls had knocked on their doors, asking for someone. They kept changing the name of the person they were asking for as they went down the floors, and since Madame Bodé was not home they or someone else working with them broke into her apartment. I imagined Mohammed wearing Madame Bodé's gold necklaces with his rapper look, but I erased the picture from my mind. I walked quickly past the scene and Madame Bodé took the opportunity to tell the police officers about all the suspected *sans-papiers* living upstairs who might be responsible for this.

"We are sorry," one officer explained in French, "but we are not connected with Immigration and are not authorized to search for *sans-papiers*."

I stayed in my room, frozen in self-pity. I felt so sad and lonely, even sadder than Edith Piaf on her deathbed . . . Okay, maybe I'm exaggerating, but that was the worst I had ever felt in my life. Luna's suicide became Altair's assumed suicide and I hadn't been able to save either one of them. I couldn't even rescue myself from the abyss of depression I was sliding into. Not knowing what had happened to Altair was worse than knowing that she'd died at the hands of her husband or by her own hands. I felt ashamed for interfering with Altair's life. I cried for hours, until my eyelids burned. I wanted to drink, but then I realized that since I'd gotten to Paris I drank every time I felt pain. Had I become a high-functioning alcoholic without even noticing it? The saddest part was that this realization didn't stop me from drinking. I drank a bottle of wine and when I reached the bottom of it I thought I heard Altair calling out my name to buzz her in. I went out to the balcony and looked down. There was no Altair. I wondered how it would feel to jump off the balcony. Would my spirit fly out of my body as it was falling and crashing to the pavement? As drunk as I was, I knew that if I ever committed suicide it would be painless. Why kill yourself painfully when the whole point of dying is to escape pain?

I remembered trying to talk Luna out of committing suicide a couple of times. She would begin to describe the hot bath she would make for herself, as her final resting place. I would try to convince her that she could have a wonderful life even if she couldn't have children. I felt sad that all she wanted was to have children, she had found her reason for living, and here I was a fertile, healthy woman who never wanted to have kids, feeling sorry for myself because I had lost my passion for life.

I got up and my hands, independent of my body, were turning the water knobs in the bathtub. Or was it La Calaca Flaca inside of me doing it? I looked around the room, searching for her. Why wasn't she here to remind me that I wanted to die? Maybe because at that moment I didn't need to be reminded . . . because I really wanted to die. I stared at my hands doing what felt natural to them. I searched in the medicine cabinet and found Rosemary's sleeping pills. This was the first time I had seen them, but my hands knew they were there. I swallowed the first pill. Painless. I took the next one and a smile slipped out of me. I swallowed a third and I was horrified inside to see how peaceful my face looked. Then, finally, when I swallowed the fourth one, a tear slipped out. I prepared my hot bath and got in the tub. I felt like I was already floating out of my body, but I imagined people criticizing me for trying to imitate Jim Morrison. I wasn't even a fan, but people might make that comparison. I hadn't even gotten to see his tomb in Père-Lachaise while I was here in Paris—on earth, I told myself.

I felt so relaxed, and my eyes began to close. I saw Luna coming to my side and presenting a letter to me. I was sinking and my hands could not reach up. She smiled at me and asked me, "Aren't you going to read it?" I opened my eyes and she was not there. I got a flashback of being in Chef Sauber's bathroom. Luna had been in the mirror holding a letter. Luna had left a letter for me. That was the letter Tía Lucia had passed to my mother at the wake. I jumped out of the bath and called my mother for the first time in almost eight months.

The phone rang a couple of times before my mother picked up.

"¿Sí?" she answered.

"It's Canela," I announced.

"¡Que milagro!" she said sarcastically. "To what do I owe this miracle?"

"Hello, Mama."

"I carried you in my womb for nine months and you don't call me in eight months? That's not right," my mother said, beginning her guilt trip.

"Did Luna—?" I was about to ask when my mother cut me off.

"So how are you?" she asked, completely disregarding my urgency.

"I'm ah . . . I was calling—"

She cut me off again. "I haven't been feeling well. I've been so worried about you—"

I cut her off this time. "Ama, I was calling to ask you if—?" I tried asking.

"You don't do this to your mother. You don't just get up and go and not call for months—" she admonished me before I cut her off again.

"Did Luna leave me a letter?"

My mother was silent for a moment. "Who told you? Did your sister tell you? She promised she wouldn't say anything!"

"She didn't tell me. Luna did," I replied.

"Ay, ay, ay, I knew that Luna would figure out a way to let you know. She was always too clever for her own good," my mother recalled.

"Tell me what the letter says!" I demanded.

"No. You come back to Los Angeles and I will give you the letter!" she shot back at me.

"I will never forgive you for this," I told her and hung up. I was so angry with her I vomited. My body went into convulsive vomiting and out came the pills dissolved in my bile. I was so pissed I couldn't go through with the suicide because I had to live to go get that pinchi letter and find out what it said!

"Wanting to die is not normal," an overentitled white male college friend had once told me—he who didn't have a concern or any kind of social responsibility to make a difference in the world. I knew I was missing whatever chemicals in his brain were overflowing . . . I always knew I was not normal; the thought of being normal kills me.

SUPERIOR
CUISINE

CHAPTER 16

Spanish Omelette

After ten weeks away from cooking school I was looking forward to socializing with Americans again. Sage hadn't returned any of my phone calls after our night out. Bassie filled me in on the rumors about Sage in the courtyard, before I started Intensive Superior. Sage had been spotted by Françoise, also rumored to have been involved with all the chefs, on a romantic rendezvous with Chef Sauber. Chef Sauber's soon-to-be ex-wife—it turned out they weren't yet divorced and she was trying to mend things with him—found out about Sage and made it into a big scandal, getting her kicked out of school.

"But I heard from Henry that he saw her doing an internship at a three-star restaurant," Bassie added. "I think Chef Sauber got it for her." I nodded my head in agreement with Bassie and said a silent prayer of thanks that my name had not been mentioned in the scandal.

"So what have you been up to?" Bassie asked.

"Just working on my French," I lied, sparing her the details of my depressing life. I excused myself and sat in the demonstration room, waiting for my intensive course to begin. I had been warned that the students in this particular class were highly competitive because they were attempting to do in fifteen weeks what the regular students do in thirty. Despite the warning, I was looking forward to meeting my new classmates and hoping to make a friend or two. A group of students came in and some joked around, speaking Spanish. One was from Argentina and another, named Miguel Angel, was from Mexico. A Spanish woman named Pepa, who seemed like she should be in an Almodóvar film with her erect nose and witty comebacks, and a Spanish girl named Bianca, who acted like Chicken Little, said "Hola" to me and welcomed me to their group. Minutes later another woman from Peru came in. I introduced myself to her in Spanish and she told me her name was Blanca. She was dark and indigenous-looking with large brown eyes and a smile that sparkled like the sun. There was also a short student from Greece named Alexandros with spiky blond hair, and a student from Israel named Akiva who was too tall to be in a small kitchen.

An American student sat behind me and introduced himself as Richard. "But call me Dick—I prefer that," he said kindly, revealing a Tennessee accent. He was small-framed and looked like he couldn't hurt an ant. One minute before class was to start another American, Craig, ran in taking deep breaths. On any other day his good looks and defined jaw would have gotten him the admiration of all the women, but since his plane had arrived late his whole schedule had been thrown off. He was jet-lagged and as frazzled as a cat left out in the rain.

Chef Papillon, who reminded me of Popeye, and who hopefully didn't remember me from my horrible hollandaise sauce experience, welcomed us in French to Intensive Superior Cuisine. Akiva looked to his classmates and asked in a Hebrew-accented English, "Where is the translator?" Chef Papillon reminded him in French that Superior is not translated. Akiva got up from the back and sat in the front row next to me, because he assumed I spoke French.

"In Superior Cuisine we will be doing French dishes with influences from around the world," he declared. I inspected the demonstration recipes and was appalled to see that the chef was going to demonstrate how to make guacamole with butter! We were also making salmon with Indian spices and spinach.

When the dishes were done and I tasted the French guacamole I had to admit it was pretty good. I could never do this dish for my family and friends back in the United States, but it was rich and creamy.

The class was dismissed and, to Craig's horror, he and Blanca were the assistants for the week.

I got to the practical room early and set up at my favorite cooking station. Dick came in after me and set up on the other side of the counter. We quickly did our prep routine and waited for the supplies to make their way up the elevator. Since Craig was tired I went ahead and started setting up the metal bowls and other people's *planchettes* so everyone would have one when they arrived. Craig and Blanca distributed the supplies and the group was off and running at their usual pace. Blanca and I were new, so we tried to adjust to the pace and routine of this competitive group. Craig finally arrived in class and discovered that the space left for him was the worst station.

"Oh, great." He tried to set up and asked Dick, who was taking up a lot of space, to move down so that he could settle in.

"No, I'm not going to move," Dick said coldly.

"I know you don't want to move, but I have no space left," Craig said nicely, trying to avoid a confrontation. The other students noticed Craig's discomfort at being mistreated, but everyone was too busy to interfere.

"Why don't you move down to the corner?" Dick suggested with some annoyance at being interrupted. Craig shook his head and just moved down to the corner, too tired to debate.

We finished the class and had another demonstration to go to for the day. I looked through my schedule and was shocked to discover that we were actually going to have four classes one particular day. From eight-thirty in the morning until nine P.M. I counted the recipes, knowing these were going to be five long weeks.

In Superior the chefs were kinder; that didn't tell you much, because if you had made it to Superior you had already proven yourself. My Intermediate class had been laid-back and had had a lot of newcomers, but in this group everyone aside from Bianca and me had worked at a restaurant or had professional cooking experience. Bianca was there because her parents wanted her to be in charge of their kitchen at their resort. Blanca was already a professional chef back in Peru and was just getting her diploma to work at better restaurants. She was calm, fast, and organized. I quickly became friends with her by asking her to be my mentor. Blanca was so generous with her advice and always tried to help me out.

On the third day of class Bianca confided in me that she hated her station because Akiva always took up too much space. The guy just didn't understand that even though he was so tall and had long arms, he wasn't entitled to more space on the counter than everyone else. She had been having nightmares about him suffocating her. I told her to tell him to move and she cowered like a little bird and said she was scared to do it. I felt sorry for her and switched stations with her. I set up my *planchette* and my supplies at the center of the counter and began my work. Akiva always came in late and was the first to finish. He took a lot of pride in doing that. So he set up next to me and told me to move down the counter.

"No. I'm not going to move. This is exactly where I am supposed to be," I said assertively.

"You're too close—I have no room," he insisted. I knew he was trying to be a gentleman about it, but being nice didn't make him right.

"You see this line in the marble?" I asked. "This line indicates that this is exactly the center. Since there are five people on this counter, the third person should be right in the center of the line. Do the math and you'll see." It was like I was defending Texas before it was stolen from Mexico. Akiva stopped requesting that I move. The next day he stationed himself on my right side, thinking he would get more room there. The guy was like an octopus, chopping meat and slicing vegetables with no grace at all. Next to him I looked like a ballerina. I know you've heard me complain about the space, but they put us in an unfair situation: fourteen people in a tiny kitchen. It's just very bad planning by the architects, who had no clue about cuisine or people's tempers when things in the kitchen get too hot. There wasn't even a place for the chef to station himself and taste the sample dishes. They would probably argue that working in a tiny hole was part of the education.

The fact that six of the students in our tiny class were Spanish speakers made most of us close, like a community. We joked in Spanish and cussed in Spanish, and whenever we needed something everyone in our little group would share. Craig mostly kept to himself, feeling completely left out. I spoke to him in English and tried to help him along. He kept burning his food and I couldn't believe he had actually placed number one in his Intermediate class. Later, when he got to know me better and trusted me, he revealed that there had only been five students in his class.

"I'm a food whore. I'll do anything for caviar, truffles, and champagne," Craig said, and I knew we would be friends for life.

I befriended everyone in class and realized that, in this group, I had no chance of placing, so I might as well enjoy it and not stress out about my scores or the things the chefs told me. I was determined that no matter what the chefs said I was going to finish and get that diploma and relish the experience. I decided I would laugh at how bad my food was instead of taking it personally.

I tried to be Dick's friend, until I realized that he was a Republican who'd voted for "W" and that he wasn't interested in being friends with anyone. We were making a dish that required us to stuff spinach inside phyllo dough. Just like in Basic and Intermediate, we would not get enough ingredients, but at the end of the day everyone shared. I was busy frying something when I realized I had forgotten to get my spinach. Everyone else already had theirs and there was no more left.

"Where's the spinach?" I asked Pepa.

"There's no more," she replied. I turned around and saw a bowl overflowing with spinach on the counter next to Dick. I assumed it was available, so I went back to my station and reached over to get some. Dick snapped, "That's mine!" like a two-year-old in day care. I was stunned at first, then tried reasoning with him like an adult.

"Clearly that's not all for you because there's none left. You don't need that much. We're only going to need four or five leaves and you've got like—"

"They're mine," he insisted and turned back to his stove.

"But you're not going to need all that. There's no way you could possibly use all that spinach," I said in a loud voice so he would respond.

"Well . . . after I get my spinach you can have some, but you have to wait," he snapped. I was actually shocked that an adult male didn't know how to share. People kind of noticed and Blanca leaned over and said in Spanish, "Don't worry, we'll find some for you." But I wasn't worried that I wasn't going to get some; I was flabbergasted that someone could be so thoughtless and selfish. By now I should have gotten used to it, but it took me several minutes to get over it. Dick couldn't care less about sharing; he wanted to come in first. Suddenly I felt sad for Dick, that he had to win to feel good about himself. He wasn't bad-looking; his thinning hair and thin body were not unattractive. Maybe he had been an abused and neglected child left in the closet, or maybe he was a repressed homosexual (also left in the closet), even though he claimed to be married. *Stop it*, I told myself. "Just because someone has been mean to me doesn't give me the right to think bad thoughts," said the angel on my right shoulder. The devil on my left shoulder insisted that Dick had tortured animals before coming to cooking school and was someday going to shoot up people at the post office.

The spinach incident was just the tip of the iceberg lettuce. As the weeks progressed, his passive-aggressive ways also scared Blanca and Craig. He was like a poodle with fangs. Every time I would eye him stealing herbs from people's trays like a sneaky squirrel, I would debate whether I should tell him what a jerk he was. Chances were he already knew it and didn't care. I knew he was not just competitive but rotten too.

During a practical class Blanca finished cleaning her stove and moved to the sink to wash her knives. I was about to call Blanca's name when she looked at her stove and noticed a small pot on it.

"Who put this pot on my stove?" she asked. Dick was stationed next to her and said nothing. She grabbed the pot by the handle, then yelled and dropped it. The pot had come straight out of the oven and had burnt her hand. I turned to see Dick's face at that second and caught his eyes sneaking a peek. He remained emotionless and continued packing his knives. Everyone else stopped what they were doing to sympathize with Blanca and to ask how her hand was doing. Craig almost hugged her, feeling her pain. Dick snapped shut his tool case and left without looking back.

"It was probably Dick who did it," I said to her in Spanish and described his look. Any conscious and kind human being would have reacted with sympathy or even admitted that they were sorry they had accidentally left the hot pot on her stove. The fact that he'd left made him evil in my eyes. Blanca practically cried as she passed her hand through cold water for several minutes. Her hand was badly burnt and she had trouble cutting for the rest of the day.

The next day Blanca was missing celery from her tray and I told her I'd seen Dick take it, which he had.

"Dick, did you take my celery?" asked Blanca.

"No," he responded without blinking or taking the time to consider her accusatory question.

"Dick, are you sure you didn't take my celery?" she asked. He denied it again. I no longer wanted to find a reason to feel sorry for Dick. I wanted to kick his ass, but we were stuck with him until graduation.

I was so stressed out already by being thrown into a competitive environment that I wondered whether I wanted to choose that battle. I just kept telling myself to ignore Dick. When it's over I'll just laugh at his pathetic existence.

I woke up at three in the morning to catch a taxi and pick up Blanca at her apartment. We arrived at a spot near the metro stop by the school and got on the chartered bus to Rungis, the world's largest food market. It hadn't been on our schedule, because our class was too fast-paced, but I'd insisted and we'd been given the same opportunity to visit Rungis that the regular Superior cooking classes got. We were made to wear white lab coats and hairnets in order to enter the food markets. I had never seen so many gutted pigs and cows in my life. There were cheeses the size of tractor tires, weighing over two hundred kilos, a large selection of rotting cheeses, and roosters and poultry of every shape and size. After about two hours of this food tour I was ready to fall asleep, but this was just the beginning of our day.

We were supposed to have a nine-hour day, but by the middle of the practical I was brain-dead. When I said good-bye to everyone, Pepa couldn't believe my audacity. She wished she could do the same; she had no choice but to finish her classes. Pepa had started the intensive courses thirteen weeks ago, and she was burning out. She desperately needed the diploma because she was planning to open a cooking school in Spain.

Bassie invited me to her graduation and I debated whether or not I should go. On Fridays the last thing I wanted to do was go out. I told her I would attend her graduation because I heard in her voice that it meant something to her if I went. She had no family coming and Henry was history. I promised I would be there and would try not to fall asleep. I bought flowers for Bassie and congratulated her on passing her final exam. No matter how incompetent they wanted to claim she was, she'd finished the exam on time and her food was actually good.

"Henry still has feelings for you," Bassie admitted.

"No. We just had fun," I said.

"I'm sure you did, but he kept bringing up your name. I just know he still cares about you and I feel like a jerk for being with him," she confessed.

"Yeah, I wouldn't feel right being with someone who I thought had feelings for someone else," I concurred, then added, "But you are not a jerk, Bassie . . . I know how cold a bed can be in Paris."

Bassie shrugged. "I'm returning to the States next week. My ex-boyfriend wants me back."

"Not the guy who was a jerk to you, then became nice, then went back to being a jerk?"

Bassie shrugged again. "Same one."

"Has he changed?" I had to ask.

"No, I have." Bassie looked up proudly and smiled.

Sunday night, when I was sleeping, I heard a knock at the door. It was only nine P.M., but I'd been exhausted and had gone to bed early so I could be ready for my practical class. I got up and answered the door wearing my skimpy see-through camisole. It was either that camisole or no clothes at all, because I can barely sleep with clothes on. If an earthquake ever happened I would run out naked, I don't care . . . Besides, I figured it was probably just Marina, since she was the only person in the building who would talk to me. All the other immigrants, like the Filipina housekeepers or the African chauffeurs, just smiled but never spoke.

I pulled open the door and found two police officers. They looked at me, and simultaneously their eyes headed south, where my nipples were saying hi to them. I slammed the door like a criminal and they pounded on it, demanding that I open up right away. I'm sure they threatened to break down the door in French, but I threw on a robe and opened my door again before they had a chance to kick it in. They began to ask me questions in French, but I asked them if they spoke English. They said they spoke a little. My other neighbors, as well as Marina, had surrounded my door, wanting to know what was going on. I asked the police officers to come in so the neighbors would stay out of my business. I offered them chairs, but they preferred to stand. They took in my room and asked me for identification. I handed them my *carte de séjour* and they asked me what I was doing in France.

"I'm studying cuisine at Le Coq Rouge," I said, but they had never heard of the school. I wondered how that was possible if it was supposed to be so famous. They told me they wanted to ask questions about the robbery. I told them I knew nothing about it except that it had happened to Madame Bodé. I sat down on my bed and looked up at them. They went on to say that Madame Bodé had filed a police report and on her report she'd claimed that she'd seen me with a young Arab male a few days before the robbery.

"Madame Bodé claims she saw you with a man one night on the stairway having sex. Is that true?" Officer Sansgene asked. His question surprised me and I regretted letting Mohammed convince me to do it on the stairway. But what the hell had Madame Bodé been doing on the stairway at three A.M.? She lived on the first floor and there was never a reason to come upstairs . . . unless she'd been visiting her chauffer in the middle of the night . . . Hmm, so she'd caught me and I'd caught her. Must be why she'd seen us and, yet, said nothing to me. I would have expected her to chastise us and make a scene, but she'd quietly passed us and slipped away into the night.

"Yes," I said, trying to reveal as little as possible.

"Was this man a *maghrébin*?" Officer De la Corbeille asked.

"What is that?" I said, feeling so ignorant for not knowing.

"An Arab." Officer Sansgene slipped in. *Maghrébin* was their P.C. term.

"Yes," I said, wondering what kind of trouble I was in for having sex with an Arab.

"Who was this man? Is he your boyfriend? Does he live with you?" Officer Sansgene continued his probing.

I didn't want to give them any information because Mohammed would think it low of me to do so. "No. He is not my boyfriend and he does not live here. I was seeing him for a few weeks and then we had a fight and I kicked him out and I have not seen him since," I said, trying to imagine the officers naked. It was a technique I'd used so often to keep from being intimidated by people in positions of power who I was interviewing that it had become automatic. As soon as they began their interrogation I saw them naked and imagined the shorter one with a huge penis to explain his inner confidence. I recalled making love to Mohammed on the stairway . . . then I fantasized about the two naked officers joining us. They would handcuff me and take turns penetrating me as I—. I shook my head and smiled, trying to erase that image. God, why do I have such inappropriate thoughts at the most awkward times? They stared at me with more seriousness and continued with their questions.

"How long ago did you stop seeing him?" Officer Sansgene asked. They took turns drilling me with questions. Reluctantly, I gave them all the information I had on Mohammed and hoped that was the end of it.

"Who was that Muslim woman staying with you?" Officer De la Corbeille asked. Madame Bodé was so nosy; why did she have to tell them about Altair? I should tell her husband about the chauffeur, I thought. Of course, he probably visits the nanny at night too.

"She was a friend who was visiting, but she went back to her country a few weeks ago," I said, casually fighting my tears. They nodded their heads, satisfied, and the short officer gave me his card. He wrote his cell phone number on the back of the card just in case I remembered any other information, no matter how small. I assured him I would call him if I wanted to be handcuffed—I mean, if I had any more information for him. They said *"Bonne nuit"* and apologized for scaring me. I turned off the lights and debated in the dark whether I should have told them about Altair. Maybe they could have given me the information necessary so I could confirm for myself if she was dead or had been deported.

That night I had a nightmare. I woke up crying when I saw Altair's corpse being pulled out of the Seine. In my dream she had been wandering by the Seine, searching for her children, and when she lost hope she drowned herself. In my dream I ran to her body and when I kneeled to look at her face it was Luna looking back at me, with sad eyes full of tears and water drops from the Seine. It took me an hour to recover from the nightmare. I felt ashamed for not having tried harder to find Altair or given her hope. I cried myself to sleep and woke up feeling like crap on Monday morning.

CHAPTER 17

No Exit

*I*n the kitchen my biggest fear was cutting myself, so when I saw Alexandros chop up his bones with his cleaver and nearly chop off his left thumb, I thanked God it wasn't me. He didn't hit the bone, but he carved enough of a cut that he had to go to the emergency room for stitches. Every time I would need my bones chopped up I would ask Akiva, who used to be in the army back in Israel, to do it for me. He took so much pleasure in doing it that I was convinced he had experience clubbing people the same way. Akiva, who had finally learned to respect the imaginary border between us, had a soft heart and dreamed of being a chef so he could provide for his little girl back in Israel. He missed her a lot, and the thirteen weeks he had been in Paris with only a little French and with even less money was taking a toll on his heart. Only when he was drunk would he show it, but I tried not to get too close to him because he also got frisky when he got drunk.

As the days continued I kept looking at the final recipes, doing a countdown like a prisoner waiting to be released from a ten-year sentence. All the recipes started to look and feel the same; how many times could we do guinea fowl? I was so tired from nearly three weeks of cooking nine hours a day that I couldn't care less about making the guinea fowl in a bourguignon sauce.

"Didn't we do this dish already in Basic?" I asked Bianca, but she was nervous about the written exam in a few days. Bianca still reminded me of Chicken Little, always waiting for the culinary sky to fall apart. That girl was so nervous and insecure about everything. No matter how bad I did, Bianca was always more disorganized, lost, and just plain worse. She was always asking for advice and begging for help. Pepa had taken her on as a mentee and looked out for her like a mother hen. I felt sorry for Bianca—how could she possibly be worse than me?

Chef Tristan was unlucky enough to finally get stuck with our class—the Le Coq Rouge orphans abandoned in the second-floor dungeon. We were the orphans because our class was always given the leftover food. Why this was, no one from the school ever explained. Chef Tristan was a stern man with sad eyes and dark circles under them. He had dark hair and a beautiful mouth. He wasn't handsome, but he had a manly presence that demanded respect. When he would address me I would shake in my skin and be aroused by his masculinity. I couldn't look him in the eyes because I felt he could see my naked soul. I quivered in my shoes, but I smiled every time I presented a dish. I'd learned to enjoy the sensation.

The day we were making the guinea fowl bourguignon I bunched up my leftover bacon into a ball and threw it into the sauce. What the hell, I figured. We're not doing brain surgery; it's just food. I'd gotten to the point in my cooking where I knew that no matter how much you mess with the recipes, it always comes down to the taste. Of course, taste is subjective. What I thought was delicious and would be a best-seller at a restaurant in California wasn't necessarily what the French chefs considered delicious in

Paris. So who the hell cares about pleasing the chefs? Ultimately, I have to please myself. Isn't that what self-esteem is about?

I presented the plate to Chef Tristan, expecting him to hate it. He tasted my sauce and looked up at me, licking his lips, savoring the flavor. I wanted him to take me right there on the counter. I could picture us on the marble surface having thrown off all the food to make room for our sweaty bodies, struggling to remove our stupid rooster-looking cooking uniforms. In my fantasy all the students would still be there cooking, oblivious to us making nasty and passionate lust sauce.

Chef Tristan tasted my sauce for a third time and said, *"Magnifique! C'est parfait!"* He said it was perfect. He gave me a score of five and said, *"Excellent travail, Chef."* This was the first time I had scored a five, the highest possible grade, and been called "Chef" by any of the chefs. I blushed and walked away all proud of myself. I'd begun cleaning my tools when Chef Tristan told Alexandros, who was being judged, that his sauce was good, but not as good as mine. He announced to everyone in the class that so far my sauce was the best. Dick smirked and continued packing his tools. I instantly turned all shades of red and lowered my head. Even with my newfound self-esteem, I had a problem accepting compliments—fighting is easy; winning is hard. Blanca congratulated me and I said thanks. I did my best to ignore Dick, not wanting to allow someone like him to ruin my moment.

Two weeks before the final exam we were given the list of all the ingredients. There were three that were absolutely required: artichokes, fava beans, and lamb. This time around we would also create an original recipe that demonstrated our cooking skills. I studied the list and came up with so many possibilities. I decided on something easy but delicious and unique. I was going to stuff the lamb. Maybe mix some mushrooms, pine nuts, crème fraîche, and then use port to make a sweet sauce. Is there an alcohol that has mint in it? I wondered. Probably, but not one we had in our kitchen. I wanted to add mint to the lamb because it goes so well with it, but they weren't going to give us mint if it wasn't on the list or already in the kitchen. They were giving us red and green bell peppers and onions, so I planned to mix them and cook them together in a *tian* ... maybe a tomato confit too. The confit stuffed with artichoke and basil would be so simple and tasty. I was more excited about this final than I had been for anything else in the class.

Wow, maybe someday I really could be a chef, I thought to myself. My mind wandered off to the future and I saw my dream restaurant, made to look like a rose garden. I imagined being the chef in my own kitchen, making exotic dishes with pomegranates and mangoes and figs and kiwis. It would be a nonsmoking restaurant and I would change the menu every season. I would have little tables for women's purses that would go under the main tables, and candies to take home in little boxes at the end of the meal. I would make rose-petal-covered tamales *de foie gras* ... Wait a minute: that's like fat covered in fat. It's a recipe for heart attacks and lawsuits.

My excitement soon dwindled when I studied my schedule and realized that I was due to be an assistant along with Dick on the fourth week. How, I asked God, could I be so unlucky? I went over to Miguel Angel, the student from Mexico, and begged him to change slots with me. He agreed to help me out and committed to getting the supplies up with Dick; then I would clean up and bring down the supplies. The first day worked out okay, but then Miguel Angel was late most of the time and Dick just thought I was getting back at him for being a jerk by not doing my part. I tried to explain to Dick that Miguel Angel had switched with me. He continued being the assistant until he came to practical pissed off. Miguel Angel was absent that day and Dick had had to get all the supplies by himself. Akiva looked around for the tomatoes and asked Dick for them.

"I just got screamed at by the pastry chef for the mess Miguel Angel made yesterday because *he* left the flour out, and *I* had to mop it up. So from this day forward I am no longer the assistant and you can all fuck off!" Dick exploded. "I resign being the assistant, so someone has to go get the tomatoes because I'm not doing it!" he declared.

Everyone just stared, silently calling him an asshole. I was happy on the inside thinking, There is a God: every jerk always has a bigger jerk stomp on him. No longer worried about having to deal with Dick, I went downstairs to the basement kitchen and brought up all the ingredients he'd forgotten. I returned to class with the supplies and everyone thanked me. When Dick needed something, I ignored him, and he was forced to go to the basement and get whatever he needed himself. I didn't like Dick, but I felt sorry for him. He was indeed the Ugly American everyone hated, not just in class but all around the world. He wanted to come in first so badly that he didn't care to share his resources, or give a shit if everyone had enough materials to succeed. And now the time had arrived when the others turned their backs on his needs just as he had turned his back to theirs. How did this sad little person get through life not understanding that it takes a global village to make a good meal?

The six-hour practical exam was a good way to experiment with our recipe and learn from all the mistakes we made because we had two extra hours to experiment. At the final we would make the same dish but everything had to be perfect and we had to make four identical *dégustation* plates. We were also supposed to have an original written recipe with all the ingredients and a detailed plan of every step of our preparation and technique. We couldn't get spontaneous at the exam because we had to show that we'd actually thought about the dishes we were making and were completely aware of everything necessary to execute them. My first attempt at making my dish was successful, except I burnt the phyllo dough. I quickly removed it and salvaged the lamb, which came out only a little overcooked.

"It is better to have it be undercooked than overcooked because lamb is supposed to be served pink; otherwise it's too rubbery to eat," Chef Papillon warned us. He advised us to cook the meat last, so it would not be overdone or cold by the time we served it.

I cleaned out my tools at the sink and heard Chef Papillon chastising Akiva for his lack of originality. Akiva could barely understand French and was always asking someone to translate. My French still wasn't great, but I felt so bad for the guy that I began to translate for the chef.

"This dish you have made is so elementary. This looks like Basic Cuisine, not Superior. You will not be able to get your diploma with this dish. You must create garnishes that show at least a two- or three-step process," I translated for Akiva. He nodded his head and grabbed his chin, trying to figure out what recipe to do tomorrow. Akiva was so fast he could work at McDonald's, but he had no originality. He was embarrassed by the chef's remarks, especially since he would brag about working at the Atelier de Joël Robuchon and the amazing things he was learning there. I was hoping that whatever he had learned he could use on his final and save his ass.

The night before the exam I had another nightmare. This time I was doing surgery on Blanca and I was cutting her in all the wrong places and she ended up overcooked. I woke up stressed, but I calmed down by telling myself, It's just food!

On the day of the final we were scheduled to have a demonstration class at eight-thirty in the morning. Only six people attended out of the fourteen. I arrived and was trying to write out my recipe while I waited for the chef to finish his demonstration, which would become my breakfast. I originally sat in the back, thinking I could ignore the chef and finish translating my recipe, but because hardly any of the students showed up I thought I better sit in the front and pretend like I was paying attention. I got busy studying my recipe, which I called *agneau à la Mexicaine-Américaine,* writing down a list of all the steps I needed to execute my process. Chef Papillon gave us advice on how to write out our recipes and reiterated not to overcook the lamb. A former graduate student gave us advice on how to keep our plates warm by using four bain-maries and setting up our dishes on top so we could dress them strategically. None of the Spanish-speaking students, including me, hid their nervousness; we can't hide our feelings so easily.

In the locker room Pepa confided that she'd got her period that day, which only added to her stress. It was all going to be over in less than five hours. She had come in first and second in the last two classes and wanted to get first place again.

"Did I have to get my period today?" she screamed in the locker room.

"Yes, God, did it have to happen to me too, today of all days?" I whispered to myself in the ladies' room.

Everyone except for Dick and Craig decided to go to the local bar, which also served strong coffee, and fill our veins with caffeine for the four stressful hours ahead. I took out my translated recipe and finished drawing my proposed dish. Blanca saw that I could draw and asked me to draw her a picture too. I drew it and it came out quite polished.

"Why don't you draw mine too? Mine is horrible," said Pepa. She showed it to me and I tried to improve what she had. The recipes and the drawing were important because as soon as we walked into the practical we were supposed to present them to the chef, and once you gave over the recipe that was it.

All the Intensive Superior students waited in the courtyard; at fifteen-minute intervals, the students were supposed to come upstairs to the large kitchen and begin the exam. Four hours later we all had to have four plates exactly alike, three for the jury of chefs to taste and one for the photo.

I was so nervous I sharpened all my knives until I could cut paper with them. I looked up at the clock. Five minutes before my exam time I started fixing my tie and hanging my hand towel in my apron, preparing as if I were a soldier going off to war. I picked up my knives and all my equipment and walked past Dick, who was studying his recipe. I prayed that they wouldn't put that passive-aggressive jerk next to me just because his last name followed mine. I took my time getting to the second floor, slowly passing the *Sabrina* movie poster in the stairway. I arrived at the designated practical kitchen and peeked in. I was still early, according to the clock on the wall in the practical room. I took deep breaths and studied my recipe.

⤚ *Agneau à la Mexicaine–Américaine* ⤙
Lamb Mexican–American Style

Okay, no way would this lamb be spicy enough to be called Mexican; but it's spicy enough for France. At least it ends up looking red and green. It's closer to an Italian dish, and the Italians are more like Mexicans, so I guess that's okay.

half of lamb shoulder with saddle, trimmed

STUFFING

100 grams shiitake mushrooms, sliced, sautéed
100 milliliters port, reduced with shallots
 50 grams pine nuts, chopped
 75 milliliters crème fraîche
  1 piece pig intestine lining, large enough to wrap
    around the stuffed lamb

DECORATION

4 basil leaves, fried
4 black olives, sliced

JUICE

1 carrot, diced
1 shallot, finely chopped
1 stalk celery, diced

BOUQUET GARNI

laurel and basil leaf

SIDE DISHES

600 grams fava beans, boiled, sautéed
  4 tomatoes, sliced, baked in oil
  4 artichokes, boiled and macerated
  2 eggplants, baked and macerated
  6 basil leaves, chopped
  4 garlic cloves, sliced and smashed
  4 olives, chopped
    Juice of 1 lemon

TIAN

1 red bell pepper, cut into sticks
1 green bell pepper, cut into sticks
1 onion, sliced

Chef Papillon finally let me in and I was calm when I handed my recipe to him. I was number seven. Lucky seven, right? I got there and everything was set up: a basket with everything I needed to create my recipe, ready to go. I had to take care of my tomatoes first because they took an hour and fifteen minutes. I went to one of the two communal ovens usually used for pastries and turned it on and got my tomatoes ready. I went to get a baking tray and Miguel Angel handed me one, trying to be helpful. I took it and a moment later realized it was hot at one end and instinctively put it down on an unoccupied stove. I looked under my forearm and saw that I had burnt my skin, in a line about five inches long. My arm felt like it was melting every time I reached over by the burners. Blanca noticed my large blister and grabbed my hand to take a closer look. She dragged me to the sink and stuck my arm under cold water.

"You have to use water to stop it from getting worse," she said. She went to the first-aid box and gave me the burn cream. I didn't want to take the time to tend to my injury because I was scared I was not going to finish, but she insisted that I take care of it. Ten minutes later, my burn was bearable and I checked the tomatoes. They seemed fine and I left them in the oven because I wanted them to be really dry and nice. An hour and fifteen minutes later, when I was finally ready to get them out, Dick was right in front of the oven, putting his fava beans in the Robot Coupe. If I went over there, I figured, he would probably refuse to move just to spite me. I decided to wait a few more minutes until he was finished and away from the communal oven.

I got caught up with other things, and fifteen minutes later I realized I had not taken my tomatoes out. When I got them they had dwindled to nothing. I debated whether I should try to do it again or settle for these. I looked at the clock and thought if I rushed I could do them again and end right on time. I proceeded forward and did my meat and sauce. I cut up my bones and put the trimmings on my pan to caramelize them along with my vegetables. The sauce I got didn't taste like anything, so I reduced it until it was savory. The fava beans were ready in two minutes, but when I sautéed them I had a little crisis trying to get aluminum foil, and ended up overcooking them and forgot the salt.

I didn't want to overcook the lamb, but it became a guessing game for me to determine how long it needed to be in the oven to be pink. Then I worked on my stuffing and I really loved it. In fact, I loved it so much that I put too much of it in the lamb. I thought it was so good, so I didn't want to waste any of it. I wrapped the lamb with crépine, or pig intestine, to seal it. I didn't want to use too much of it because it looks weird and a little disgusting. I had the lamb in my oven, but after around six minutes I panicked. I thought if I left it in the oven for nine minutes it was going to get overcooked so I turned off the oven and took it out. I discovered I hadn't used enough crépine because it burst open coming out of the oven. Now, why did I turn off the oven? I really thought it was cooked and I wanted to finish so badly. This is the one regret I will take to my grave! I took out the lamb, left it in the aluminum foil to settle, and figured if it was very pink it would still continue to cook under the aluminum foil. Minutes later I checked and I saw it wasn't cooked. I turned the oven back on, but I couldn't get it to cook the lamb anymore!

I looked up at the clock: all of a sudden I had ten minutes left to put everything together. Praying that the lamb would somehow cook just a few more minutes, I put my four plates on the bains-marie, which had gotten too hot to work on. I turned off the burners under them and began the assembly process. I took out my circular mold and put the bell pepper *tian* in it, forming nice little circles. I cut the lamb into four pieces; the stuffed lamb looked huge and was too big for a *dégustation* plate. With three minutes left I had no choice but to leave them like that. The hard part was the olives. I wanted to use flowers as my decoration on the plate and was trying to arrange the tiny olive slices in the shapes of petals. They kept sticking to my fingertips and my hands were trembling. This was the most stressful thing I had ever attempted. As if things weren't bad enough, next to me Dick casually began to assemble his plates over the bains-marie. He looked around for his mold and couldn't find it.

"Who took my mold?" asked Dick loudly so that I could hear. Everyone was too busy to pay attention to him.

"I'm missing my mold," Dick announced. I did everything to ignore him and then he walked up to Chef Papillon. "Chef, someone stole my mold."

I thought, Who the fuck has time to steal your pinchi mold, gringo!

"No one stole your mold. I'm sure we'll find it," Chef Papillon said to calm him down.

"No, someone took it! I need it," he said, practically stomping his foot like a toddler. Dick started to panic, and had I not been trembling like a freezing Chihuahua with two minutes left to finish I would have laughed in his face because his karma was kicking his ass . . . Dick walked up to my stove and pointed to a mold on the top shelf.

"Well, what's that?" he demanded. I grabbed the mold and showed him the red dot I'd made with nail polish to mark my equipment.

"It's mine, I just used it," I said, trying not to bite his head off for being an inconsiderate fucking jerk. I put away the mold and placed it on my *planchette*. I continued to work on the last of the olive slices, settling for flowers with three petals instead of four. Then Dick walked up to my *planchette* and like Inspector Clouseau, grabbed the mold off my *planchette,* and said, "Well, what about this one?"

"It's the same one I just showed you," I said. I saw his desperate look and felt sorry for that loser. "Do you want to borrow it? You can borrow it," I said with compassion, surprising myself. I hadn't known I'd had any kindness left for that ass. He shook his head and continued hunting for his mold. With one minute left I threw the sauce on the four dishes as Chef Papillon and his assistant came up to my stove like Nazis ready to take away my four children. They grabbed the hot plates and ordered me to carry the saucer with my sauce down to the first floor, where the three chefs on the jury awaited my dish. Two of the chefs on the jury were retired chefs with more opinions than white hair. Chef Chocon saw the dishes coming in with the giant pieces of stuffed lamb and immediately commented on how my dish *agneau à la Mexicaine-Américaine* was really a *dégustation* plate for Americans. I hated being there for his joke and immediately slipped out before they commented on my undercooked lamb.

Four hours of labor and the results were disappointing. I'd done the best I could, but it was a mess. I went back to my stove to clean up and saw that Dick's presentation looked great. The fact that my plates looked like a disaster would only make his shine even more, since he was the next to present. Glad I could be of service, jerk. Dick's plate was so simple. I should have done something stupid and simple like him, but my dish ended up being so complicated. I felt like such a failure after I finished, though when I saw Akiva scrounging around for leftover tomatoes, I realized that maybe my food was not perfect but I'd finished on time and hadn't burnt anything. Akiva had burnt all of his food and had had to restart, making a whole new dish that he was forced to improvise with all the leftovers from the other students. I remembered my promise to just enjoy this class and not get caught up in the competition and started to clean up my station. When I was washing my dishes I saw Bianca crying and offered to help her, since I was done. But she was such an emotional mess that she snapped at me and told me not to talk to her. I gave Bianca her space and went down to the locker room.

After I dressed I looked for Blanca, who had finished an hour before me. She was calm about the whole thing and had no mishaps to report. She was a pro and was very satisfied with her work. Blanca told me she had to run off to work and said she would see me the next day at the restaurant where we were supposed to celebrate our graduation. I walked outside with her to get some fresh air and commiserate with all the other students who had also just finished. Pepa was smoking her lungs out and got close to tears when she revealed to us that her lamb was undercooked. She reflected on her whole process like a boxer who couldn't explain how he had been knocked out when everything was going in his favor. Pepa shook her head and counted the minutes until they posted the grades on the wall. She couldn't imagine not passing the class after all the personal sacrifices she'd made. If she didn't pass she could not come back and try again. Her family life and her schedule would not permit it. This was the first time I had seen Pepa so distraught. Normally she was the fearless wisecracking mother hen who was in charge of the kitchen.

"Ten weeks is hard, but four months of this is crazy," Pepa said. I kept listening to Pepa and wanted to cry too. I'd thought that after doing Le Coq Rouge I would be able to do amazing things in the kitchen, but at this moment, despite my promise, I felt even worse about my cooking skills. I was glad I didn't want to be a chef, because it was really gut-wrenching and soul-shattering. From observing what all the students here went through, I'd learned that food is about who you are. It's like being undressed and saying, Look at me naked. Do you like what you see?

"I'm sure we all passed because they already printed the diplomas," Miguel Angel said, trying to console her.

"Yeah, but they can easily tear them up," responded Pepa.

"I'm sure we all passed." Miguel Angel insisted, trying to cheer her up. "You'd have to burn the food and set the kitchen on fire for them to flunk you. There's no way you can't pass after what you've been through."

Pepa smiled back at his kindness. "Yeah, I'm sure we all passed."

"If you didn't pass, they'll have to tell us not to show up to the three-star restaurant and the graduation," Alexandros said. We all laughed and looked at our watches, wanting time to go by faster.

"Should we go find out?" asked Miguel Angel. "They must be done by now. We can go to the jury room and ask for our grades." Pepa, Bianca, Miguel Angel, and I looked at one another and nodded and went for our scores. When we got to the jury room, we waited around, still a bit unsure if we wanted to go in. Then we were told to come in and see the plates.

There were four plates in one section and six in another. One of the retired chefs came in and saw us and welcomed us to the exciting and fulfilling world of cuisine. He explained how the four plates set aside were the acceptable ones and the other six were not. I instantly recognized my plate in the unacceptable bunch, and my heart sank. All my childhood nightmares of being an immigrant and an outsider, of not belonging and not being normal flashed through my unconscious mind and I felt a punch in my solar plexus. It's just food, I reminded myself so the tears would not come out in public. Pepa and Bianca also recognized their plates in the unacceptable bunch and lowered their heads with shame. Miguel Angel smiled when he recognized his plate in the acceptable section, and I tried to be happy for him. Our plates looked like crap, like a carcass of a cow in the desert or a decaying pigeon on the pavement. It was so humiliating. Chef Papillon came in with his head down, disappointed in us. I looked over to the acceptable plates and recognized Blanca's dish as well as Craig's and Dick's. Part of me thought, Oh gosh. I bet you Dick's going to win; he's going to come in first. I prayed Blanca would come in first and then maybe Craig and then Miguel Angel, but I was certain Dick was going to get first place. Chef Papillon commented on how the portions on the unacceptable plates were too big. When I look at it now, I know he's right, but at that moment I'd just wanted to get it on the plate and meet the deadline.

Chef Papillon grabbed the plates and started throwing the food into the garbage. We watched this and it stung because he discarded the unacceptable plates first. We'd put so much work and creativity into making those dishes and they ended up being dinner for the garbage can. As my plate sailed into the garbage, I took one last look and asked myself, What did I do right? The tomato confit, the stuffing; I loved it. It wasn't perfect, but it was part of me and I loved it.

CHAPTER 18

Au Revoir les Euros

Madame Bodé stopped me at the entrance to my apartment building and handed me a letter. I was about to open it when she informed me herself in French, "You have to move out at the end of the month."

"That's next week," I replied in French, raising my voice.

"*Oui.*" She smiled.

"You're not the landlord of my room," I reminded her.

"I spoke to your landlord and Rosemary is the only person who is supposed to live there, not you," she informed me with righteousness.

"But she said I could stay in her apartment if I paid her rent!" I yelled back. She lifted her shoulders and made a face in the usual annoying French way and said, *Ce n'est pas mon problème. Au revoir.* Madame Bodé climbed up the stairs with a smile of satisfaction. I took the servants' elevator upstairs and when I got to my floor I was in tears. Marina was waiting for the elevator and saw me crying.

"What happened?" she asked in Spanish. After I explained she filled me in on the whole situation. Madame Bodé was trying to get rid of all the servants who were *sans-papiers* before winter because

French law did not permit her to kick people out in winter. Marina lamented that it was just a matter of time before Madame Bodé and the Minister of the Interior, whose last name sounded like a disease, would find a way to kick the *sans-papiers* out.

"They are trying to get rid of us. Everyone in France hates immigrants," she said.

"No, not just in France—they hate us in the United States too," I added and made her crack a tiny smile. She asked me about the United States and I told her about how Latinos are such a large population that life is slightly easier for undocumented people there. Marina shared with me that she looked forward to the day when her daughters were old enough to apply for French citizenship and she could finally rest for a few days. Every day she had to work just to survive and carve out a miserable existence.

"When I was told I was going to be brought to Paris, I imagined a wonderful life, but life in Paris as a *sans papier* is just as miserable as being back in Colombia," she lamented. I hugged her and said, "Adios."

I didn't want to show up early to Ledoyen, the three-star restaurant where we were celebrating our graduation, looking all pretty when I knew Dick was going to show up right on time like the big nerd that he was. I walked around the restaurant, famous for being the place where Joséphine met Napoléon, admiring the many floral arrangements with burgundy calla lilies. So what if the French were rude? They knew how to celebrate beauty in every form, and therefore they were forgiven. Blanca arrived at the entrance and I walked up to her, admiring her dress. Out of uniform we were hotties. We climbed the stairs to the small but beautiful and exclusive room set aside for our graduation. I saw Craig downing champagne and we commiserated. It made me happy to know that Akiva had been allowed to graduate and that no one, not even Blanca or Dick, felt great about their dish. The sous-chef of Ledoyen welcomed us to his restaurant and posed for photos. Lunch was served, and after our four-course meal we drank more champagne and prepared ourselves to receive our diplomas.

The diplomas were large and ridiculous-looking, but they were certainly impactful and precious once received. In regular classes the students were not allowed to give speeches because all combined there were over one hundred, on average, but because we were only a class of fourteen we were encouraged to say a few words. The names were called in alphabetical order and Pepa was awarded third place. She was relieved that she had placed at all despite her undercooked lamb. She gave a heartfelt speech about the wonderful people who'd shared the same difficult journey. Craig was called to receive his diploma but refused to give a speech and feign gratitude to anyone, especially the stingy school. Blanca's name was called; she had not placed. I applauded loudly for her and was disappointed she hadn't won.

The biggest shock came when they announced Bianca's name and said she had come in second. Pepa's jaw dropped, but she quickly closed it and applauded loudly to cover up her horror. Her face wore the collective shock of the entire class. I was happy for Bianca and thought maybe she just surprised the chefs. Maybe her dish had been so great after all; it counted for 45 percent of the grade. Then my intuition whispered a thought that made me feel disgusted . . . Maybe it was the bubbles in the champagne, but I understood why Bianca had come in second. They probably mixed up Blanca's grades with Bianca's, because there is no way she could have beat me either. Her lamb had been undercooked and her plate had been judged "unacceptable." I shook my head and drank more champagne, hoping it would force me to vomit and maybe Dick would just happen to be there when I did.

Miguel Angel was called up to receive his diploma, and his parents, who had flown all the way from Mexico, cheered him on. He gave his speech in Spanish and thanked his parents for believing in him. How I wished I could have had someone special there to witness that moment for me. Françoise, whose derriere had grown into a "ghetto booty" over the course of my studies, called my name. I debated whether I should speak about Dick being a dick, but I knew that if I said anything resembling the truth my words would be considered sour grapes. I would look like a jerk bad-mouthing him. I knew Dick had won and there was nothing I could do about it. I was awarded my diploma and Chef Chocon placed the official Le Coq Rouge chef's hat on my head. Françoise placed the silver medal bearing their emblem over my neck and I got emotionally overwhelmed, like a typical Latina.

"I have worked so hard for this. I have shed blood, sweat, and tears for this . . . I even have the scars to prove it," I said, displaying my five-inch burn. "I realize now what it takes to be a chef and I know that it's too hot, and that's why I'm getting out of the kitchen," I said, trying to hold back the tears. People applauded, and I let the moment wash over me, soaking in both the celebration and the sadness.

Of course the next person after me was Dick. They called his name and announced that he had won first place. Dick got up and his wife cheered him on.

"Since I was a little kid I wanted to become a Le Coq Rouge chef," he said and started crying. Françoise and all the Le Coq Rouge staff ate that shit up and got emotional too. "This is the happiest day of my life and I feel so blessed for having so many wonderful chefs help me become who I am." Now I knew he was going to be a serial killer someday. A person like him could not possibly be that emotional and yet so thoughtless of other people's feelings. I know I have been accused of being sick, but maybe that qualifies me to point the finger. And yet this kind of person seemed familiar . . . You see, Dick always wins. He gets to be the chef, or the CEO of a giant corporation, or even the president of the United States. How wonderful that I got to see that even though I'd left the United States to avoid Dick, here he was again, giving a speech and telling lies through his teeth without a care in the world or remorse for all the damage he had done to others. Yeah, no matter where I go, Dick is there. I pray to God that I have the strength and courage to continue exposing the Dicks of this world with my writing.

After the graduation ceremony we were ushered back to the school grounds and into the courtyard for the customary class photo with our chef's hats. We set ourselves up in two rows and I positioned myself away from Dick. When the photographer said, *"C'est tout,"* That is all, I was relieved that it was over. I no longer had to feel like a dishrag.

Henry passed by the courtyard on his way to the men's locker room and saw me with a long face. He walked up to me and smiled.

"It wasn't so bad. I actually liked your food. The filling was quite original," Henry acknowledged.

"You're just being nice," I said, feeling sorry for myself.

"No, I actually tasted it," he said.

"I know you're lying, but thanks for that beautiful lie," I said and kissed him on the cheek.

"Are you doing a *stage*?" he asked.

"No. I'm getting kicked out of my apartment next week and I have just enough money left to catch a plane back to the U.S.," I told him.

"What are you doing after this?" he asked me.

"We're supposed to go drinking. Why?"

"Come to my apartment when you're done. I have a graduation present for you."

"Liar," I joked.

"I know I was an ass to you, but come to my place—I want to make it up to you," Henry insisted.

"What did Bassie tell you?"

"Nothing. I just need to see you before you go back home."

"I'm tired," I lied.

"Please, Canela. Give me a chance to say I'm sorry," he pleaded.

I agreed to meet him no matter how late it was.

I congratulated Blanca and Pepa and wished them luck in their future careers as chefs. Blanca saw my disappointment and put her arm around me like a big sister.

"Canela, you, too, are entitled to call yourself a chef," she reminded me.

"No, I'm just somebody who has a diploma that says I graduated from Le Coq Rouge. I'm not a chef."

Pepa turned to me and proclaimed, "Of course you are a chef now. You can cook just like the rest of us."

I smiled, touched by her words, but I shook my head. "You see, cooking for you is your passion. Writing to uncover truth is my passion. I had forgotten that for a while, but I remember now. I'm a writer and that's what I should be doing."

We walked to the metro and said good-bye forever.

CHAPTER 19

Last Mango in Paris

I arrived at Henry's building and hesitated before going upstairs. Why should I give him a second chance? He'd been so cold to me after I'd said, "I love you." True, I had nothing better to do right now, but I needed a better reason than boredom. I thought about it for a few more minutes and I knew I would regret not seeing him before I left Paris. I also had to see what he'd meant by a present. The curiosity was killing me, and I had to admit I did care about Henry, at least enough to know that it would be nice to say good-bye properly and complete things. I, too, wanted to see him one last time, so I was glad he'd been the one who'd made the request and insisted I see him. Yeah, sex with Henry was amazing, but now that I had distance from him I could laugh a little at how serious I'd been about having sex with a stranger and about Max and . . . it was just sex. I could finally enjoy sex for sex.

I knocked on Henry's door, hoping I was not so drunk that I was bothering his neighbor. He opened the door wearing an apron and nothing else. When I walked in he had his small table set up for dinner. He made me sit and put a chef's hat on my head.

Henry had cooked for me. He had prepared duck *à l'orange* and made *macarons* from scratch. I must have been drunk, because I started to cry. Henry put his hands on my face.

"Why are you crying, silly girl?" he said with his cute little accent. I was so embarrassed to admit to him that I was so touched because this was the first time someone had acknowledged an accomplishment by making me dinner. When I told him he didn't believe me.

"You're joking," he said, dismissing my claim. I insisted that it was true.

"What about Chef Sauber? He cooked for you," he said, pouring the sauce on my duck.

I turned to him. "How did you hear . . . ?"

"Little Henry knows everything because he has many ears and many mouths and many tongues," he said. I took a bite of the duck and complimented Henry, trying to change the subject.

"What about Mohammed—did he make couscous for you?" Henry continued.

"Did you keep track of all my lovers?" I asked.

"I don't need to; I already know you're my kind of girl," he replied.

"And what kind of girl is that?"

"One with an appetite." He poured red wine and I tried to stop him because I had already had too many glasses of champagne.

"Come now, this is a celebration, Miss Canela. Let me make a fuss, my little gourmand," he insisted until I decided, Why not? I'm already going to hell.

"You should do a *stage*, Canela," Henry suggested.

"Henry, I have no money. I maxed out my credit cards and spent all my savings and I don't have rich relatives," I went on.

"Maybe I can get you a *stage* where they actually pay you—not a lot, but enough to get by until you can prove yourself or get a better job. Would you consider staying if I got you a job?"

"Hmmm . . . I don't know . . . Maybe . . . But I'm not a good cook."

"Of course you are. Now you're a perfectionist, but you can cook. I know you can. Your sauce and stuffing today were delicious, actually."

"Honestly?" I looked up to see how sincere he was being. He knew he didn't have to lie to get sex from me.

"Canela, you have the talent to be a chef, and a good one. Now it's up to you to decide whether you want to work to be a great one." Henry's voice was so sincere, I had to turn away so he wouldn't see me blushing.

"Maybe I could work at a Mexican restaurant . . . ," I said, imagining myself working at a Tex-Mex restaurant, since that's mostly what they had in Paris. I could actually see myself in a kitchen, speaking Spanish and slinging tortillas onto plates. Maybe it wouldn't be so bad. Maybe I could do that for a while until I got a job as a writer for an American newspaper or found a way to write for a tourist paper in English.

"You know, I might know some people. I'll make some calls," Henry said, bringing me back to reality.

"Henry, I have to decide tomorrow what I am going to do," I said.

"Fair enough. Give me a day to change your mind," he requested. I was so drunk I think I fell asleep at the dining table.

"Canela, get up. I have something to show you," Henry said, waking me up in the middle of the night. I woke up hoping it wasn't an erection he was talking about. "Look at the moon." He pointed through the window. It was a full moon looking perfectly beautiful, with the Mona Lisa smiling in it.

"It's a lovers' moon. We have to go make love under it and all our dreams will come true," Henry exclaimed like Peter Pan. We put on trench coats quickly and went to Pont Neuf to kiss under the moon. He put his hands through my trench coat and caressed my naked body. My nipples were already hard from the cold. We kissed as a large boat passed under the bridge. We leaned in to watch another small boat pass by. Henry got behind me and lifted my trench coat. He penetrated me and I laughed when my derriere was exposed to the cold.

"You like it?" Henry asked, not sure if I was laughing at him.

"I love it," I said, half-giggling. We stared up at the moon, her light massaging our skin, kissing us with her rays of light.

"The moon loves Paris more than any other city in the world," Henry bragged. "So many poems written to her and lovers making love to her, she always comes to Paris dressed like a queen." Henry said all this in between loud breaths and humps.

"It's the same moon I made love to back in Los Angeles," I interjected, not convinced that his romantic observations had been authentically inspired by me. For all I knew this was his routine, his M.O. every full moon. The moon was the same, but never the woman, you know. Oh God, I'm so jaded. How many women would kill to be in this same position, pun intended?

"Ah, but Paris to the moon is the shortest ride. You can go there at the same time you French-kiss," he said, kissing me, then dying in my arms. Minutes later Henry recovered from la petite mort and we headed back to his apartment just as the sun was rising.

Henry stopped at a farmers' market and picked out fresh fruit and vegetables, fish, and a baguette. I was surprised to find mangoes out of season and all sorts of tiny fruit I had never seen before. He had no translation duties that day and spent the morning making me an English breakfast. He was so sweet to cook for me that I didn't have the heart to tell him I didn't care too much for it. It didn't matter—he could tell by the way I ate.

"I love that about you; you can't lie," Henry chuckled.

"Oh, you'll hate that real soon," I warned him.

He kissed me lovingly and took my hand. "Let me show you the Paris no one will take you to see.

For the next twelve hours we challenged ourselves to have sex in all the tourist places in Paris. I would take mental pictures of all the sights as he penetrated me, and I knew I would never forget him or the hidden places for lovers in Paris. We almost got caught in the bathroom at the Louvre. It was so exciting, the idea of getting caught in a men's bathroom by security guards. Would I negotiate my way out of it or would I just say, "Handcuff me," half-dressed?

Henry took me dancing at Barrio Latino in the Bastille to show me I could be as Latina as I wanted to be in Paris. He surprised me with a few dance moves and I knew he had probably dated a lot of black women to dance like he did. He bought me drinks and told me dirty stories about doing it in the bathroom. We sat at the bar discussing what I loved about being Mexican. Yes, France may be the culinary capital of the world, but what kind of a world would it be if Mexico had never produced chocolate or vanilla or salsa or tequila? He poured me more tequila and I quickly forgot all the reasons why I yearned to go back to the United States.

At the end of the night Henry reminded me why I couldn't leave Paris: "It's the most beautiful city in the world!"

"Henry, there is more to life than Paris. I have to go back to the U.S.; it's my home," I said, sincerely calling it *home* for the first time. People say if you hate America you should leave it, but I think you have to leave it to love it again.

"Canela, you can start a whole new life here. You can finally have the life you want," Henry declared. "With me." I rolled my eyes, dismissing him. Henry saw me and quickly interjected, "Look, I know you have no reason to believe me since I didn't treat you so well at the beginning."

"What do you mean? I thought we were just having fun and that we meant nothing to each other," I replied. I was proud of myself because I could say that out loud and mean it. When I first had sex with Henry, I'll admit, I was hooked into him and wanted something more than sex. Now that I knew how to ride his roller coaster I could sit back a happy passenger, knowing it was just temporary.

"Canela, you know I care about you!" I was so touched by Henry's sincerity that I wanted to kiss him, but I held off, knowing that I couldn't lead him on or fool myself into thinking anything serious could develop between us. Instead I studied his funny pale face.

"If I stay here I will always be an immigrant. I will always be treated like an outsider, and I've already been through that. As bad as the U.S. is, I still like it better than France. I'm a Latina and I want to live in a country where I feel I belong and in a city where I get some respect."

"It's not that bad," Henry interjected.

"Need I remind you, you are a white male—" I said, about to give him a lecture, until he cut me off.

"Fine. Go back to your lousy country and have a nice life." Henry tried to be funny, but he was too hurt to make either one of us laugh.

"Yeah, it's fucked up what the U.S. is doing . . . but I have to go back and try to do something about it . . . even if I can't make a difference."

That night Henry cooked for me and we had sex one last time, but it was more of a release for him. I was still sore from our sexual tour of Paris.

Henry was kind enough to go with me to the airport. I began to cry when I saw the Eiffel Tower and the merry-go-round from the taxi window. To keep myself from crying I sucked on a mango. I ate it because I knew I couldn't take it with me on the airplane. I thought about all the beautiful things I was going to miss about Paris, the roasted chickens and the aroma-filled street named Belles-Feuilles, the crepes by the metro stop, the fresh bread at the corner of my street, the *macarons* and the chocolate at Maison du Chocolat on place de Victor Hugo. It was mostly the food I was going to miss. I was certainly not going to miss the dog poop or the urine stains everywhere, which looked like Rorschach tests revealing to me my miserable existence in Paris. I definitely would not miss the wannabe model hostesses at the few fancy restaurants I got to go to, or the anorexic waitresses laughing at me for asking for tea as my aperitif, or the arrogant waiters sick of American tourists practically throwing the menu at me and rolling their eyes because my French sucked. Still, I started crying. How could living in Paris have made me so miserable? No, wait—Paris didn't make me miserable. I'd left Los Angeles and the United States so I wouldn't be miserable under the leadership of an idiot, but I'd arrived and was leaving the same miserable person.

I shook my head. No, I wasn't the same miserable person. I'd come to Paris already dead. I was leaving Paris almost alive. Henry and Le Coq Rouge had revived me and awakened my senses. I was alive again . . . Maybe I should take medication, like my mother has been insisting, so I won't be so cynical and pessimistic and I can finally replace my urine-stained glasses for pretty rose-colored ones and see *la vie en rose* wherever I go. Maybe it will help me. I don't want to leave Paris feeling this way. If Luna were here she would be so happy to have finally seen Paris.

I shouldn't have thought of Luna, because I couldn't stop crying after that. Henry misinterpreted my crying and held my hand and said, "We could turn around."

"No, it's . . . It's nothing . . . Los Angeles . . . I have to go home," I told him, trying to be strong. I decided my last hours in Paris were going to be happy ones, even if it killed me. I was going to be happy because I was at least alive to enjoy Paris on Luna's behalf.

At the airport Henry walked with me to the security gate and embraced me, not wanting to let go. "I could fall in love with you," confessed Henry. "I hope you can come back soon." Then he kissed me.

"I don't know if I'm ever coming back," I told him, then kissed him good-bye on the cheek. Henry was a man I could love and love madly, but all great loves end in tragedy or sometimes they end in marriage; and that's the tragedy.

CHAPTER 20

Canela's Feast

I landed at the airport and almost cried when I saw a Latino mayor welcoming me to Los Angeles on a large billboard. My little sister Rosie picked me up at the airport, and as we rode in her car I could tell life had changed while I'd been gone. There were many more Spanish stations on the radio and reggaetón was the hottest thing on the charts. Rosie was hooked on it and played Daddy Yankee, Zion, and Calle 13 the whole ride to her house. Rosie had invited me to stay in her guest bedroom as long as I needed to. I didn't want her to tell my mother or any other family members that I had returned. She swore she would not tell anyone and that she would not gossip about it either, so it wouldn't get to my Tía Bonifacia. Only when I was ready was I going to go over to my parents' house and confront my mother about the letter.

I assumed that since I had been away and had abandoned my apartment, all my belongings had either been thrown out or donated. I had only two suitcases and my LV purse to my name. It felt liberating to know I had so few belongings and no money.

I borrowed money from Rosie and bought a new outfit to wear to Rosemary's wedding. I didn't want to go alone to her wedding, but I'd promised I would be there.

Rosemary looked pregnant in her wedding dress; either that or she'd gotten a boob job. When I had a chance to talk to her privately in the ladies' restroom she revealed to me that she was four months pregnant and happy about it. She was so in love and happy that I was able to share this precious day with her. Rosemary got all teary-eyed when she started thinking about her mother not being there. She quickly changed the subject and said she couldn't wait for me to find my true love and get married. At the reception I forced myself to make small talk with the other guests and had to explain why I was alone and no, nobody would be coming later to join me. I debated whether I should sneak out early or stay until the cutting of the cake. I loved her reception and wondered if I could see myself in a wedding dress or making dinner for someone. It felt good knowing that I could cook, but I never had to. I bet Henry would never expect me to make dinner or clean up. Yes, but Henry would never be the kind of guy who would propose or promise love for a lifetime; he could never lie like that. But I will never know now what a life with him would have been like.

Rosie came into my room and asked me what I was planning to do for my thirtieth birthday party. My birthday was before Christmas and my family usually combined the two; yeah, I would get cheated on the presents. I told her I honestly didn't know what to do. She walked past my suitcase and saw a giant cardboard envelope and asked me what it was. I told her it was nothing and attempted to hide it. Rosie knew me well enough to know it was important because I got nervous talking about it. She insisted that I show it to her, so I figured, what the hell, and showed her my giant diploma. She didn't understand why I had a diploma for cooking when I'd been studying journalism. I told her the truth and she practically laughed. See, that's why I did it. Rosie stared at the diploma and smiled.

"Wow, so are you going to cook for me?" she asked, savoring the imaginary French food I would make for her. I made a note to myself not to mention cooking school ever again to anyone.

"Why don't you make a dinner party for your birthday?" Rosie suggested. I considered her suggestion and almost dismissed the idea until Rosie added, "Maybe I can invite all the family to dinner and then surprise them with you coming out of the kitchen. Do you have a chef's hat?" Rosie always had her heart in the right place, but I wasn't sure I could go through with it. But, after much urging from Rosie, I agreed to try.

I went shopping and bought all the ingredients. I wasn't thrilled about doing all the work for my birthday party, but this would be a nice way to be welcomed back. Plus, I could live out my cooking fantasy, which would be a nice present. I debated whether to make fish or meat. Should I make the monkfish wrapped in bacon or the *saumon farcie en feuille de chou vert* or the *truite farcie aux morilles?* Or should I make my *agneau à la Mexicaine-Américaine* and finally get it right? What kind of dessert? Should I attempt to make a chocolate soufflé with Chantilly cream or something really fancy with caramel decorations? When I was paying for the groceries I picked up the newspaper and read an article about a proposed wall along the border between Mexico and the United States being approved by Congress. I asked Rosie about it and she told me, "They're even proposing to make it a crime if anyone assists an undocumented person. Something called the HR no se que cochinada something. It sounds like hemorrhoid medicine."

Rosie made her husband set up the table all fancy and forced him to use the fine china that was typically just for decoration. When the family arrived they were impressed by the table settings and asked who was cooking and why the early celebration; Christmas was still days away. Rosie said that she had hired a professional chef and forbid anyone from going into her kitchen. I ran around like a madwoman getting the veal ready. Finally I was satisfied with my dish; it was done as it was meant to be prepared and presented. Rosie ran into the kitchen to check on me and asked me if I was ready. I put the chocolate soufflé into the oven and I put on my chef hat and fixed my tie. I grabbed the veal and walked out of her kitchen holding the platter. It took a few seconds for everyone at the table to notice that it was me under the chef's hat. Collectively my whole family said, "Canela, is that you?" I announced my dish and began serving. When I got to the end of the table I almost dropped the platter when I discovered that Armando was one of my guests.

"Armando? What are you doing here?" I blurted out tactlessly.

"Your mother invited me."

"He's practically a part of the family," my mother interjected. She stared at me defiantly, her eyes gleaming with pride that she had outsmarted me. I gave her a dirty look and went back into the kitchen, Rosie following at my heels.

"Did you tell mama about this?" I snapped at her.

"No! But . . ." Rosie hesitated. "I think my husband might have accidentally let it slip out." I went to the sink and stared at the dirty dishes. I was so annoyed at my mother for what she'd done, but I also knew that it was not fair to Armando to embarrass him or make him feel unwelcome.

I gritted my teeth and took the platters with the tomato confit and the bell pepper *tian* into the dinning room. I finished serving my guests and said, *"Bon appétit."* My family began to eat. My mother took a bite and stared at me, incredulous. "You made this?" I nodded. I stared at everyone as they ate my food and wanted to cry. Not because I was angry about Armando or afraid of what my family thought, but because I was relieved to be back home and to see all my siblings and my parents. Being away for nine months had helped me remember I loved them.

"It's delicious," my mother said approvingly. "Don't you think so, Armando?" He smiled at me and agreed with her. After several bites I was showered with compliments and questions about my life in Paris. I tried to give as little information as possible without making it obvious that I was trying to be vague.

"I went to cooking school," I said, and no one laughed.

"Wait, didn't you tell Rosie you were studying journalism?" my sister Reina interjected.

"I did . . . I wanted it to be a surprise," I told them, and they all thought that was sweet. "Excuse me, I have to finish dessert," I said and went into the kitchen. I finally understood what that female chef named Babette felt after she made her fabulous feast for those sexually repressed Danes. I felt like an artist. Like in some small way I had contributed to enriching my family's life. I danced around victoriously and stopped the second Rosie walked back in. She hugged me and said, "You did it! Happy birthday." I took the chocolate soufflé out of the oven and it looked like a beautiful hot-air balloon. I felt so proud of myself. All this and my soufflé had risen to great heights, looking perfect—there is a God! I took the soufflé to the table and everyone looked at it. Reina's husband didn't know what the black thing was and I educated everyone on the fine art of making soufflés. My father finally spoke up. He commented that maybe now that I knew how to cook and was a "hot commodity" I could be a real woman and settle down. The table fell silent. Everyone was waiting for me to explode, to scream and yell so they could roll their eyes and share "you know how Canela is" smirks. And it's true, I wanted to tell him the thirty reasons his comment was sexist, but I forced a smile and let his sexist comment slide; I wasn't going to let him ruin my fantasy. I had accepted that machos don't evolve and that you can't teach an old macho a new trick.

I sliced the soufflé as best I could and handed the pieces out before the soufflé was reduced to a flattened ball. I added the Chantilly cream and powdered sugar to the slices. I handed my mother a big piece and put tons of cream on it. It was so rich and delicious I salivated just serving it to her. One of my sisters asked me if I got to eat frogs and snails.

"*Escargot*, as they call snails, and *grenouille*, as they call frogs, don't taste bad. Drown them in butter and they taste like chicken." Reina asked me what I thought about the French—were they really snobs like everyone says they are? I tried to be diplomatic, but I couldn't lie either.

"They are so arrogant; who do they think they are?" Reina said loudly. I didn't want to generalize, so I explained how I had heard people in the south and in the country were so much nicer than the Parisians. "I'm glad I went, but I wouldn't want to live there again," I confided. "But at least they stood up against the war in Iraq," I said on France's behalf, forgetting that my sister was a Republican.

"Yeah, that's because they had an arms contract with Saddam—" Reina interjected. I was about to argue with her when my mother tipped over the pitcher of water. Everyone stared at her, but she continued searching for the water with her hands, like a blind woman.

Armando reached over to her and my mother passed out. Quickly gathering her into his arms, Armando carried her to his car and we rushed her to the emergency room.

CHAPTER 21

Bitter Truths

*Y*our mother has lost her sight. Her diabetes—" explained the doctor before I cut him off.

"She has diabetes?" I asked.

"She's had it for a long time. It has to be severe for her to lose her sight," the doctor told all of us.

"Are you sure she's blind? Maybe it's temporary?" my father asked, almost angry at the doctor for delivering the bad news.

"No. It's permanent."

My brothers and sisters started crying. My father just got up and left. We figured he needed time to process it by himself, so no one chased after him. I couldn't stop crying. I felt so angry no one had told me she was a diabetic. I felt so angry with myself for not speaking to her for almost a year. Talk about guilt; I felt terrible serving her a chocolate soufflé! I'd never felt like a bad daughter until that moment. Armando handed me a tissue for my tears, but I buried myself in his chest. He hugged me and I smelled his beautiful scent. He was such a good guy; why had I left him? The hours passed and my brothers and sisters said good-bye because they had to get up early for work. I had no place to go so I stayed until visiting hours were over. I kissed my mother on her forehead as she slept.

Armando offered to give me a ride back to Rosie's place or continue talking to me if I needed to talk. Aside from his long hours as a doctor and his annoying mother, Armando was a catch, but by now he was sure to have a girlfriend. Probably a nurse who was always by his side. I sat in his Mercedes crying and he invited me over to his apartment and offered to make me a root beer float or an ice cream cone. I was so touched by his gesture, but I warned him that I might need to cry the whole night.

His apartment had not changed much since I'd broken off the engagement. I carefully surveyed the living room, waiting to find a photo of his new girlfriend. I even excused myself so I could go to the bathroom and inspect his medicine cabinet for signs of a new woman. I closed the mirror and caught myself snooping. So what if he has a girlfriend, I don't care, I told myself. None of my business, I scolded myself.

Armando made me a bowl of ice cream with whipped cream on top and I felt so joyous to be with him again. Maybe my mother was right; maybe he was too good to pass up.

"So how are you?" I asked.

"Busy as usual. More responsibilities, but happy overall."

I took this to mean that he was happy about our breakup. I looked at my watch and saw it was two in the morning.

"I better go back to Rosie's place; I don't want to get there much later because her door is squeaky."

"Why don't you stay here?" he suggested.

"Armando, I don't deserve your kindness. I know you want to be supportive, but I did not treat you right."

"Neither did I. I should have defended you better. My mother should not have interfered, but I allowed her."

I cried, realizing how much I'd missed him, and we embraced until we could both hear each other's hearts beating at the same time.

"How is your mother?" I asked, trying to be nice.

"She nags me about having kids and sets me up on bad blind dates that I have to cancel. She's all right."

"So none of the blind dates worked out?"

"No. I am not interested in anyone else but you."

"So this last nine months you didn't date and you waited for me?"

"No, I didn't say that. I went out with some women for a few weeks here and there, but they were more interested in marrying a doctor than actually getting to know me ... Canela, I know you, so don't tell me what you did in Paris. I don't need to know."

"Aren't you at all curious about my life in Paris?" I teased him.

"Only if it doesn't include men," he said.

He made his bed on the couch and told me to take his bed. I insisted that he let me sleep on the sofa and pretty soon a pillow fight ensued that led to both of us in the same bed, making wild and passionate makeup sex. If only wars could be resolved the same way.

I stared at the ceiling after Armando was sleeping. Could it be that I'd just needed time to explore the world, play around, "sow my oats," and come back to finally be a responsible married woman?

No one had heard from my father in two days, so I asked Armando to take me to my parents' house. I inspected the house and put together the pieces of his disappearance. He had taken enough clothes and all the money under the mattress and all my mother's jewels. I didn't want to assume the worst—that he had taken off to Mexico with his mistress—so I pretended my father just needed time to think. Perhaps, like me, he needed time to live life before returning to commit himself to being my mother's full-time nurse. How could my father leave her after all she'd put up with to be with him?

I suppose I should say more about my father; otherwise you'll assume he was an insensitive macho jerk who only made sexist comments. He was obviously more than that and actually had good qualities too. Like many immigrant men he came to the United States without papers and was deported many times until he was able to get a green card and bring his family here. He could have been a real macho jerk and abandoned my mother in Mexico with their ten kids and never returned, but he did return for her and even sent money. He was an extraordinary worker and had many heartbreaks, like my mother, but this isn't his story.

As I closed the drawers in my parents' room I came across a white envelope with my name on it. It was written in Luna's handwriting and I could tell by her lines she'd been shaking when she'd attempted to scribble my name. She'd probably penned it just as her body was starting to go into shock. I could not pick up the letter. I thought I was strong enough and ready, but a tiny voice still screamed from within, "She's gone forever." I was frozen for a few minutes until Armando approached me cautiously, as if he were treating a shock victim.

"What is that?" Armando asked when he saw me staring at the letter, unable to pick it up.

"Nothing," I said, shaking my head and myself back to reality and left the room.

"¿Canela, eres tú?" my mother called out to me as soon as I walked in. After three days of being in the hospital I was her only full-time visitor and she could tell it was me by the sound of my footsteps.

"Si, Mama, soy yo." Yes, Mom, it's me, I replied in Spanish.

"So did he leave me?" my mother asked. My mother always got to the point and could see through everyone. It might be the only trait we shared. I hesitated to answer her and was about to make up a lie when she turned to me. Blind or not, she looked at my soul and I could not hide.

"Did he take off with his mistress?" she asked matter-of-factly.

"Yes," I replied, not wanting to bullshit her.

She cursed, said every possible obscenity in Spanish, and when she was done she took a minute to reflect.

"Hmm, donde el va, yo ya vine." Where he is going I've already been was my mother's way of saying she had already planned for betrayal.

"Why did you let it get this bad?" I asked her.

"Because he would have left me sooner. I already knew about the latest one, and when I refused to go back to Mexico after he retired I could tell he was itching for something different. I never told anyone about this so no one would worry and get all emotionally traumatized like you . . ."

"I'm not traumatized!" I lied.

"Yes, you are! That's how come you never trust men. You'd rather control them, manipulate them to be the jerks you don't want, than surrender to love." She said it like a wise woman on the mountain. I wanted to respond to her but instead I stayed silent for a few minutes, letting her words sink in. I remember being naked and blindfolded and Henry on top, kissing me. I had surrendered to love and that's why "I love you" had slipped out of me. I thought about Henry at the airport and it was clear for the first time that we did share love. It started out as sex, but I did love him.

"Don't worry about me. I'm blind now, but I can see every-thing," she said proudly. "Did you sleep with Armando last night?" she asked, her voice telling me she already knew the answer.

"Why do you care so much about Armando?" I whined.

"So am I right?"

"None of your business . . ." I took a deep breath and changed the subject. "You were so mean to withhold the letter from me . . . but thank you for not opening it."

"I wanted to, but I was scared Luna's ghost would show up and haunt me. You know how those tortured spirits can be, tu sabes. So what does it say?" my mother asked casually, as though she were requesting the plot of last night's telenovela.

"I haven't read it," I said, cutting off that inquiry.

"¡No te creo!" She shook her head incredulously. "Why haven't you opened the letter?"

"I can't get myself to do it. What if she blames me?" I confessed.

"Don't be a pendeja. She would never do that. You did nothing," my mother said, trying to console me with her tough talk.

"I know . . . I did nothing," I said, studying the worn tiles on the floor. I took a deep breath and looked out the window, trying to think of something else to talk about.

"So what are we going to do now?" my mother asked, also taking a deep breath.

"What do you mean we?" I asked.

"Pues, we. You're not getting married; I'm not getting any younger or prettier . . . It looks like our destinies are tied together." I started laughing when she made that assumption.

"So? This isn't *Like Water for Chocolate*. I don't have to take care of you; I'm not the oldest or the youngest. That's what con-valescent homes are for," I said jokingly. My mother burst out crying and I felt ashamed for making that joke. I hugged her and told her I was only teasing and of course I would take care of her. I held her in my arms like the child I would never have.

Later that day Armando and I went to the cemetery and I placed a basket of different tamales on Luna's grave, including ones with raisins, and her favorite desserts. I apologized to her for not coming to visit her sooner, but since she'd visited me so often in Paris I knew she didn't mind. I also apologized for not having the strength to read the letter yet. I felt like such a coward. I looked over at Armando playing along with me and thought, What a wonderful man—how could I have left him like I did? Now I could understand how Rosemary must have felt when her mother died and her ex-boyfriend was there. Having someone next to you at your most painful time can make you fall in love with him again.

CHAPTER 22

Cinnamon Souls

$\mathcal{A}$rmando and I pushed my mother's wheelchair into his Mercedes and we took her back to her house. He folded up her wheelchair while I escorted her by the hand up the stairs and through the front door. We walked through the living room and flashes of the past appeared. I saw my parents arguing in the doorway. My mother accused my father of cheating and wanted to open the door so she could walk over to her neighbor's house and go kick the shit out of his mistress. My father blocked the door so she wouldn't go make a scene and embarrass his mistress in front of her children. My mother slapped him and pushed him furiously and he cowered and took it, trying to hold her hands down. She threw thunder and lightning at a man who had no umbrella.

We continued walking into the kitchen and I saw more flashes of my past. While my parents argued about the affair, I stuffed myself with corn drowned in butter and wished his mistress would die, but not her daughter, who was my best friend. My mother stopped walking and placed her hand on the counter. Another flash in the kitchen, where I saw my mother telling me, "If you are not going to do it with love, then don't do it at all." Then she kicked me out of the kitchen and banned me from coming in. This time I found it funny and laughed out loud.

"Why are you laughing?" my mother asked.

"You kicked me out of the kitchen," I told her.

"No, I didn't," she snapped, embarrassed to be outed this way in front of her potential son-in-law.

"Yes, you did," I told her and reminded her of all the details. She remembered the incident and apologized to me for all the bad she had ever done to me. I felt embarrassed finally getting her to admit it. I felt like an ungrateful daughter and was ashamed to hear my mother humiliate herself on my behalf.

"Stop. I know you always meant well. Like they say, the road to hell is paved with good intentions."

"Yes, I was a devil to you; but I just thought in the end you would appreciate what I was doing. Tell me, did I do wrong getting you and Armando back together? It's just a matter of time before he proposes," she said, loud enough so he could hear. I shook my head, knowing my mother would not change. What did I do to her in my past life to deserve this? I thought to myself.

After we placed my mother in bed, Armando showed me how to give my mother insulin shots and explained to me how to read her numbers on the meter. I didn't want him to go, but I was her nurse, not him.

The next morning I dressed my mother and saw her naked for the first time since I was five. On her body were so many stretch marks, like a road map of her life, displaying all the ways she'd tried to stretch and mold herself for everyone else, trying to be all things to all people.

"It's good your father left me," my mother said to me when I was brushing her hair. "I was turning into a bitter old woman. Who would want to be married to me?" she confided, feeling sorry for herself. I tried not to agree or disagree with her and just listened compassionately.

"I gave your papa everything," she said in Spanish. She began to cry, recalling her life of pure sacrifice. "I never did anything for myself. Never gave myself pleasure . . . That's why I began to hate him so much. He never sacrificed himself for me the way I did for him. I don't blame him for his affairs. I should have had one too, but like a dummy I thought I would go to hell. Hell is living the life your mother and the Catholic Church tell you to live," she said, practically spitting.

I was at the Louis Vuitton store with Henry, dressed all in black. The store was closed, but somehow through a back door we had managed to break in without setting off the alarm. We quickly made our way to the second floor. With flashlights we searched for the burgundy crocodile bag on the second floor. I grabbed the purse and ran to the section with the suitcases. Henry ran alongside me and kissed me ferociously on top of the suitcases. The smell of leather and crocodile made my nipples erect. Henry tore off my blouse and licked my hard nipples. We continued to take off our clothes and played around naked on top of the suitcases. Henry took the burgndry crocodile purse and stimulated my clitoris with it. The sight of the purse between my legs made me even wetter. I closed my eyes while Henry continued where the purse left off. When I opened my eyes to look for Henry, he was gone. I searched around the store naked, holding my flashlight. I saw some leather coats moving and knew he was hiding in the leather coats. I dug in and caught an ankle. I fell on top of him and started kissing his legs and worked my way to his face. On my way to his face his body had transformed into a woman's body and I found myself French-kissing a woman. I stopped, pulled away, and saw myself naked on the floor. I looked at my hands and at my body and wondered what was going on. The shock was too much and I yelled.

"What's wrong?" Armando said, next to me in bed. I awoke from my wet dream to find Armando shaking me to wake up. I stared at him blankly, wondering what had happened to the burgundy crocodile bag, before I realized it was a dream.

"What were you dreaming? You had a nightmare," he informed me as he studied my pupils.

"I had a . . . I was having a dream that I was making love to a . . . woman," I divulged. Armando's eyes lit up with excitement.

"Tell me more," he urged.

"Well, it started out being an androgynous body and then it became a woman and then it was me. I was making love to myself." I didn't want to reveal that before it was a woman it was Henry. "What do you think it means?" Armando thought about it for a few seconds and smiled playfully.

"It could be that you have lesbian tendencies . . . or that you want to have more intimacy with yourself," he concluded. "So which do you think?"

"It's probably that I've never really loved myself—that's why the thought of making love to myself was so frightening," I confessed.

"I make love to you and it's beautiful; you're beautiful," he added and put his arm around me to comfort me. We fell back on the bed with my head buried in his armpit like a little kid hiding from La Llorona. Armando turned off the lights and I was still frightened, shaking in my soul, wondering what it really meant.

Armando was too perfect; his only flaw was that he loved me too much. When he proposed I pretended to be surprised and took back the original ring he had bought me for his first proposal.

The news quickly spread and a date not too far into the future was set. Armando had arranged for my mother to have a nurse who would do most of the injections and spare me that painful duty. One night while we were cuddling he said he would go crazy if he ever lost me again. I shared with him my suicide attempt and he convinced me that I needed to talk to someone about that. He had a psychiatrist friend who owed him a favor and that doctor was able to fit me in.

"So how often do these thoughts come to you?" the psychiatrist asked.

"I've had them ever since I can remember. When I eat, especially something creamy and sweet, they tend to go away . . . temporarily," I admitted.

"So you've had this chemical imbalance since birth?" he asked.

"A chemical imbalance? That's what it is?" I asked. He told me that wanting to die was not normal, not even when you've lost hope of ever getting justice for women, the poor, immigrants, the exploited, and oppressed. Not even when you've lost your cousin and best friend.

"It definitely sounds like depression with some hyperactivity," he said, writing down a prescription. At the end of the session he said he was confident the medication would make all those depressing thoughts fade away. I would be the first person in my family to take antidepressants. Before that, generations of women in my family had eaten their way out of their depression.

Two weeks later, after taking the medication, I found that the world was finally not miserable. I could see how people could live in the suburbs with their SUVs and their 2.5 kids in a house with a white picket fence. I felt numb. I've no doubt this was someone else's version of happiness, but I just felt numb and apathetic. Why should I let other people's misery get in the way of my happiness? was my mantra. Even Armando's mother didn't annoy me. When she found out through the grapevine that I was on medication she wanted Armando to break off the engagement, claiming she was concerned that her future grandchildren were going to end up retarded. Armando told her to stay out of his personal life and said that if his kids ended up retarded he would love them just as much.

One morning I cooked my mother a diabetic-friendly breakfast and she praised me for being such a good daughter and a good cook.

"Why don't you open up a Mexican restaurant?" she suggested. "Maybe I could do tortillas for you by hand. I don't need my eyesight to make tortillas," she said proudly. I dismissed her idea and told her I wouldn't be opening a restaurant anytime soon, but if I ever did I would take her up on her offer. My mother told me to come close to her and to stick out my hand. She put a gold bracelet in my hand and closed it for me to indicate it was a gift for me.

"I wanted to give you this at your wedding, but here, it's yours. I'm proud of you," she said. I was so touched I wanted to cry, but the antidepressant wouldn't let me. I remembered Altair offering me her gold bracelet after I helped her escape, and I just had to sit down. My mother rolled herself to my side and then I surprised myself. Despite the antidepressant, tears were still capable of escaping out of me. It felt good to cry, even if it was only three tears.

"Don't you like it?" my mother asked, confused.

"Yes. I love it. Thank you, Mama," I said.

A month before the wedding I saw flyers on the street announcing an immigrant march to protest the building of the wall between the United States and Mexico, and also against a bill to criminalize anyone aiding undocumented immigrants. I kept one with me and told my mother about the march. She was so outraged by the wall.

"Que pendejos. Don't they know they need us?" she muttered.

I had been so preoccupied with the wedding I hadn't contacted any of my old friends to ask them about the march. I was waiting to decide what to do about my writing career. I knew I was a writer and that's why I was put on earth. Writing chooses you; you don't choose it. Whether I wanted to make my living off my writing was another thing. I was so numb, happy, whatever you want to call it . . . "nuppy" . . . let's call it that . . . that I couldn't imagine putting myself through the stress of being mistreated or meeting impossible deadlines and, frankly, who needs an adrenaline rush when you're taking anti-depressants? For someone like me who was used to being miserable, I was having a hard time recognizing myself. I didn't crave sugar anymore or food or sex . . . Yeah, that was the big drawback. I couldn't come anymore. Armando worked tirelessly to satisfy me but I just lay in bed like a happy idiot, unattached to a result. I stopped making sarcastic remarks about mediocre people getting ahead or all the things I would observe not being right in the world. I could finally understand how a president who'd never gone to war himself could send thousands of soldiers to their deaths, or an immigrant turned governor could praise the works of vigilantes abusing other immigrants as they crossed the desert without documents. Everything was great now; but that was the problem. Life had no edge and I had no opinions of my own.

Armando had agreed that I would get to decide the kind of menu I wanted for the reception, but I didn't even care about that anymore. Whatever he wanted was fine by me. He would forsake all others, including his mother, for me. He was even going to let my mother move in with us once we got a big house with a guest-house in the back.

The day of the appointment with the caterer I could not find my antidepressant pills. Had I run out of them or had someone hidden them? As I searched for them, my mother told me to come over to her bed.

"Don't do it," she whispered.

"Do what?" I asked.

"Don't marry him if you don't want to. I know everyone says you're happy now, but I don't see your light anymore," my mother confided, trying to outline where she used to see the light around me.

"What do you mean?" I asked.

"I know you want to marry him so you can take care of me. I can tell you feel guilty about not calling me and then . . . making me blind—"

"I didn't make you blind!" I interrupted her.

"I know, I'm joking . . . I can see this is a sacrifice for you. Don't go sacrificing yourself for me. Look where it gets you."

"No, that's not true," I said and dismissed her. I continued looking for the pills.

"Ten!" she said in Spanish and threw them at me. I grabbed them and went to the bathroom to take one. I saw my unhappy face in the mirror, knowing that in a second I would return to being a happy idiot. I stared at the pill and thought about all the hard work some wonderful person had put into capturing happiness in a pill, and here I was debating the value of this pill in my life. I thought about all those poets and great artists who were depressed who could have been spared their misery or could have avoided suicide if this pill had been around hundreds of years of ago . . . Yeah, but then we would not have been able to see their beautiful paintings, or heard of their beautiful poetry.

Yes, I can finally smile and not carry the weight of the world on my back, but what about the moments when I feel people's pain so deeply that it becomes my own, and those moments when I feel people's joy so beautifully that it too becomes my own? What about those highs and lows that make me feel alive? But when I take this pill I don't overeat and I've lost twenty pounds, a little voice shouted back at me. Hmm, that was true; if I stopped taking it I would gain back the twenty pounds and maybe even gain another twenty and go back to being a human yo-yo . . . I seriously considered that objection before thinking how pathetic it would be if my greatest contribution to humanity was losing twenty pounds. I put the pill down and saved it for later, after I had answered my own questions.

My mother's nurse arrived and I got ready to go out with Armando. My mother handed me Luna's letter.

"How come you haven't read it? It's been in my drawer all this time and you knew it was there. Why don't you read it now?" she challenged me.

I went to the bathroom and locked myself in. I opened the envelope and saw that there were tearstains on the paper and some of the words were almost illegible. I began to read it.

"Canela, I'm sorry I am not as courageous as you. Adios."

That's all it said. Damn, why can't suicide notes be longer! After my burst of anger I cried, picturing Luna drinking from the Coke cans, knowing that little by little she was killing herself softly, sweetly.

Armando honked when he arrived at my mother's house and waited outside for me. I quickly told my mother good-bye as I ran past her nurse. I got in his Mercedes and we took off; on the radio a disc jockey on a Spanish radio station encouraged everyone to march and take a stand against HR 4437, the proposed immigration bill. Armando was about to turn off the radio when I told him to stop the car. He pulled to the side of the road and looked at me with concern.

"I can't do this," I said. "I know I love you, but I'm not ready to commit to you or anyone," I continued courageously, knowing that I couldn't sell out. For another woman this would be happiness, but for me it was selling out on my dreams. Sure, I would have financial security and a nice husband and all the wonderful things in life called the American dream, but this was not my dream.

Armando looked at me and sadly asked, "Don't you get lonely?"

"Yeah, I do . . . but even chocolate, as good as it is . . . gets boring. There are too many flavors to settle for one," I confessed, wondering if he thought I was a heartless bitch for putting it that way.

"All right. Give me back the ring," he said casually. I gave it back. "So you think I'm boring?" he said sadly and put the ring away in his pocket without looking at me.

"No, you're not boring, but I know that you can't live life through me. You have to go live it for yourself. I have a lot of living to do still."

"And you can't do that with me?" he asked. I thought about it for a long time and knew that the answer was private. I can't be monogamous; I don't want to be some man's property or responsibility, or have to ask for permission to take on a cause or a mission in life.

"No," I answered. I kissed his hand and got out of his car.

"Canela, this is the last time I'll do this. I will not pursue you again," he warned me.

"Thank you," I said and closed the door to his Mercedes.

When I walked into the house my mother could tell by my step that I was sad.

"What happened? What did he tell you?"

"I can't go through with it." I started crying.

"So why are you going to cry? You got what you wanted. You should celebrate—you are a free woman again, que no?" my mother said a bit sarcastically.

"You're right." I grabbed her jacket and our purses.

"We're going for a little walk." I pushed my mother's wheelchair out of the house and into history.

"Where are we?" my mother asked in the midst of a sea of humanity made up of over four hundred thousand conscious objectors clad in Mexican and American flags, millions of cinnamon souls marching throughout the United States for a piece of the American pie.

"We are among friends," I answered her and continued to push her wheelchair very slowly, shoulder to shoulder with immigrants of every color. I heard people shouting all sorts of things, like: "America, you need us. We clean up after you and feed you and take care of your children, and soon we'll take care of your parents too." I swear I even heard someone yell in Spanish, "Respect and dessert!" Maybe that should be our version of "Bread and Roses."

"Why are people shouting, 'Today we march, tomorrow we vote'?" asked my mother.

"Because we've had enough," I proclaimed.

Epilogue

*M*onths after I arrived in Los Angeles I got a letter from Altair. She'd gotten my address from Marina and apologized for not contacting me sooner. She informed me that she had called her bodyguard to turn herself in, but because she had escaped from him he'd been fired. He had decided to stay in Paris to look for her and they'd found each other. They are both living in Paris *sans papiers,* trying to start a new life together.

Frenchwomen don't get fat and Japanese women don't grow old or get fat ... but Latina women do. We get fat and we wrinkle, but our wrinkles come from laughing and crying. We know how to feel and eat; we know how to love and to come; we know how to live ourselves to death.

Everything is about food and hunger, whether it is hunger for the body or hunger for the soul. As long as I am alive I will always be hungry for revolution, for justice and truth, but I am no longer hungry for my soul the way I used to be. I have plenty of beautiful memories and life-inspiring moments to nourish my soul for many lifetimes ... I hope this was delicious.

Glossary of French and Spanish Words and Terms

Allez, allez (F): Come on, come on

à l'orange (F, cooking): prepared with an orange sauce

Ama (S, slang): Mom

Amuse-bouche (F): a tiny appetizer before the appetizer; literally, amusement to the mouth

Apéritif (F): a drink before dinner to whet the appetite

¡Apurate! (S): Hurry up!

Arrondisements (F): neighborhoods of Paris

Au revoir (F): Good-bye

Au revoir les euros (F): Good-bye to the Europeans

¡Ay, que vergüenza! (S): How embarrassing!

Bain-marie (F, cooking): a metal bowl that is placed over boiling water such as when heating eggs in hollandaise sauce

Banlieue (F): outskirts, also a connotation for 'hood, projects

Batons (F, cooking): sticks

BCBG, bon chic, bon genre (F): well dresssed, stylish

Bienvenu (F): Welcome

Blanc de barbue poêlé (F): pan-fried brill fillet

Blanquette de veau à l'ancienne (F): traditional veal stew

Bonjour (F): Hello, good day

Botânica (S): Latino shop offering cures for the spirit; sells herbs, candles, saints, and the like

Brunoise (F, cooking): finely diced carrot, celery, leek, or zucchini

Bueno pues (S): Well, then

Buñuelos (S): Mexican pastry consisting of a fried flour tortilla with sugar and cinnamon

Caliente (S): hot, horny

Callate (S): Be quiet, shut up

Calle (S): street

Canela (S): cinnamon

Carte de séjour (F): a residency card

Casa chica (S): small house, the small house for the mistress

Ça va? (F, slang): How's it going? Are you all right?

Ce n'est pas mon problème (F): It's not my problem

C'est facile (F): It's easy

C'est fini (F): It's finished

C'est fou! (F): It's crazy!

C'est ma vie (F): It's my life

C'est parfait (F): It's perfect

C'est tout (F): That's all.

Chambre de bonne (F): a nanny's or servant's room, usually a small room on the upper floor of an apartment building

Chérie, chéri (F): dear, darling

Chicana (S): A female of Mexican descent; also, a woman with a Chicana consciousness

Chismosa (S): gossipper

Cochina (S): pig, dirty girl

Confit (F, cooking): a sieved purée or sauce, often made with tomatoes or fruits combined with a sweetener and a small amount of lemon juice

Corranle (S): run

Curandera (S): a female healer

Crépine (F, cooking): intestine lining from a pig used to wrap around meat or food to seal it in the oven

¿De dónde es usted? (S): Where are you from?

Deux Magots (F): a famous French restaurant where Hemingway and notable French people like Sartre hung out

Doña (S): Madam

Donde el va, yo ya vine (S): Where he is headed, I've already arrived

¿Eres tú? (S): Is that you?

Escargot (F): snail

Es una locura (S): It's insanity

Et voilà (F): And here it is

Foie gras (F): goose liver

Grenouille (F): frog

Haricots verts (F): green beans

Hola (S): Hello

Je m'appelle Marina, et vous? (F): My name is Marina, and you?

La Calaca Flaca (S): The skinny skeleton

La Llorona (S): The crying woman; a character from a ghost legend, she roams the rivers of Mexico looking for her children, whom she drowned

Madame Bodé (F): Mrs. Nosy

Macaron (F): a French pastry, round with a sweet and creamy center made in just about any color and flavor

Magnifique (F): magnificent

Mais de quoi tu parles? (F): But what are you talking about?

Mais pourquoi? (F): But why?

Mais, vous êtes mexicaine, n'est-ce pas? (F): But you are Mexican, aren't you?

Merci (F): Thank you

Metiche (S): nosy

Mexique (F): Mexico

Migra (S, slang): Immigration authorities

Mira (S): look

Mirepoix (F, cooking): vegetables cut into half-inch lengths and roughly diced (traditionally carrot, onion, celery, and leek), used to flavor sauces, soups, and stews

N'est-ce pas? (F): Don't you think? or Isn't it so?

¡No mas corta, corta! (S): Just cut, cut!

No te creo (S): I don't believe you

Omelette à la crème de la Mère Poulard (F): omelette made with Mother Poulard's cream

Paleta (S): icicle

Paysane (F, cooking): mixture of vegetables cut into small squares, triangles, diamonds or rounds

Pendeja (S, slang): idiot

Phyllo (Greek, cooking): a special dough developed for Greek cuisine and also used in French pastries

Pinche, pinchi (S, slang): damned, stupid

Planchette (F): cutting board

Por favor (S): Please

Pues (S): well

Puta (S): whore

Que milagro (S): What a miracle

¿Qué no? (S): Isn't it so?

Qui? (F): Who?

Qui sont les assistants? (F): Who are the assistants?

Rapido (S): Hurry, fast

Sans-gêne (F): rude, overly forward

Sans papiers (F): without papers, undocumented

Saumon farcie en feuille de chou vert (F, cooking): stuffed salmon wrapped in green cabbage

S'il vous plaît (F): Please; if you would like

Sí, Mamá, soy yo (S): Yes, mother, it is me

También (S): also, as well

Terrine (F, cooking): paté

T'es folle (F) You are crazy

Tía Bonifacia (S): Aunt Bonifacia (Goodface)

Travail (F): work

Truite farcie aux morilles (F, cooking): Trout with morel mush-
    rooms

Tú de veras estás loca (S): You are truly crazy

Une minute, s'il vous plaît! (F): Just a minute, please.

Vámonos (S): Let's go

Viva México (S): Long live Mexico

Voilà l'apéritif (F): Here is the aperitif (the drink before the
    meal)

Voulez-vouz danser avec moi? (F): Would you like to dance
    with me?

Ya ves (S): you see

Reading Group Guide

1. Compare and contrast Canela's immigrant experiences in the United States and France. Have you ever lived in another country? If so, how did your experience compare with Canela's?
2. Chart Canela's romantic and sexual relationship with Henry. How does her relationship with him compare to her relationships with other men, like Armando or Yves?
3. Why is Canela so hungry and depressed? Do you think there is just one reason or many reasons? Do you think she knows why she is depressed, or could there be something outside of what she shares with the reader that is causing her pain?
4. What are the different types of hunger Canela experiences throughout the novel? How does she satisfy her hunger?
5. What is the significance placed by Canela—and many young women in the United States—on turning thirty?
6. When applying to school, Canela tells the admissions woman that she wants to open a French restaurant in the United States so that people can experience French

culture. Do you agree that food communicates culture? Why or why not? If so, then how does food communicate culture?

7. Do you think Canela's journey to France is an act of courage, fear, or both?

8. How does Canela's experience in France fuel her to return to Los Angeles to continue fighting for what she believes in? What did she discover—or rediscover—while in Paris to enable her to do this?

9. What role does diabetes play in the lives of Canela, her mother, and Luna?

10. Compare and contrast Canela's expatriate experience with that of other famous American writers, such as Ernest Hemingway, Gertrude Stein, or Mark Twain.

Guía de lector

1. Compare la experiencia de Canela de ser inmigrante en los Estados Unidos con su experiencia en Francia. ¿Ha vivido Ud. en otro país? ¿Cómo compara su experiencia con la de Canela?

2. Siga la relación romántica y sexual de Henry y Canela. ¿Cómo es diferente la relación con Henry a las relaciones con otros hombres como Armando e Yves?

3. ¿Por qué tiene tanta hambre Canela? ¿Y por qué está tan deprimida? ¿Cree Ud. que hay solo una razón o muchas razones?

4. ¿Cuáles son los tipos de hambres diferentes que Canela tiene en la novela? ¿Cómo las satisface?

5. ¿Qué es el significado a Canela—y a muchas señoritas en los Estados Unidos—en cumplir trienta años?

6. Cuando aplica a la escuela Le Coq Rouge, Canela le dice a la mujer de la admisión que ella quiere abrir un restaurante frances en los Estados Unidos para que la gente allí pueda conocer la cultura frances. ¿Está Ud. de acuerdo que la comida comunica la cultura? ¿Por qué o por qué no? ¿Y sí la comunica, en cual manera?

7. ¿Cree Ud. que el viaje de Canela a Francia es un acto de valor, de miedo o de los dos?

8. ¿Después de vivir en Paris, Canela tiene la fuerza para regresar a Los Angeles y luchar para lo que le importa a ella? ¿Cómo le auyda su experiencia en Francia regresar?

9. ¿Qué parte juega la diabetes en las vidas de Canela, su madre y Luna?

10. Compare la experiencia de Canela en Paris con otros escritores Americanos famosos, como Ernest Hemingway, Gertrude Stein y Mark Twain.

About the Author

Josefina López is best known for authoring the play and coauthoring the Sundance Audience Award–winning film *Real Women Have Curves*. Although *Real Women Have Curves* is López's most recognized work, it is only one of many literary works she has created since she began her writing career, at age seventeen. Born in San Luis Potosí, Mexico, in 1969, Josefina López was five years old when she and her family immigrated to the United States and settled in the East Los Angeles neighborhood of Boyle Heights. She was undocumented for thirteen years until she obtained amnesty in 1988 and in 1995 became a United States citizen

Josefina attended the Los Angeles County High School for the Arts, graduating in 1987. She obtained her bachelor of arts degree in film and screenwriting from Columbia College, in Chicago, in 1993. She then obtained her MFA in screenwriting from UCLA's School of Theater, Film, and Television. She is currently pursuing an MA in spiritual psychology.

Josefina is the recipient of a number of other awards and accolades, including a formal recognition from U.S. Senator Barbara Boxer's seventh annual Women Making History banquet in 1998 and a screenwriting fellowship from the California Arts Council in

2001. She and *Real Women Have Curves* coauthor George LaVoo won the Humanitas Prize for Screenwriting in 2002, the Gabriel García Márquez Award from the Los Angeles mayor in 2003, and an artist-in-residency grant from the NEA/TCG for 2007.

Even though she is best known for the success of *Real Women Have Curves*, Josefina has had more than eighty productions of her plays throughout the United States. Josefina is also a poet, performer, designer, artist, and lecturer of women's studies, and Chicano theater and film. She is the founder of the Casa 0101 Theater Art Space in Boyle Heights, where she teaches screenwriting and playwriting and nurtures a new generation of Latino artists. Josefina is presently workshopping the musical version of *Real Women Have Curves*, and writing her second novel, *You'll Never Eat Tacos in This Town Again*, and a self-esteem book for women, *Real Women Love Themselves*.

Josefina lived in Paris for almost eighteen months and graduated with a diploma in cuisine from Le Cordon Bleu, Paris. She lives in Silverlake, California, with her French-American husband, Emmanuel, and her two little Fren-chican (French-Chicano) sons, Etienne and Sebastian. *Hungry Woman in Paris* is her first novel.